CHAINED TO THE STREETS 2

**Lock Down Publications and
Ca$h Presents
Chained to the Streets 2
A Novel by J-Blunt**

Chained to the Streets 2

Lock Down Publications
P.O. Box 870494
Mesquite, Tx 75187

Visit our website
www.lockdownpublications.com

Lock Down Publications
Like our page on Facebook: Lock Down Publications @
www.facebook.com/lockdownpublications.ldp
Cover design and layout by: **Dynasty Cover Me**
Book interior design by: **Shawn Walker**
Edited by: **Jill Duska**

Stay Connected with Us!

Text **LOCKDOWN** to 22828 to stay up-to-date
with new releases, sneak peeks, contests and more…

Submission Guideline.

Submit the first three chapters of your completed manuscript to ldpsubmissions@gmail.com, subject line: Your book's title. The manuscript must be in a .doc file and sent as an attachment. The document should be in Times New Roman, double-spaced and in size 12 font. Also, provide your synopsis and full contact information. If sending multiple submissions, they must each be in a separate email.

Have a story but no way to send it electronically? You can still submit to LDP/Ca$h Presents. Send in the first three chapters, written or typed, of your completed manuscript to:

LDP: Submissions Dept
Po Box 870494
Mesquite, Tx 75187

DO NOT send original manuscript. Must be a duplicate.

Provide your synopsis and a cover letter containing your full contact information.

Thanks for considering LDP and Ca$h Presents.

Chapter 1

The request was too much.

That's what Desmond thought as he stared into the grief-stricken face of Polo. He could see the pain and determination in the whites of the snake's eyes. Polo had showed up with Scooter and another goon at one o'clock in the morning. The shooters held assault rifles at their sides. Polo wasn't showing a weapon, but Desmond knew he was armed. They wanted Quaysha, his girlfriend's daughter, and Desmond couldn't allow them to take her. The child was innocent, had nothing to do with whatever happened to Polo's niece. And he would lay down his life for the toddler, if necessary.

"I can't let you do that," Desmond spoke.

"She ain't yours," Polo tried to reason. "You still owe me, nigga."

Three against two weren't the best odds. Plus, they had choppers. But Desmond couldn't allow them to take his girl's daughter. "Ain't nobody getting nothing up outta here. It's time for y'all to leave now. Y'all gotta go," he refused, gripping the pistol tight in his fist.

Polo's mug gave away his intentions. It was on. When he went for the pistol at his waist, his shooters followed the lead and made a motion to lift their rifles.

And the Navy SEAL was ready. Desmond had been trained for close combat. Even though he still wore a cast on his injured forearm, the rifles were useless when you were too close to someone with his skill. As soon as the thugs made their move, Desmond made his. He moved with the speed and precision of someone trained to kill, lifting his right leg and pistol at the same time, kicking Scooter in the chest while shooting the other man in the face. Both men went down.

At the same moment, Lucky grabbed Polo, trying to stop him from pulling the weapon from his waist. A wrestling match began and the men fell on the ground, rolling around in the grass.

Desmond took his eyes off Scooter and looked over at the scuffle on the lawn. Polo rolled on top of Lucky and looked to be gaining an advantage. Desmond was about to turn his pistol and kill Polo, but motion from Scooter got his attention. The shooter lay on his back and pointed the chopper at Desmond.

Brrrrreaaaaatttt!

The chopper erupted, sending a volley of hot lead towards the spot where Desmond had been standing. When Scooter realized that Desmond had moved and the bullets missed, an ice cold panic entered his body. He looked to the right just in time to see Desmond recovering from a tuck roll and standing to his feet. Scooter moved to turn the chopper upon him again, but the war-ready soldier was already pointing the pistol at him.

Pop, pop, pop!

Bullets to the face and chest silenced Scooter for all eternity.

Desmond turned back to the scuffle on the lawn just as Lucky rolled on top of Polo and took the pistol. He pointed it in Polo's face, anger and the desire to kill flickering like a fire in the ex-con's eyes.

"Lucky! Lucky! Are you okay?" Melissa called, the high-pitched female voice cutting through the night as she ran onto the porch. She stopped in her tracks when she saw her man on top of Polo pointing the gun in his face and two dead bodies in the grass. Shock and fear made her voice rise another octave. "LUCKY, NO!"

"Don't do it, brah," Desmond said, kneeling next to Lucky and reaching for the pistol.

Lucky refused to give the gun. "Move, Des. This bitch-ass nigga just tried to kill us. I'ma kill him."

"Desmond! What happened?" Lasonya asked, walking up next to Melissa and surveying the scene. "Oh my!"

Desmond ignored his woman, giving all his attention to Lucky. "C'mon, brah. Gimme the gun. Let me take care of it. You can't go back to jail. I got it."

Polo lay on the ground remaining stiff as a board, the fear of death making the whites of his eyes wide with terror. Lucky's arm shook from the desire to kill, and he didn't want to give him a reason to shoot.

8

"C'mon, Lucky. Don't do me like this, my nigga," he pleaded. "I wasn't gon' hurt nobody. I just wanted the - "

"Shut the fuck up, nigga!" Lucky yelled, slapping him across the face with the pistol. "You lucky my girl out here or I woulda offed yo' bitch ass."

"Melissa, is everything okay out here?" a neighbor called, stepping outside holding a cell phone. "The police are on the way."

"Gimme the gun, Lucky. It's over," Desmond said, gripping the gun. "The police on the way."

Lucky allowed him to take the pistol. After he was disarmed, Polo pushed Lucky off and ran for his ride.

◆◆◆

Detective Larry Johnson wasn't a fan of the graveyard shift. He preferred to be at home snuggled up next to his wife during the late night hours. Plus, the city slowed down at night. During the day, the call for detectives was constant and it kept him on his feet. Late night was the opposite. There were two or three calls a night. Hardly any excitement. And at twenty-eight years old, he preferred excitement. But moving to a new district meant that you had to fulfill whatever was available, and the only thing available was late nights. So when the call came through about a double homicide, he jumped in the car and sped to the east side. When he pulled onto the scene, blue and red lights blazed in the night, lighting the quiet neighborhood. Neighbors stood around watching the police. Yellow tape surrounded the crime scene. Forensic experts took pictures and gathered evidence.

"What do we got?" the detective asked the female police sergeant as he ducked under the crime scene tape.

"Two black male victims. We have the shooter and weapon. He stayed on the scene and claims self-defense."

"Where is he?"

"In the back of my car."

"Okay. I'll talk to him after I look around. Have we gotten statements from witnesses?"

"Yes. They all say he was defending them."

The detective nodded. "Okay. Let me take a look at the bodies."

Two bodies lay on the lawn covered with white sheets. Both had gunshot wounds to the face. "Damn. He looks like a good shot."

"He's a Navy SEAL."

The detective shot the sergeant a glance. "Bullshit. You serious?"

"That's what he says."

"Where is your car? I want to see him."

When they got to the car, the sergeant opened the back door so the detective could see the suspect. Desmond sat in the car without a shirt or shoes. He wore a set of cuffs. The detective noticed the cast on his wrist as well as the muscular frame. When he and Desmond locked eyes, he noticed the scar.

"You did that?" the detective asked, nodding towards the dead bodies.

"Yeah. It was self-defense. They tried to take my girlfriend's daughter."

The detective raised an eyebrow. "Why would they want to take your girlfriend's daughter? How old is she?"

"She's five. It was a misunderstanding."

"Two people dead sounds like more than a misunderstanding. Why would they want to take a five-year-old?"

"I told you, it was a misunderstanding."

The detective was silent for a moment, searching Desmond's face and demeanor. "You seem pretty calm for a man that just killed two people. I heard you're a Navy SEAL."

"I am. Am I being arrested?"

"I don't know. Probably. Two people are dead and all you've told me is there was a misunderstanding. I need more than that, so we're going to have to take you in so we can talk about it."

Desmond nodded. "Okay. I don't want to answer any more questions. I want a lawyer. Also, a shirt and pair of shoes, if you don't mind."

◆◆◆

Desmond hated being locked up.

He paced the small cell, going from the cell bars to the sink in four steps before spinning around and taking another lap. He had been walking for almost an hour. Every time he tried to sit on the thin green mattress, he got antsy and had to get up again. It seemed as if the walls were closing in on him and the only way to make the room bigger was to get up and walk. So he paced. The thought of being charged with murder was playing heavily on his mind. He couldn't help but think that he had traded his life for Lucky's. At the time it seemed like the right thing to do. He loved his brother and wanted to protect him from any hurt, harm, or danger. But now that he was in jail and faced the uncertainty of going to prison, he wasn't sure if he made the right choice. Plus, he had killed his only ally on the police force. He regretted that decision like heroin addicts regret their first taste of the deadly and highly addictive powder.

"Desmond, you got a visitor," a police officer called as he walked up to the cell. "Your lawyer is here."

A little bit of relief filled Desmond when he heard those words and the door was unlocked. He was escorted to a small room. A tall, clean-cut, brown-skinned man sat at the table. When the door was opened, he stood to greet Desmond with an outstretched hand.

"Desmond, how are you doing? I'm your attorney, Brandon Williams."

Desmond shook his hand eagerly. "I'm okay, I guess."

"Have a seat," he said before turning to the officer. "I'd like to have a moment with my client, please." When the door closed, Brandon sat across from Desmond and got right down to business. "I got a call from your brother, Larry, and he told me a little about the situation before the shooting. The police aren't saying much just that you admitted to shooting the guys and claim self-defense. How does all of this sound so far?"

"It sounds about right."

"Okay. I still don't have all the information to do a good job representing you, so I need you to fill in the blanks. Did you know the people you killed?"

"One of them was named Scooter. I didn't know the other guy. They came over with Polo. They wanted to take my girlfriend's daughter and I wouldn't let them. I killed them in self-defense. They had automatic weapons and tried to kill me. I don't understand why I'm being arrested."

"You aren't being arrested, yet," Brandon clarified. "Why did they want to take a kid? Did you owe them something?"

Desmond let out a gust of hot breath, wondering how much he should say.

"C'mon, Desmond. Now is not the time to decide how much you want to tell me. If I am to properly represent you, you have to be honest with me. I've represented some of the baddest dudes this city has ever seen and won those cases. You have to trust me. That's the only way this will work."

Desmond could see genuine sincerity lighting the lawyer's eyes. Brandon wasn't a silver spoon in the mouth type. He looked like he worked hard to get his spot, like he came from where Desmond came from. So Desmond decided to trust him.

"I've known Polo since I was a kid. Ran the streets with him and my brother back in the day before I joined the military. He and my brother recently did some bullshit and Polo got some leverage over him. I knew Polo was a snake so I made a deal with him to protect my brother. Because I'm a Navy SEAL, he wanted to use my skills and we agreed on three favors. I did the first two. Yesterday his niece was killed. They were trying to get him, but hit the girl. The man who called the hit is my girlfriend's daughter's father. Polo wanted to kill the girl to get even with the man that called the hit. I killed the two guys in the grass, but Polo got away."

Brandon looked impressed. "You're really a Navy SEAL?"

Desmond nodded.

"Okay. I'm not going to tell the police everything you've told me, but I'm going to try to get you released. Is there anything more that I need to know before I go out here and get in they asses? Are you wanted for anything or being investigated for anything?"

Desmond thought about the deal he made with Detective Perry. He wondered if it was still important, considering the detective was now dead. "Nah. That's all. I told them what happened and gave them the gun. That's all."

"Okay. Hang tight. I'll see what I can do."

J-Blunt

Chapter 2

Lucky felt like shit.

The police had taken Desmond into custody and it was all his fault. If he hadn't started fucking with Polo, none of this would've happened. He had to find a way to get Desmond out and get even with Polo's snake ass, but was clueless as to how he was going to do either.

"Where are we gonna stay? I don't want to sleep here tonight." Lucky looked up from the couch and saw Melissa standing in the threshold to the living room staring at him. "I don't know. I'm not really concerned about where I'ma sleep. The only thing I'm thinking about is my brother."

Melissa let out a huff. "So, you're not thinkin' about your family? About your girl and the kids? What about us? People came to our house with guns. We have bullet holes in the house. Two people died! What do you mean you not concerned about nothing but your brother?"

Lucky lowered his head and massaged his temples. Melissa's voice was irritating. High-pitched and whiny. The sound was making his head hurt. "I didn't say I was only concerned about Desmond. I said I'm not concerned where I'ma sleep. Stop putting words in my mouth. If you don't feel safe here, go stay with your mother."

"Why you gotta say it like that? I heard what you said. You supposed to be my man and I'm bringing our problem to you for you to figure out. Your brother is the one that brought this shit to our house. You should - "

"Bitch, shit the fuck up!" Lucky exploded, shooting to his feet with a deranged look in his eyes. "All the fuck you do is complain and talk shit. I'm tired of yo' fuckin' mouth. Desmond didn't bring the problem here. I did. Desmond saved all our asses by killin' them niggas, and yo' bitter ass is too fucking stupid to appreciate that he just traded his life for mine."

By the time he finished speaking, Lucky was in Melissa's face, his eyes wide, fists clenched like he wanted to hit her. Melissa cringed under his intimidating presence.

Raised voices brought Lasonya from the bedroom just in time to stop Lucky from doing something stupid. "LUCKY, STOP!" Lasonya screamed, holding Quaysha in her arms.

Lucky and Melissa had an angry stare-off. A part of him was thankful that Lasonya had showed up when she did to stop him from ending up back in prison. "I'ma pick up my shit later. Fuck you. I'm out this bitch!" he spat before walking away.

"Lucky! Lucky, wait!" Melissa called after him.

He didn't turn around or break a stride as he walked out the front door.

"Don't chase him, Melissa. Just let him go. I'll talk to him," Lasonya said before taking Quaysha outside. Lucky was walking to his Mustang. "Lucky, hold on. I need a ride."

He didn't look up or stop. He unlocked the door and hopped in the car. Lasonya had just made it to the door when the engine started.

"Damn, man. Let me get my daughter in the car," she complained as she sat in the passenger seat with Quaysha on her lap.

Lucky finally stopped being mad long enough for his passengers to get situated. "My bad. I'm just tired of her bullshit. My brother just put his life on the line to save all our asses, and she act like she don't see it. We all good, but he in jail. She tripping."

"Mommy, Uncle Lucky said another bad word," Quaysha whispered.

"I know, baby. Uncle Lucky is mad right now," she told her daughter. "I'm just glad you didn't hit her. I thought you was for a minute. We don't need you back in jail over nothing stupid."

"I was just so mad. I'm tired of her sh- I mean, stuff. All she did was complain, and it's draining my energy. I got other stuff to worry about than a nagging girlfriend. I'm worried about Desmond. They might be charging him with two homicides."

"I can't believe they took him to jail. What happened to self-defense? What happened to the detective that was supposed to help us?"

"I don't know. I didn't trust that fag anyway. Forget the police. They can't be trusted either. None of them. I called him a lawyer and I'm just waiting to hear back. Hopefully he tells me something soon. Where you wanna go? I'm not going back to Melissa's house. I'm done."

"I don't know. I really don't know what to do. Polo looking for my daughter. I can't go back home because Desmond killed Wacco's friend and he might be looking for me. I don't really feel safe nowhere without Desmond. Where you going?"

Lucky took a moment to think. "I don't know. I don't really got nowhere to go either. I put all my eggs in one basket staying with Melissa. But I'ma have to make my way to see my P.O. before the day is out. I gotta let him know what happened."

The car became silent for a few moments. "Can you take me to my mother's house? You can probably stay there for a little while. At least until you figure out where you're going to stay. My mother loved you and Desmond. She used to let y'all spend the night when we was little."

"I got you."

Twenty minutes later, Lucky parked the Mustang in front of Marcy's house. Lasonya's mother ran from the porch to embrace her daughter and granddaughter.

"Oh, thank you Jesus for protecting my babies! Thank you, Lord!" she praised, grabbing Quaysha from Lasonya's arms. "Hey, Lucky. Y'all come on in the house."

"Hi, Marcy." He nodded as he followed them into the house.

As soon as they were safely inside, Marcy turned to Lasonya, a motherly scold upon her face. "Why the hell didn't you come over after that boy got killed at yo' house? Why you wait til more bodies got dropped before you came to see me? Got me in here worried about you and my grandbaby. I should crack you upside yo' head for having me up in here worried."

"I couldn't, Mama. I couldn't come to where nobody knew me. The police that was supposed to help us told me to stay with Desmond."

"So what's supposed to happen now? What they gon' do with Desmond?"

"We don't know. They took him to jail."

"I got him a lawyer, so hopefully he'll call me and let me know something soon," Lucky spoke up.

"What about self-defense? Them niggas had guns and tried to take my grandbaby. Did y'all tell 'em that?"

"They know."

"Damn, Desmond is my nigga," Marcy lamented. "I hope they don't try to send him to prison. And why is this nigga tryna take my grandbaby? Who is he?"

"It's Polo. Tony's people killed his niece yesterday and now he wants her," Lasonya explained.

Marcy got indignant. "Ain't nobody gon' touch my grandbaby, I swear to God! Where that nigga at? I'll pop a cap in him right now. Let me go get my heat. I got thirty-eight bullets with Polo's name on it. Let him try."

"I don't think we gotta worry about him for a while. Desmond messed his boys up and got him hot," Lucky explained. "He probably laying low for a while."

"Good. When he come out of hiding, let me know, 'cause I'ma put him in a Ziploc bag," Marcy promised. "And you not going back home, Lasonya. You and Quaysha staying here with me. I wish a nigga would try to run up in here. I bet they gon' limp out that door or leave on a stretcher, and I put that on everythang I love."

"Yes, ma'am. Lucky might need somewhere to stay, too. Him and his girlfriend just broke up."

Marcy turned to Lucky. "I'm sorry to hear that. I only got two bedrooms, but you can have the couch if you want it."

"I was thinking about renting a hotel room," Lucky said.

Marcy shrugged. "Just let me know. My door gon' be open."

"Granny, I'm hungry. Can I have some cereal?" Quaysha asked.

"You sure can, baby. What kind you want? I got Captain Crunch and Fruity Pebbles."

"I want Fruity Pebbles!" she sang before running towards the kitchen.

"You don't have to stay in a hotel. You can stay here," Lasonya said.

"I know. But I think I need to be by myself for a li'l while. Figure some things out and get my mind right. You good?"

She nodded, looking sad to see him leave. "Yes. Call me if you hear something about Desmond."

"I will. And call me if you need anything," he said, opening his arms for an embrace. "Tell Marcy I had to go."

"All right, bro."

After leaving Marcy's house, Lucky hopped in the Mustang and called his P.O.

"Probation and parole. This is Gary."

"Gary, this is Larry Harrison. You got a minute?"

"Sure, Larry. What's going on? You good?"

Lucky let out a long breath. "Nah, not really. I had some police contact about one o'clock this morning. My brother killed somebody at my house and I had to give a statement."

"Whoa, Larry. Hang on. This sounds serious. I might need you to come in. Where are you now?"

"I'm in my car driving. I got into it with my girl and I have to find a new spot to live. I'm thinking about a hotel."

"Damn, Larry. You have a lot going on this morning. Um, yeah. I think I need you to come in so we can talk."

"C'mon, Gary. I know how this finna go. I was locked up with a million niggas that got they parole revoked for being in the wrong place at the wrong time. Don't tell me you finna lock me up, man. I didn't do nothing. I did the right thing by calling you and letting you know. The police didn't arrest me. I'm good."

"I need to find out what happened and how you was involved in this. I can't promise you that you won't be locked up. You just told me that your brother killed someone. I have to find out what happened. This is serious. Were you involved?"

Lucky paused to think about a response. If he admitted to being involved in the shooting, he would be locked up for sure. And the one thing he didn't want is to go back to prison. He still had ten years left on parole and hadn't even been out a full three months. But if he lied or didn't turn himself in, he would be locked up for sure. Damn. He was stuck in between a rock and a hard place.

"Larry, talk to me. I need you to come in," Gary spoke when Lucky didn't answer.

"Okay. I'm on my way. I'll be there in thirty minutes."

After hanging up the phone, Lucky closed his eyes, laying his head against the headrest. He couldn't turn himself in. He didn't want to go back to jail. Not even for a day. He had seen niggas get revoked and sent back to prison for situations way less complicated than this. Scorned girlfriends called P.O.'s all the time and alleged an attack. Even though no crime was committed, niggas got sent back up north for allegations. This morning two people died and he was involved in the situation up to his ears. A prison sentence was certain. Damn.

The ringing of his phone brought him from thoughts of a prison cell and back to the moment. It was his daughter.

"What up, Laronda?"

"I need a ride. Come get me."

Lucky pulled the phone away from his ear and looked at it like he was staring in Laronda's face. "You asking me to come get you, right?"

She smacked her lips. "Yeah."

"Well, ask me then."

She huffed and puffed like he was getting on her nerves. "I need a ride. Can you come pick me up? Please," she said, her voice dripping with attitude.

Lucky knew he had to put her in her place and he wasn't about to do it over the phone. "You finna watch how you talk to me. Where you at? I'm on my way."

"I'm on 64th and Silver Spring. In Westlawn."

Lucky was only five minutes away from the housing project. When he pulled onto 64th, he sent a text letting her know he was outside.

A few moments later, the adult teenager walked from one of the row houses. She wore next to nothing for clothes. Her cleavage spilled from the halter top and ass was hanging out the bottom of booty shorts. She power walked towards his Mustang like somebody was chasing her from the house. Right when she got to the passenger door, the front door of the row house opened and a tall, dark-skinned nigga with wild dreads stormed outside.

"Ay, bitch! Get'cho ass back in here right now!"

"Fuck you, Troy. You bitch-ass nigga! You ain't finna keep hitting me," Laronda snapped as she snatched open the passenger door.

"Who is that?" Lucky asked, eyeing the man as he speed walked to the car.

"Fuck him. Can you pull off? Hurry up," she said, with fear in her voice and in her eyes.

Seeing his daughter's fear pissed Lucky off.

"Bitch, you tryna fuck wit' anotha nigga? Hell nah! Get the fuck out the car!" the jealous man yelled, snatching the passenger door open.

"Get the fuck away from my car, nigga!" Lucky snapped as he jumped from the car and ran to the passenger side.

Troy let go of the door and poked his chest out. "You betta get'cho bitch ass back in the car 'fore I fade you, nigga," he mugged, grabbing his nuts.

Lucky didn't have time to think about his actions. He just reacted and started throwing punches. Troy caught a couple in the face before going down. Instead of stopping, Lucky began stomping the young nigga. All of the frustration he'd felt since coming home was released on the youngster. All the times he got into it with Melissa. His hatred for Wacco. His desire to kill Polo. His frustration at not being able to help Desmond.

"Lucky, stop! You gonna kill him!" Laronda screamed, grabbing his arm to pull him away from Troy.

When Lucky came to his senses, he saw the damage. Troy was laid out on the ground, unconscious, and bleeding from several facial wounds.

"Shit," he panicked. "Get in the car! We gotta go!"

◆◆◆

"Oh, my God, Lucky! I think he might be dead!" Laronda panicked.

"He a'ight. Who was that nigga?" Lucky asked, trying to act nonchalant but hoping he hadn't killed the man.

"Troy. A nobody. Damn. You fucked him up."

"He had that shit coming. Why you and him fighting?"

She cut her eyes at him. "Damn. You nosy."

He took his eyes off the road to mug her. "I just went out my way to pick you up and whooped somebody's ass over you. I ain't being nosy enough. What was the shit about?"

"A jealous and insecure nigga. Think he a pimp or my daddy."

"So them the kinda niggas you deal with? The ones that don't got no respect for you?"

Laronda smacked her lips and rolled her eyes. "I know you ain't finna try to play the daddy role after you been gone my whole life. It's too late for that shit. I'm good."

"I didn't even know you was my daughter until a couple days ago. Don't be mad at me. Be mad at yo' mama. I was just tryna see about yo' situation. But if you wanna be like that, I don't give no fuck. Just don't be callin' me and making demands. Ask me. Where you wanna go?"

She didn't respond right away. She folded her arms over her chest and sucked the back of her teeth like a spoiled child. "Take me to my mama's house."

They rode in silence for a while, Lucky thinking about his upcoming incarceration. "I might have to go away for a li'l while."

"Where?" she asked, her voice filled with attitude.

"I think my P.O. finna lock me up. My brother, your uncle Desmond, killed some people at my house this morning. Since I was there, my parole officer wanted me to come in. I think they gon' lock me up. I was on my way to his office before you called."

Compassion shone in the young girl's eyes. "Why he locking you up? You didn't do nothing, right?"

He shook his head. "It don't matter. I'm on parole for killing somebody. They be locking niggas up for less."

"Damn. That's bogus. How long they gon' keep you for?"

"I don't know. I got ten years parole. If push come to shove, they can give me the whole ten."

Her eyes popped. "Ten years!"

"Yeah. I just got out from doing fourteen. I can do it if I have to, but I don't want to."

Laronda was quiet for a moment. "Can I come see you?" she asked, a childlike tenderness in her voice.

Lucky glanced at her, surprised by the show of emotion. "Yeah. I hope you do."

When she smiled, Lucky's heart melted. There was something growing between them. Some kind of bond was building, and he liked it. For the first time since he met her, he saw the child that she was.

"My mama said you wrote some books. Can I read one?"

"Yeah. I got some in the trunk. I'ma give 'em to you when we get to the house."

"I don't think you should turn yo'self in. I know I wouldn't. Why not just run until they catch you, since they gon' lock you up anyway?"

Lucky thought on the answer. "I'm trying to do the right thing. I don't wanna be on the run for the rest of my life. Having to always look over your shoulder ain't free."

"Being in jail ain't free either," she countered.

"You smart." Lucky laughed.

When they pulled up to Laronda's house, he went to the trunk to get her some books. "I want you to tell me what you think. Make sure you be honest. Don't spare my feelings."

"I won't." She smiled.

An awkward moment passed between them. Lucky wondered if they were supposed to hug or if he should maybe tell her that he loved her.

"Make sure you call me if they lock you up so I can have your address. I'll write you too."

Lucky nodded. "I will. Wait. I want to give you something. This was your grandmother's. This is the only possession I got of hers, and I want to give it to you," he said, taking off the small gold chain and crucifix and giving it to his daughter.

She twisted her face at the cheap piece of jewelry. "What is this?"

"Don't think about the price. Think about what it means, and that makes it worth more than diamonds."

She smirked. "You blowin' me, Lucky. But okay. Thank-"

Her words were cut short by the loud revving of a car engine. The father and daughter looked up just as a black G6 skidded to a stop a few feet away. Two tall, skinny niggas jumped out brandishing semiautomatic handguns. They ran at Lucky and Laronda.

"Get in the car, bitch!" one of them yelled, yanking Laronda by the arm.

"Stop! Let her go!" Lucky attempted, grabbing the man roughing up his daughter.

"No! Stop, Quest! Let me go!" Laronda resisted, dropping the books and the chain.

"Quit fighting, bitch!" he yelled, slapping the girl across the face.

"Sit cho bitch ass down, nigga!" the other man yelled, slapping Lucky upside the head with his pistol.

Lucky's lights went out and he fell down.

"And gimme yo' keys and phone!" the man yelled, going in Lucky's pockets and taking his possessions.

"Stop! Leave him alone!" Laronda yelled, struggling to get free of the man's grasp and protect her father. Her attempts were useless. They dragged the teenager to the car and sped away.

Lucky lifted himself up from the street slowly, trying to gain his bearings as he stumbled up on Sharday's porch and began beating in the door.

"Sharday! Sharday, open the door! They took Laronda!"

"Wait a minute. Hold on," Sharday called from behind the door. When the door opened, Sharday stood swaying like a tree blowing in the wind, her eyes low like she was sleepy.

"Somebody took Laronda!" Lucky screamed.

The words seemed to barely have an effect on Sharday. "What? Where she at?" she asked groggily, leaning against the wall.

"I don't know. She said his name is Quest."

Sharday didn't seem the least bit concerned. She waved a hand and blew him off, her head rolling around on her shoulders like it was about to fall off. "Quest is Polo's friend. She okay."

"Nah, they had guns. She in trouble. She - " Lucky stopped talking when he realized Sharday was barely listening to him. He took a second to study how she was acting and realized she was high. The sight reminded him of Cookie and pissed him off. He grabbed her face between his hands and began squeezing her jaws. "Listen to what the fuck I'm telling you, bitch! Them niggas just kidnapped our daughter!"

Sharday pulled away from him. "Damn, man. I heard you. But she a big girl. She got it."

Lucky pushed past her and walked in the house, pacing the living room, stressing about the whereabouts of his daughter. Did Polo send his boys to take her, or was this all some kind of misunderstanding? And if he did send them to take her, why didn't they take him? And how did Polo find out she was his daughter?

"You sure Quest took her?" Sharday asked, trying to fight the foggy mind created by sniffing heroin.

"Yeah. This is serious, Sharday. I need you awake. Do you know where Quest live or where he be at?"

"Yeah." She yawned. "I told you he Polo's friend. Ain't you and Polo friends? Polo my nigga, I know he wouldn't do that. You sure?"

"Listen. Desmond killed Scooter and another one of Polo's niggas this morning. They doing this to get back. Did you tell Polo she was my daughter?"

Sharday's head drooped for a moment before she nodded away. "I don't know. What you say? I'm sorry, I didn't hear you."

Lucky lost his cool and reached his arm back like he was trying to touch another state. He brought it forward with all his might and slapped the shit out of Sharday. Then he grabbed her by the collar of her shirt and lifted her from her feet until they were face to face. "Bitch, listen to what the fuck I'm saying! Where the fuck do Quest and Polo be at?"

"Damn, Lucky. You didn't have to hit me," she mumbled, the high not really allowing her to feel pain. "They be over on Florist. Ouch. That shit hurt."

When Lucky released Sharday, she fell to the floor like dead weight. He was halfway to the door when he remembered that he didn't have a phone or car keys. He ran back to grab Sharday's phone and called Lasonya.

"Hello?"

"Lasonya, this Lucky. Polo just had his niggas take my daughter. I need a ride."

Chapter 3

"Why didn't you tell me you were being investigated by the police?" Brandon asked, staring at Desmond angrily. Confusion lit Desmond's eyes. "I don't know what you're talking about. I'm not being investigated. Am I?" Brandon let out a sarcastic chuckle. "So this the game you wanna play?" he asked, giving a nod. "One thing I don't do is play games. Find somebody else to represent you," he said before spinning for the door. "Wait!" Desmond called, sounding like a desperate man as he leapt from his chair. "I swear to God I don't know what you're talking about. I didn't know I was being investigated. For what?"

Brandon paused, turning to study Desmond. He saw the sincerity in Desmond's eyes and realized he was telling the truth. The lawyer relaxed and sat down. "The detective that was killed the other day was working with the district attorney investigating your connection with Polo, the same guy you said tried to take your girlfriend's daughter. This ain't making no sense to me, Desmond. I need you to clear up some things if I'm going to move forward representing you. What the hell is going on?"

Desmond thought for a moment. The news about him being investigated for a connection to Polo was new. How? Why? It didn't make sense. He was working with Detective Perry to get Polo. How could he be getting investigated for what he was helping the cop with?

"Honestly, I didn't know I was being investigated. It don't make sense because I was working with Detective Perry to help get Polo. He promised to make another situation disappear if I helped."

Brandon looked like he was about to have a stroke. "Wait a second. Are you saying you were working with Detective Perry to get Polo while also working with Polo to save your brother?"

Desmond nodded. "Yeah. It was complicated, but my brother being out here with me means everything. He just did fourteen years for fucking with Polo and I wanted to protect him."

27

Brandon nodded, finally understanding. "Okay. I need you to tell me the exact terms of you and the detective's agreement. And what situation was he supposed to make disappear? I need to know everything, so start from the beginning."

"Okay. My mother got killed a couple months ago. Niggas in a turf war on Clarke got into a shootout and she got hit. Detective Perry is the one who called and told me she was dead and that her killers would probably never be found. I came back to the States to bury her and ended up running into some of the Clarke Street Goons. I killed one and fucked the other one up while also learning who actually killed my mother. Somebody seen what I did and CSG put a green light on me. Somehow Detective Perry found out and approached me with the deal to help him get Polo. That was before my brother and Polo did what they did. That forced me to make a deal with Polo to clear my brother."

"What did your brother and Polo do? What happened?"

"Polo helped find the trigger man that killed my mother. My brother shot him and Polo kept the gun to use it as leverage. I went to get it, and me and Polo made a deal. Three wishes."

"And the three wishes were?"

Desmond looked at the door nervously. "I'd rather not say."

"C'mon, Desmond. You gotta trust me, man. I need to know everything."

"I want to tell you, but not in here. What if they're listening?"

Brandon could see the look in Desmond's eyes and knew he was onto something monumental. He pulled out a small notepad and pen. "Okay. Write it down and rip it up as soon as I read it."

Desmond took the pen and began writing.

3 kills.

"Who?" Brandon asked, feeling his body grow warm with excitement and anticipation.

Made Nigga Mario. Detective Perry. And my girlfriend's daughter.

Brandon's eyes grew as wide as a full moon on a clear night. "Shit! Rip it up! Hurry up!"

Desmond ripped the sheet of paper from the pad and ate it, making sure there was no evidence.

"Can you be connected to them? Obviously you didn't do the third one, right?"

Desmond shook his head. "Nah. That's why I had to kill them. And I don't think I can be physically connected anything. I was careful."

Brandon took a moment to think. "Damn, Desmond. This is some deep shit. Sounds like a movie plot. Damn. I'm really confused on how to make my next move. This is serious. Okay, is there anybody that knows about the deal you made with Detective Perry?"

"Yeah. My girlfriend Lasonya, and my brother. They were at one of our meets and my girl was supposed to help with the investigation as well."

Brandon nodded. "Okay. That could help. I'll contact them and get some statements. The district attorney wants to interview you. I will be in the room with you. My guess is it's about your connection to Polo and the killings this morning. We'll see. I'm going to let him know we're ready. If I tell you not to answer, don't say a word."

Mitchell Sellers looked like a politician. Mid-forties, tall, and portly around the midsection. He had graying hair, sharp eyes, and a serious face. He wore a tailored gray suit and walked with the air of an important person. He entered the room followed by another important-looking man wearing a police uniform with a lot of medals on the breast. Captain Morales had been the police chief for less than a year. Ten months and fourteen days, to be exact. His presence was required during this interview to make sure all procedures were followed.

"Good afternoon, gentlemen. I've heard a lot about you, Brandon." The city prosecutor nodded as he extended a hand to the attorney.

"Nice to meet you." Brandon nodded.

"Desmond, I'm District Attorney Mitchell Sellers and this is the Chief of Police, Captain Morales. I want to ask you some questions about the shooting this morning. Is that okay?"

Desmond looked to Brandon. The attorney nodded.

"Yeah. That's fine."

"I'm going to record this. Is that okay?"

"Yeah," Desmond agreed.

Mitchell set a recording device in the middle of the table and pressed record. "Okay. I'd like to ask you some questions. I looked into your background a little and see that you're in the military. What branch?"

"I'm in the Navy."

"You a sailor?"

"Not exactly. A SEAL."

The district attorney didn't look surprised. "Tell me what happened this morning."

"I was in bed when I heard the doorbell. It was late and we weren't expecting any visitors, so I grabbed my gun. I looked out the peephole and seen three people on the porch. Two of them were armed."

"Did you know them?"

"Yeah. Two of them. Polo and Scooter."

"And how did you know them?"

"I knew Polo since we were kids. I just met Scooter a couple weeks ago through Polo."

"Okay. Continue. What happened next?"

"When I stepped outside, Polo told me that his niece got killed and that he wanted my girlfriend's daughter."

Mitchell looked confused. "Why would he want your girlfriend's daughter? Did you kill his niece?"

"No. Polo said my girlfriend's daughter's father did it and he wanted Quaysha to get back at him."

"Is his niece the child that was killed at the mall the other day?" the chief asked.

Desmond shrugged. "I don't know. He didn't say."

"Okay. And then what happened?"

"When I told him they weren't getting Quaysha, they tried to shoot us. I shot the guy I didn't know in the face and kicked the other one. When I took my eyes off him to check on Polo, he tried to shoot me and I shot him. Polo ran away."

The police chief looked skeptical. "And you did all this by yourself? With one good eye and a cast on your arm? You didn't have any help?"

"No. I did it all by myself."

"Where was your brother while all of this was going on?" Mitchell asked.

"In the house with our girls. They didn't start coming outside until the shooting," Desmond said, delivering the story they'd rehearsed. If possible, he wanted to take all the blame.

"What if I told you I knew you were lying?" Mitchell smirked, staring Desmond dead in the eyes with a smug look upon his face.

"I'm not lying. That's what happened," Desmond said, meeting the district attorney's stare. He could tell Mitchell knew something, but Desmond stood strong and stuck to the script.

"Okay," Mitchell smirked. "We'll come back to that later. Do you know Detective Perry?"

Desmond looked at his lawyer. Brandon nodded. "Yes. He told me my mother died."

"Did you kill him?"

Desmond remained stone-faced, not showing any emotion. Brandon wasn't so stoic. He jumped to his feet like he was in court. "Whoa, Mitchell! What kinda shit is that?"

The district attorney didn't even acknowledge Brandon's overreaction. He stayed focused on Desmond. "The detective was killed by someone throwing knives from a hundred feet away. I don't know too many people with the skill to pull that off. But there is one in this room."

"Don't answer that, Desmond! This is bullshit!" Brandon huffed and puffed. "My client is not under arrest, nor do you have any evidence that he killed the detective, and I would strongly advise you not to bring any unnecessary allegations into this interview.

We agreed to talk about the shooting this morning. That's it. This is not an interrogation."

Mitchell continued to stare at Desmond with an "I know you did it" look in his eyes. "Fine, Counsel. Okay, Desmond. I'm going to stop the bullshit. Detective Perry told me about the deal you and he made for the murder investigation into Billy Cannon, a.k.a. Big Man, to disappear. And I'm here to tell you that since Detective Perry is no longer with us and he never got official authorization from his bosses to make such a deal, that investigation is back on and you will be arrested for the murder of Billy Cannon. We have a witness putting you there. Would you like to make a statement?"

"No, he doesn't want to make a statement," Brandon interjected. "Matter of fact, this interview is over. If you're going to arrest him, then do it. If not, I want to leave with my client right now."

Mitchell nodded towards the Chief of Police. Captain Morales stood and pulled out his cuffs. "Desmond, you are being arrested for the murder of Billy Cannon. Anything you say can and will be used against you in the court of law…"

Chapter 4

"Who took Laronda!?" Lasonya asked, her eyes wide with alarm.

A pained look played across Lucky's face as he climbed in the passenger seat of the blue Ford Explorer. "A nigga named Quest. It's one of Polo's niggas," he said mournfully, like it hurt to say the words. "He took her right in front of me and it wasn't nothing I could do about it."

"Are you sure it was Polo's niggas? Why didn't they do anything to you?"

"I asked myself that, and I don't know. I never seen them niggas before and they never seen me. Maybe they wasn't looking for me because they don't know what I look like. I think they just came for her. I gotta get her back. Take me to they hood."

Lasonya didn't drive away. She looked at him like he was crazy. "For what? What are you gonna do if they try to hurt us? Do you have a gun?"

Lucky's body shook with anger and frustration. "Nah, but I gotta do something. I can't just let them niggas get away with taking my shorty. Just head over on Florist so I can see if they outside. I just wanna see."

"Lucky, I don't think - "

"JUST TAKE ME OVER THERE SO I CAN LOOK!" he exploded.

The display of anger made Lasonya shrink back a little. When Lucky realized his outburst had scared her, he calmed down and spoke a little softer. "My bad, Lasonya. I'm frustrated and mad as fuck. I need to see the scene. I need to see how I'ma make my next move. Please."

Lasonya reluctantly pulled away from the curb. She didn't want to go into the lion's den, especially when they wanted her daughter too. But the pain in Lucky's eyes made her want to help. If she was in his position, she would be trying to do all she could to get her daughter back. "What did Sharday say? Did she know that Polo had something to do with this?"

Lucky ran a hand over his face. "She laid on the couch high on dope. I had to slap her ass just to find out where these niggas be at. She gone."

Lasonya shook her head. "Damn. That's so fucked up."

The drive was short. Five minutes later Lasonya turned onto Florist and Lucky sat up in the seat, looking around in all directions. "Just ride down the block so I can see if I see something."

Lasonya drove slowly. There was a group of men standing on the porch of a green and black house that caught Lucky's eye. One of them was Quest.

"That's him," he breathed, wishing he had a pistol. The men on the porch eyed the truck as it drove by and Quest pointed a finger gun like he was shooting.

"Did they see us?" Lasonya asked.

"I'm not sure. You can keep going. I just wanted to see the hood. Now I know where they at."

"What are you going to do? I hope you don't do nothing crazy."

Lucky looked at his hands as if they were covered in blood. "Shit, me too."

When Lasonya pulled to the stop sign at the corner, she glanced in the rearview mirror. The men were running from the porch. "I think they about to come after us."

Lucky looked over his shoulder and saw them getting in a white Charger. "Shit. Pull off!"

Lasonya mashed the gas pedal, making the Ford Explorer's tires screech as she sped away. "I got a gun in the glove box!"

Lucky yanked the compartment open and found a fully-loaded Glock inside. He checked to make sure there was a bullet in the chamber and clicked off the safety. "Where you get this?"

"From my mama. She didn't want me to leave without it," Lasonya said as she whipped the truck through traffic. The Charger caught up to them quickly and rode the bumper. Lucky spun in the seat to watch out the back window. That's when he saw the passenger lean out with window with a Draco.

"Shit! Duck down!" he called as shots rang out.

Brrrrreaaaaatttt!

34

The back window exploded, sending glass flying as bullets thudded into the frame of the truck. Lasonya got low, barely able to see over the steering wheel while continuing to whip the truck. Lucky spun around and crouched low in the seat, trying to get a good shot at the passenger. The nigga with the Draco continued hanging out the window, firing shots. Lasonya whipped the truck in a hard right turn, attempting to elude the Charger and giving Lucky the opportunity he needed. When the sports car turned behind them, the gunman stopped shooting to hang onto the car so as not to fall. Lucky stuck his arm out the window and let the pistol ride.

Pop, pop, pop, pop, pop, pop, pop, pop, pop!

The shooter caught a couple bullets to the body and fell out of the window, rolling in the street like road kill. Feeling a desire to spill more blood, Lucky pointed the pistol at the shattered back window and began squeezing the trigger until all the bullets were gone.

Pop, pop, pop, pop, pop, pop, pop, pop, pop!

The Charger dipped to the side of the street and stopped chasing, its windshield riddled with bullets

"We good. You can slow down," Lucky told her, falling back in the seat and breathing a sigh of relief.

Lasonya lifted her head slowly, checking the rearview mirror. "Damn, that shit was crazy!" she panicked.

"We good." Lucky nodded. "That just let me know how real shit is. We gotta get off the street. Need to hide yo' truck. Take us somewhere we can duck off."

Lasonya drove for five minutes before parking the truck in an alley behind a black and white house on 47th and Congress.

"Who live here?" Lucky asked as they climbed from the truck.

"My friend, Annie. She cool. C'mon," Lasonya said, leading the way to the back door. After a couple knocks, she waited.

"Who is it?" a female called from inside.

"Lasonya."

The door opened and a heavyset white woman with brown box braids answered. She had very large breasts and her smile showed off a bottom row of platinum teeth.

"Hey, bitch! What'chu doin' 'round these parts?" she yelled excitedly as the women hugged.

"I need some help. Can I come in?" Lasonya said, her serious demeanor curbing the excitement at not seeing a friend in ages.

Annie's jolly attitude changed to serious. "Yeah, come in. You okay?"

"Nah. This is my brother, Lucky. We need somewhere to chill for a li'l while," Lasonya said as they walked in the house.

Annie nodded at Lucky before taking a look around outside and closing the door. "Sit down." She gestured towards the kitchen table. "What's going on?"

"For starters, I need somewhere to hide my truck. Somebody just tried to kill us."

Annie's green eyes grew wide as two sunny side up eggs. "Shut the fuck up! You serious?"

Lasonya nodded. "I'm not playing. Girl, you wouldn't believe all the shit we been though the last couple days. This nigga Polo tried to take my daughter this morning and my boyfriend killed some of his niggas and got locked up. Then some more of his niggas just shot up my truck."

Annie's eyes remained wide in disbelief. "Dayum, bitch! What the fuck you got goin' on? How the fuck you get into it wit' Polo? Why they tryna take yo' daughter and kill y'all?"

"It wasn't me. It was my baby daddy. His niggas killed Polo's niece. Now he wants my daughter and he just took my brother's daughter."

"Oh, my God!" Annie shook her head. "Damn. You can hide yo' truck in my garage, I guess. I ain't seen yo' ass in forever and then you show up wit' all kinds of drama. This is some crazy-ass shit. So, what y'all finna do? You know Polo heavy out here. He not gon' stop coming at y'all."

"I don't know," Lasonya mumbled, looking to Lucky.

"You know Polo?" Lucky asked.

"Shit, er'body on the north side damn near know Polo. I don't know him personally, but my man do. He out in the streets right now, but he gon' be back later."

"You talkin' 'bout Trevor?" Lasonya asked.

"Yeah. Who else would I be talking about? He ain't goin' nowhere and I ain't either."

"Yo' man know him personally? Like, they cool?" Lucky asked.

"I wouldn't say they cool, but they do business every now and then."

Lucky looked to Lasonya. "How you feel about this?"

"Trevor is cool, man. We good."

"My man gon' do whatever I say, and one thang he ain't gon' do is touch my girl, Lasonya," Annie said confidently. "Y'all good. I gotta go to work at two o'clock, but y'all can stay here. I get off at ten. I'ma text Trevor and let him know y'all here."

"Thanks, sis. I owe you for this one."

"Don't even lean on it, baby gurl. I got you. I got some loud and black label Jack Daniels. Y'all look stressed. Y'all want some?"

"I'll take a drink," Lasonya said, looking to Lucky.

"I'll take 'em both," he said.

Annie left the kitchen to get the libations.

"What about your P.O.? Don't you have to see him?" Lasonya asked.

"I think he tryna lock me up. I'm not going in until I find Laronda."

"C'mon, Lucky. You sure you wanna do this?"

He let out a stressed breath. "Not really. But I can't go in when my daughter missing. Ain't no telling when I'ma get back out or what Polo might do to her. I gotta stay out here and try to get her back."

Annie came back in the kitchen and set a bottle of liquor and a blunt on the table. "Here you go. Come out here with me and put that truck up."

After Annie left for work, Lucky and Lasonya sat around smoking and drinking. It had been awhile since Lucky had mixed the weed with liquor and the combination had his mind wandering. Specifically about Lasonya. Even though he was in drama up to his eyeballs, he couldn't deny that his brother's women was fine and thick. She made him think of the pretty young woman he met at the book signing, Natasha with the green eyes. Trying to fuck Lasonya had never crossed his mind, but he had also never been home alone with her while they were buzzed. And now that he thought about fucking her, he couldn't stop thinking about it.

"Why you looking like that?" Lasonya asked, interrupting his lustful thoughts.

Lucky's eyes grew wide like she could read his mind. "What? What you talking about?"

His reaction made Lasonya bust out laughing. "What the fuck wrong with you, nigga?"

Seeing her laugh made Lucky laugh. A few moments later they were both doubled over, laughing their asses off.

"Damn, that shit was smoking!" Lucky managed after their laughter subsided. "I'm high as a mu'fucka. I gotta find out if she got some more of that."

"I know. I'm so high." Lasonya giggled, stretching her arms over her head and poking out her chest.

Lucky's eyes zeroed in on her nipples poking through her T-shirt.

"You know what I need now?" Lasonya asked, staring at Lucky intently and licking her lips.

Lucky's dick stirred in his pants as a quick picture of fucking Lasonya from the back flashed in his mind. "Is you thinkin' what I'm thinking?"

She nodded, her smile growing wide. "I'm hungry as fuck. I got the munchies. Let's go see what they got to eat," she said before heading to the kitchen.

Lucky didn't follow her immediately, taking a few moments to gather his thoughts and adjust his dick through his pants. He was hard and horny as hell. "Damn, I'm tripping. My daughter got kidnapped and my brother in jail. What the fuck is wrong with me?" he questioned.

"Lucky, come here! Oh my God!" Lasonya screamed excitedly.

When he walked into the kitchen, Lasonya was bending over, digging through the refrigerator. Her ass looked better than any food that was in the icebox and he couldn't take his eyes off of it.

"They got pineapple upside down cake!" she said excitedly, spinning around and catching Lucky looking at her ass. They had an awkward stare. In Lasonya's mind, she was wondering if she had really just caught him looking at her ass.

Lucky's eye's reflected his true feelings. He had been caught. He was down to fuck if she was.

"You want some?" she asked, breaking the awkward silence. Lucky allowed the lust to overtake good judgement. He knew she was talking about giving him some pussy and he was ready. He closed the distance between them quickly, leaning forward and kissing her lips. Lasonya froze, lifting her hands in the air and refusing to touch him. But that didn't stop Lucky. He grabbed her hips and pushed her backwards until she was against the sink.

Lasonya wanted to push him away and tell him to stop, but couldn't get the words out. The danger of the shootout and seeing Lucky in action was exciting. Plus, the weed and liquor had her horny. The risk of getting caught added to the excitement and the next thing she knew, she was kissing him back. Lucky reached down, unbuttoning her pants and trying to get them past her wide hips.

"Wait, Lucky," Lasonya broke the kiss. "We can't do this."

"Yes we can," he breathed, kissing her again. He was already past the point of no return and wanted to finish.

Lasonya turned her face and tried to push him away. "No, Lucky. We can't. Stop."

Lucky didn't stop. He became more aggressive, rubbing her breasts, gripping her ass, and kissing her neck. Lasonya gave in to the lust and went for the bulge in his pants. She unbuckled them, freeing his throbbing meat stick and stroking him roughly.

"Mmmm, yeah!" Lucky groaned. "Turn around. Bend over," he said, spinning her around and snatching her pants and panties down to her ankles.

Lasonya bent over the sink, biting her lips and looking back over her shoulder while Lucky slipped inside her. "Oh shit!"

When Lucky stuck his dick in her treasure, he almost busted a nut. He imagined she had a wet shot, but didn't think it would be this good. Her goodies were tight and wet as the ocean. He didn't even wait for her to adjust to him. He just started hitting it hard.

"Oh yeah! Oh yeah! Hit it harder. Hit it harder!" Lasonya cried, throwing her ass back against his pelvis.

Lucky used one hand to grab the back of her neck while gripping her hip with the other. He drove into her as hard and fast as he could, watching her ass bounce and jiggle. When he felt his nut building, he didn't even try to prolong it. He went harder.

"Aw shit!" he groaned, going stiff as he exploded inside of her.

The sex act lasted about two minutes. Lucky pulled out of her and stumbled backwards like a drunkard, guilt and regret gripping him instantly.

Lasonya was speechless. She pulled up her clothes and stood against the sink like she was stuck. Then a key being inserted into the lock on the back door got their attention. Both of them adjusted their clothes and ran into separate parts of the house, Lasonya in the living room, Lucky in the bathroom.

A short white man in his early twenties walked in the house. He was average height, a stocky build with dark eyes. His black hair was cut low with a taper, no facial hair except for a small beard. He walked in the living room and saw Lasonya sitting on the couch.

"Trevor, what's up, man?" Lasonya greeted, standing to give him a hug.

"Lasonya, what's good, baby?" He smiled, speaking with a slight lisp. "My girl said you was having some issues."

Lucky walked out of the bathroom wiping his hands and paused when he saw Trevor. Recognition flashed in both men's eyes at the same time.

"Trev?"

"Lucky? What's good, fool?" He smiled, walking over to shake Lucky's hand.

"Aw shit! My nigga, Trev!" Lucky laughed momentarily, forgetting about his indiscretion with Lasonya as the men embraced.

"When you get out, fool?"

"Couple months ago, man. How shit been for you? You been out here all this time?"

Lasonya watched while the men interacted long like long lost friends.

"Hell yeah!" Trevor smiled proudly. "I told y'all I wasn't goin' back. I'm out here to stay. I'm holdin' court in the street if them fags ever run up on me," he said seriously.

Lucky didn't fully agree with him, but he remembered hearing him boast proudly of killing a couple police before he died if they ever tried to send him back to prison. "I hear you, my nigga."

"How y'all know each other?" Lasonya asked.

"Lucky saved my ass when I was in Waupun. Fools tried to jump me for some shit that happened in the streets and Lucky wouldn't let 'em. We was smashing them hoe-ass dudes, huh Luck?" Trevor laughed. "So what kinda trouble y'all in? Annie said y'all had an issue. Y'all need some help?"

"Man, Trev, this shit so crazy out here. The nigga Polo had my daughter kidnapped a couple hours ago."

Trevor's eyes popped. "What? Seriously? You talkin' 'bout Polo off Florist?"

Lucky nodded. "I went through there and his niggas tried to get at us. I got down on them niggas and got 'em off our ass."

Trevor looked surprised. "Damn, Lucky. How the fuck you get into it with Polo? I thought you was writing books and shit. Fuck you get caught up in some street shit?"

"I knew Polo back when niggas called him Sammy D. Shit, that nigga was the reason I did all that time. He popped a nigga we robbed and I got caught. Took that case. Right before I got out, my OG got killed. He helped me catch the nigga that did it. I put in work, but he kept the heat and tried to have his niggas take the body."

"What? He did that after er'thang you sacrificed for that fool?"

"I know. I thought loyalty meant something, but apparently I'm a dinosaur. Niggas selfish and the game so fucked that niggas playing for keeps and thinkin' 'bout they own shit."

"That shit still means something to some of us. But you right, most dudes only thinking 'bout how they can get ahead or get out of a jam. I fuck wit' Polo a li'l bit, but that snake shit got me feelin' some type of way."

"That ain't even the worst. My li'l brother knew Polo was a snake and tried to warn me, but I was blinded by the nigga givin' me a Patek and helping me get the nigga that clapped up OG. But bro wasn't goin'. He holla'd at the nigga and got the burner, but Polo wanted three favors. Desmond did two. For the third one, he wanted her daughter."

Trevor looked at Lasonya. "Fuck he want your shorty for?"

"Wacco is my baby daddy, and I guess some of his niggas killed Polo's niece the other day. Polo wanted to kill my daughter and he wanted Desmond to give her over as the last favor."

Trevor looked blown away by the story. "This sound like some mobster shit. Damn."

"But that ain't it," Lucky added. "My brother a Navy SEAL and killed two of Polo's niggas when they showed up at my crib this morning. Now he locked up. Plus, we into it with them CSG niggas, too. That body that I caught with Polo was Wacco's nephew, Draco. The li'l nigga is the one that killed my OG."

Trevor laughed. "What the fuck, Lucky? You fools out here going crazy! Damn. Y'all don't need my help. Y'all need an army."

"I know." Lucky nodded. "But this where we at. I'm on the run from my P.O. too. Nigga tryna lock me up, but I ain't going until I get my daughter back."

"Fa'sho." Trevor nodded. "I normally don't get into somebody else's shit, especially wit' muthafuckas like Polo and Wacco. But I fuck wit' Lasonya the long way and I'll never forget the real-ass shit you did for me when I was on lock. I got you, and I gotta couple killas that get down for real. We gon' get yo' daughter back or paint they block red with them fools' blood."

The ringing of Lucky's phone got everyone's attention. "Damn," he mumbled.

"What happened?" Lasonya asked.

"It's Desmond's lawyer," he responded before answering. "What's going on, Brandon?"

"They're charging Desmond with murder."

"What? How? It was self-defense."

"It's not for the shooting at your house. They said he killed a guy named Big Man. I'm working on it. I'm going to do everything I can to get him out."

Chained to the Streets 2

Chapter 5

The Attic was where Polo and his most trusted teamsters met to discuss important issues. The meeting place wasn't an actual attic, but an apartment on the top floor of the Washington Heights Apartment Complex. Present at the meeting was the clique's inner circle: Polo, Mace, Lala, and Cash. Seated on a chair across from them was Trice. His timid demeanor showed that he didn't belong in a room amongst bosses. He was here for one reason: a grilling.

"How the fuck you let him get away? Didn't you say it was four of y'all?" Polo breathed angrily.

"Yeah, but we didn't expect the nigga to roll on the block. When I realized it was him, we got on they ass. He killed Squirt and almost killed me. The nigga wasn't sweet."

"We got the nigga's daughter," Mace spoke. "He gon' come to us eventually."

"Why don't we get his girl and her kids? That'll bring his ass out for sure," Lala added.

Cash sat in silence watching the situation unfold, listening to everyone talk and gathering all the information available before speaking. "I think we need to let Lucky do him. What's done is done."

Everyone in the apartment looked at Cash like he had committed high treason.

"You sound crazy as fuck!" Polo spat. "Our niggas dead because of these fuck niggas, and I ain't letting that shit go."

"On the real," Mace added.

"This ain't about our dead niggas. This about bringing heat to the team. I seen the shit online and that nigga screaming self-defense. That means he gotta tell the police what happened and who was involved. Polo, you went to these niggas house and tried to take a li'l girl. Fuck you think was gon' happen? And when the police ask questions, you think they gon' lie? I don't. I think yo' name all through the police paperwork. These ain't no street niggas. These working people. I think you should leave it alone before yo' name get too hot and get all of us hot. Them niggas ain't kill yo' niece. Wacco did. That's who we should be focused on," Cash countered.

"Hold up, brah. Watch yo' step," Polo warned.

Cash waved off the implied threat of violence. "Get out cho feelings, nigga, and listen to what the fuck I'm tryna tell you. Fucking with these niggas is bad for business. You bringing unnecessary heat to the team, and that's gon' fuck up our paper. And I ain't finna let you fuck up the food on my plate."

"So what you saying, nigga?" Polo challenged, the tension in the room ratcheting up several notches.

"Exactly what the fuck I been saying. Pipe down, nigga. Leave Lucky alone and focus on Wacco. He the one that violated. Lucky n'em did what they was supposed to do. Let it go."

"Now that you put it like that, I agree with Cash," Mace said.

"Me too," Lala echoed. "Problems with them people can fuck up the hustle, and you know a bitch 'bout her coins."

Polo looked around the room with disgust in his eyes. "So, we just gon' let them niggas get away with killing our niggas?"

"That blood is on yo' hands," Cash said.

"Y'all niggas ain't shit," Polo huffed as he stood to his feet. "If you want something done, a nigga gotta do it hisself. C'mon, Trice. You wit' me," Polo said before heading for the door.

"Where I'm going?" Trice asked as he followed Polo down the stairs.

"You my new shooter. For now on, you with me er'where I go. And right now I need to get out here and find this nigga Lucky so I can get his bitch ass missing and find Wacco's daughter."

"But what about Cash n'em and what they said?"

Polo paused on the stairwell to glare angrily at Trice. "Do I look like a worker to you, nigga? I'm a boss! I don't answer to no nigga. I said what I'ma do, and that's what gon' happen. Fuck what Cash n'em talkin' 'bout. Now you got any more stupid-ass questions, or can we get the fuck outta here and find Lucky's bitch ass?"

Trice cowered under the anger of his leader. "Nah, I'm good."

"Let's go then, nigga. We in my Infiniti truck," Polo said as they stepped out into the night. They were headed to the SUV when

Polo went in his pocket and pulled out his vibrating iPhone. "Yeah. What's good, Trev?"

"What's good, fool? You know you got the best hand. My man got some shit that I think you might like. You got a minute?"

"Not really. I'm kinda in the middle of somethin'. But what you got?"

"C'mon, fool. You know I don't do these phones. In person." Polo let out a breath. "I really don't got the time right now. Can it wait til tomorrow?"

"Nah. My boy tryna hit that E-way ASAP. The fool he made the move for already bugged and bro tryna get outta town. This is a now or never, my dude. And trust me, you need this. You gon' be kickin yo'self in the ass if you let this one go."

Polo paused outside the Infiniti truck to think for a moment. "Okay. Meet me at the shop. I'ma be there in like twenty minutes."

"Bet."

♦♦♦

"Shit too easy." Trevor smiled.

"How you wanna hit 'em?" Lucky asked, anxious to get on the move.

"Me and my boys going in first. Let us do some recon."

"That's what I'm talking about." Tyler grinned, stroking the 12-gauge riot pump like it was a fine woman. The big white man stood 6'3" and 230 pounds. He wore a large T-shirt that showed off the hard workouts he did during his ten year bid. The gray-eyed blonde-haired man was one of Trevor's closest friends.

"C'mon, man. I don't need y'all to get too deep in my shit," Lucky said. "Just find out where my daughter at and I got it from there."

"Are we killing some fools or what?" a tall light-skinned man with long curly hair asked impatiently. Miguel was Trevor's other goon. Like Tyler, he had also done a bid, just six months removed from a five year bid for trying to kill his baby mother. "If I don't kill me a motherfucker soon, I'ma go crazy."

Lucky looked to Trevor, wondering if Miguel was serious. "What's up with yo' boy?"

Trevor smiled wickedly. "He's a killing machine. One body a day keeps the demons away."

Lucky began to have second thoughts about the sanity of Trevor and his goons.

Tyler busted out laughing. "Killing makes us happy, bro. Don't worry. We're not crazy. Just fucked up in the head."

◆◆◆

"What's so important that it couldn't wait?" Polo asked. He was in the back of the barber shop meeting with Trevor and Tyler.

"Show 'em what you got," Trevor told his boy.

Tyler unzipped the soft gun case, revealing a black semiautomatic 12-gauge.

"Oooh shit!" Trice moaned like he had busted a nut in his pants.

"Lemme see that bitch!" Polo said, a lustful look in his eyes as he fondled the gun.

"That's a 12-gauge riot pump. You can tear a building down with that mutherfucker. Semi-automatic, cooling system, infra-red beam, and a drum on that bitch. My boy got ten of 'em. He tryna get rid of 'em right now. Ten G's. What you wanna do?"

Polo looked up from the gun like he was hearing Trevor for the first time. "Come down on that price and I'ma get 'em all."

Trevor shook his head. "That's what he want. They worth more and I ain't even getting a cut."

Polo thought for a moment. "Okay. I got something important going on right now and it gotta be handled. But come back and I'ma take these off yo' hands tomorrow."

"Nah. He need to get back on the highway. This is now or never. Don't let this opportunity slip by. Ain't no serial numbers on 'em or nothing. These bitches is too good to pass up."

Polo looked caught between a rock and hard place. "Okay. Fuck it. Where the rest of 'em?"

"At my spot. All I gotta do is make a call and he gon' bring 'em."

"Make that call. We gotta pick up the money from one of my traps."

Trevor gave Tyler a nod to make the call.

"What you got going on that's important? Need some help?" Trevor offered.

Polo smiled like he was the devil. "As a matter of fact, I do. I need a couple more shooters."

It was Trevor's turn to smile. "You know how we do. Just point me in the right direction."

"I got two situations that I'm looking into. My issue with Wacco, I'ma address personally. But I need help with this nigga, Lucky. He just got out, so he ain't really connected to nobody. Him and his brother fucked over a few of my niggas, and I need that taken care of. I got his daughter at one of my spots and I was about to go holla at her right before you called. I talked to her earlier and she wasn't talking, but I wanna revisit."

"Well shit, lead the way, my dude. I wanna have a conversation with her, too. I bet I can make her talk."

"He ready with the guns," Tyler said after hanging up the phone.

Trevor nodded to Polo. "I'm ready when you is."

After leaving the barbershop, Trevor and Tyler hopped in a Yukon with tinted windows. During the drive, he called Miguel's phone.

"Are we whacking some fools, or what?"

"Chill, fool," Trevor admonished. "Where is Lucky?"

"I'm right here."

"He still got her. We on our way over right now."

"How we playing it?"

"They think Miguel coming with the merch. Once he inside, it's going down. They think it's a buy, so make sure y'all bring that case in."

"Hell yeah! I'ma blast me some fools!" Miguel celebrated.

"Just gimme a chirp when y'all ready to come in," Trevor said, ending the call and continuing to follow Polo's Infiniti to a black and white brick house on the south side. They parked in the alley and made their way to the back door. After knocking, they waited.

"Who dat?" someone called from inside.

"Polo. Open the door."

The door swung open and a tall, skinny, dark-skinned nigga answered with a pistol in his fist. "What's good, fam?" he asked, stepping aside to let them in the house.

"Where that li'l bitch at, Quest?" Polo asked.

"She in the room."

Polo nodded for Trevor and Tyler to follow him. They walked through a living room where a couple young niggas lounged around smoking weed and playing a video game.

"What's good, Polo?" Bliss nodded.

"What good, li'l nigga?" Polo saluted before heading up a flight of stairs.

They walked down a hall and heard voices coming from a bedroom. It sounded like an argument between a man and a woman. Polo walked in without knocking and saw a young nigga choking Laronda. He wasn't wearing a shirt and his pants were unbuttoned, exposing his underwear.

"Fuck you doing, Beans?" Polo laughed. "No means no."

The young sex offender looked embarrassed. "Uh, I was just tryna see something," he mumbled, buttoning his pants.

"Well, go see something somewhere else. And no means no, nigga. I ain't bailing yo' bitch ass out if you catch a rape case," Polo called after him.

Laronda moved to the corner of the room, crossing her arms over her chest. Fear and uncertainty was written on her face and body language.

"Chill, shorty. We ain't on that rape shit," Polo spoke up. "I told you we can make this easy if you tell me where yo' daddy at."

"I told you I don't know."

Polo looked to Trevor. "You wanna give it a shot?"

Trevor looked over the young girl, pausing at her thick thighs and big breasts. "Man, I see why that fool was in here tryna get his. Shorty is strapped, huh?" he asked, nodding to Tyler.

"Li'l too young for me," the big man said, looking uncomfortable.

"Good thing pussy don't got no face." Trevor laughed as he walked closer to Laronda. He pulled a pistol from his waist and put it to her face. "I wanna have a word with you in private. Is that cool?" Laronda didn't say a word.

"Polo, can you give me a minute with her?"

Polo laughed and shook his head. "You a nasty mu'fucka. Just make sure you find out where her daddy at," Polo said before turning to Tyler. "You coming with me or staying to watch?"

"I'm with you," Tyler said, giving Trevor a long stare before heading for the door.

"I got it, brother. Trust me." Trevor winked, closing the door behind them. He turned back to Laronda and began whispering. "I'm with your pop, Lucky. I need you to trust me."

Laronda remained in the corner, skepticism in her eyes. "You think I'm stupid? I know Polo told you to say that. And I'ma tell you just like I told them, I don't know nothing. I just found out he was my - "

"I don't give a fuck about none of that! Listen to me. Yo' daddy is coming in a few minutes. My phone gon' ring when they outside."

Some of the skepticism left her demeanor. "You for real?"

"Yeah. My name Trevor. I met him when we was doing time. That's my boy. We finna get you up outta here."

She smiled. "I swear to God, you bet' not be playing with me, man."

A knock on the door made them freeze.

"Y'all good in there?" Quest called.

"Yeah. I'm good." Trevor called back. "Get away from the door."

"Make sure you get some head, fool. Her shit fiya!" He laughed.

Laronda looked scared. "We gotta do something. C'mon."

Trevor's frowned. "What!? Hell Nah! How old is you?"

"I'm old enough," she said before dropping to her knees and tugging at his pants. "C'mon before they come in. It's a camera on the wall by the door."

Trevor looked around and saw a small Ring camera latched to the wall near the door. "Aw, fuck!"

♦♦♦

"Am I good?" Lucky asked, pulling the black wool knit cap over his head.

Miguel glanced over quickly. "Yeah, yeah. You good. It's dark out so they won't see you until it's too late," he mumbled before turning back to the AR-15 he was stuffing inside a duffle bag. "Send that text to Trevor so he know we're coming in."

After sending the warning text, Lucky checked the safety on his Glock before tucking the pistol and climbing from the car. They were parked in the alley behind Trevor's Yukon.

Miguel grabbed the duffle bag and took long strides towards the house. "As soon as I'm in, I'm busting these mutherfuckers' shit open. I ain't playing with these fools. You hear me?"

"Yep." Lucky nodded, looking around nervously for signs of life or witnesses. It was pitch black outside and hardly any movement from the surrounding houses, but Lucky knew that would change once the shooting started.

When they got to the back door, Lucky remained in the background while Miguel rang the doorbell. A few moments later Quest appeared.

"Who dat?"

"Fred. I'm looking for Trev," Miguel said.

When the door opened and Lucky saw Quest holding a pistol, anger shot up through his bones. He remembered him hitting Laronda. The pistol tucked in his waist burned against his hip, but he didn't think he would be able to draw before the young'un fired a shot. Quest checked out Miguel then glanced at Lucky before turning back to Miguel.

"Who is you?" Quest asked.

"C'mon with the fucking questions, my dude," Miguel said impatiently. "I just said I'm Fred. I got some hot-ass shit in this bag. Polo and Trev know we here. Let us in."

Lucky expected shots to start flying. Miguel talked slick as fuck and the young'un's face showed he didn't take kindly to the words. But surprisingly, Quest stepped aside.

"My bad. They in the living room."

Miguel walked in like he owned the house and Lucky brought up the rear. When he walked past Quest, they locked eyes again. Recognition shone in Quest's eyes and in that moment, Lucky knew he had been busted. He reached for his pistol as Quest began speaking.

"Ay, don't I know - "

Pop, pop, pop!

Quest fell to the floor with three bullets in his chest. He died with the pistol in his hand, never getting the chance to fire a shot. Miguel pulled the AR from the bag and turned to look upon the dying man. "C'mon, bro! I wanted to kill that mutherfucker!" he whined.

"Let's see if it's some more in the living room," Lucky said, not wanting to waste time debating about who killed who.

Commotion by the kitchen foyer made them look up as Bliss came to check out the shooting. A killer smile flashed on Miguel's face as he squeezed the trigger on the chopper. The high-powered bullets tore into the youngster's torso, blowing the li'l nigga against the wall. Miguel kept squeezing the trigger until he fell to the ground.

When Polo heard the shots come from the kitchen, his street instincts kicked in. It was some kind of set-up. He looked to Tyler and saw the smile of a killer clown, murder in the white man's eyes as he lifted the riot pump. Polo thought quick and shoved Trice in the line of fire. The shotgun erupted, sounding like thunder.

Boom, boom, boom!

Trice's body flew through the air, hitting Polo and knocking him to the ground. Tyler wanted to kill Polo, but he was covered by Trice and the two young niggas that were playing video games had pulled their guns. He turned the gauge towards one of them and blew him to smithereens. The other was able to get off a couple of wild shots as he tried to hide from the fire-breathing dragon. Tyler ducked into the hall as bullets whizzed by his head.

Polo used the time the young shooter brought him to throw Trice's body off him and make a break for the window. Tyler peeked his head from the hall just in time to see Polo about to leap out the window. He turned the riot pump and was about to shoot him in the back when he saw Beans taking aim at him out of the corner of his eye. He knew that he was done.

"Shit!" He flinched.

Prrraaaattttt!

Bean's body jerked like he was having a seizure as he stumbled backwards, firing wild shoots and falling to the floor.

"Wooo!" Miguel cheered as he ran into the living room, still firing at Bean's dead body. "Fuck yeah!"

When Tyler realized that he was still alive and his boy had saved his life, he breathed in relief. "Damn. He almost got me."

"Ain't nobody getting your blonde ass while I'm here, mutherfucker." Miguel laughed, his eyes wide like he had taken an illegal drug. "Are there any more of these mutherfuckers? I'm ready to kill some more!"

"That's all, man."

"Where Polo?" Lucky asked.

"Fucker jumped out the window. I had his ass too," Tyler said regretfully.

"What about my daughter?"

"Up those stairs. Trevor's got her."

Lucky tore up the stairs just as Trevor and Laronda emerged from the room. When he saw his baby girl, tears came to his eyes and his heart swelled inside his chest. "Laronda! Hey, baby girl!" he choked, opening his arms.

Laronda ran to him and drowned in her father's embrace. "Lucky! You came!"

"I was gon' come wherever they took you. I'ma always be here for you, baby."

"Uh, I hate to break up the moment but we gotta go," Trevor said. "I already got the camera. Make sure y'all take they phones."

Chapter 6

The heat was sweltering. Fire danced around the compound like orange and red hula dancers as the building went up in flames. Smoke filled the air and dead bodies littered the ground. Desmond crouched low and moved steadily across the room, staying close to the wall, trying not to be seen. He had been separated from his team and enemies surrounded him on all sides. He had already killed more enemies than he could count. The ground was slicked with blood and he had to walk carefully to keep balance. He paused when he happened upon a woman wearing a purple dress lying on the ground. He couldn't see her face because she was on her side, her back to him, but something about her build looked familiar. After checking his surroundings to make sure he wouldn't be jumped by an unseen enemy, he bent down to check the woman for signs of life. When he saw her face, ice cold terror shot up through his bones. It was his mother, Cookie.

"What the fuck?" he startled, jumping backwards and slipping and falling on the blood-slicked floor.

Cookie's eyes shot open and her head turned 180 degrees so that her head looked like it was put on backwards. "Why didn't you save me?" she asked, her voice deep and booming with bass. She didn't sound like his mother, but some kind of demon.

"I-I couldn't," he stammered, sliding in the blood as he struggled to stand. "I had to get away to save myself."

Cookie's body levitated to its feet, head twisting completely around, defying the limitations of the human body. When she spun to face Desmond, there was a hole in her neck and blood covered the front of her dress. "I never loved yo' ass, anyway. You hear me, Desmond? I hate you. You was a trick baby. You fucked up my life! I HATE YOU!"

Desmond's eyes shot open, his surroundings instantly changing from a burning warehouse to the white brick walls inside a jail cell. He ran a hand across his face and sat up on the cheap, thin mattress. He'd been in jail for two days and the dreams had gotten worse. Every time he dozed off, a nightmare was waiting behind his eyelids.

He needed to talk to somebody about them, but he didn't trust anyone with his thoughts and what went on in his head. He didn't want people to think he was crazy, so he suffered in silence. He no longer had the distractions of the outside world to keep his mind occupied. All he had was his thoughts and books and the cell. And he felt like the cell was driving him crazy, so he left for the dayroom.

Outside his cell was a phone bank with six phones. They were all being used, so he sat at an empty table to wait for one of them to open.

"What's going on, young blood?"

Desmond looked over and saw an older man sitting at a nearby table looking in his direction. His name was Clarence, a lifetime criminal that had spent fifty of his sixty-three years on earth inside a cell. He wasn't bad company and Desmond had picked his brain about the jail rules during his first night on the pod.

"You got it, Clarence. Having a hard time getting used to being locked up. I don't see how you do it."

Clarence let out a hearty laugh. "The journey of a thousand miles begins with a single step. You often don't realize what you can do until you already done it. Next thing you know, twenty years done went by and you looking back tryna find out where the time gone. Just don't think about it. I know it's easier said than done, but that's how you do time. You don't think about it. Find something to do to take yo' mind off it. You play chess?"

"I know how the pieces move," Desmond mumbled. "But how can you not think about being locked up while you locked up? That don't make sense."

"Its mind over matter. If you don't pay it no mind, then it won't matter."

"You make it sound way too easy. My brother did fourteen years and I'm having a hard time doing a couple days. I don't know if I can get used to this."

Clarence laughed again. "You would be surprised what you can do if yo' back is against the wall. Great men have come out the belly of this beast. Nelson Mandela. Malcolm X. Chef Jeff. You might be next."

"Sounds good." Desmond laughed and shook his head. When he noticed the phone open, he got up. "Lemme check this phone, OG. Grab a chess board."

Desmond had just grabbed the phone receiver when another man's hand grabbed the top of his. JP was as big as a refrigerator. 6'5", 320 pounds. Bald head. Scar on the right side of his face.

"I had the phone next," he said in a high-pitched voice.

Desmond was surprised the big man had a squeaky voice and had the situation not been so tense, he would have laughed. But he remained serious as thoughts of Lucky going to court for beating up someone trying to phone check him flashed in his head. "Nah, big man. I was here first." He stood, refusing to back down.

JP's eyes reflected his thoughts and emotions. He couldn't believe that someone had stood up to him and it pissed him off. "I said, I had next!" he yelled, trying to sound intimidating and snatching the phone away.

JP failed at both attempts. His voice didn't get any deeper, only louder. And he couldn't snatch the phone away from Desmond's grip. He only succeeded in pulling it closer to his body with Desmond's hand still wrapped around the receiver.

"C'mon, big homie. I ain't giving up the phone and I ain't tryna go there with you. Just get next," Desmond tried to reason with him.

"Hey! What's going on over there?" the correctional officer called.

Desmond didn't take his eyes off JP. He knew better than to look away from the enemy. JP turned to look at the CO walking over before turning back to Desmond. "If I catch yo' bitch ass in the gym, I'm beatin' yo' ass," he threatened, shoving the phone into Desmond's chest and walking away.

"Hey! Both of you lock in your cells! You're done for the morning!" the CO yelled.

"I didn't do nothing," Desmond said.

"I don't care! Lock in right now! That's a direct order!" the guard yelled.

"For what? I just said I didn't do nothing." Desmond continued.

"Lock in your cell right now or I'm calling a white shirt and you're going to the hole!"

Desmond paused for a moment to consider what just happened and his options. He didn't do anything wrong, but he was being punished. And if he didn't accept the punishment, he would be in the hole.

"Young blood, this ain't a fight you can win. I'll catch you at the next Dayroom," Clarence advised.

On the strength that Clarence was a veteran in the system, Desmond took his advice and hung up the phone. He mugged the CO on the way to his cell and slammed the door. After snatching off the orange smock shirt, he hit the floor to do push-ups. His arm was still in the cast and hadn't fully healed, the weight of his body causing sharp pains to shoot up his left arm and wrist. He ignored the pain and continued to do push-ups. He was too pissed off to care about a little pain. He had visions of putting the correctional officer in a guillotine choke hold until he passed out and breaking every bone in JP's body, starting with his nose. Desmond knew that he needed to work off the anger before he left the cell again for fear that he might hurt someone and make his situation worse.

Twenty minutes later, the lock on his door clicked.

"Harrison, attorney visit!" the CO called.

Even though he was still hot from the unprovoked encounter and unfair punishment, he was happy to get off the pod for a few minutes. And hopefully Brandon would have some good news. After putting on the smock top, he left the cell and headed for the pod exit. The big mechanical door jarred open and he walked out to the control desk in the hall.

"Who you?" the CO at the control asked.

"Harrison."

"Jamison, this one is yours," the officer spoke to a coworker.

"C'mon, Harrison. We gotta take a ride," he said, walking towards the elevator.

"Where we going?" Desmond asked, expecting a meeting with his lawyer.

"Downstairs. I don't know much, but anytime you go downstairs, the important people wanna talk."

During the elevator ride, Desmond thought about these "important people" that wanted to talk, wondering who they could be and what they wanted. A couple minutes later, he got his answer when they stopped at the door of an interrogation room. Inside, two white men wearing suits were sitting at the table. One of them was District Attorney Mitchell Sellers.

"Thank you for the escort, Officer. You can take a load off for a few minutes. Desmond, come in," Mitchell spoke up, motioning for Desmond to sit down.

Desmond eyed both men as he sat at the table.

"Hey, Desmond." Mitchell said, closing the door. "I don't know if you remember me, but I'm the prosecuting attorney, Mitchell Sellers, and this is a colleague, Assistant District Attorney Brian Schick."

"Okay," Desmond said wearily.

"You can relax, soldier. I know this is a tense situation, but we come with good tidings. We want to offer you an opportunity."

Desmond raised an eyebrow. "What kind of opportunity?"

Brian spoke up. "We want you to work with us."

Desmond laughed.

"We're not kidding," Mitchell said in a serious tone.

Desmond let out a stressed breath. "How you gon' lock me up for protecting my family and not give me bail and then try to get me to work with you? If you wanted my help, you went about it the wrong way."

"I'm sorry, but this is the way the law works sometimes." Mitchell shrugged. "Nothing happens the way we want, but this is an opportunity to get back to your family. I talked to Detective Perry before his passing, and I want to reopen the investigation into Polo. And we also want to take a look at Wacco. I hear you had a run-in with him as well. These two are at the top of the food chain in Milwaukee and if you can help us bring charges against them, all charges against you will be dropped. I'm talking about the murder of Big Man and we'll give you self-defense for defending your family."

Desmond took a moment to think, looking back and forth from each man's face. They were eagerly awaiting his answer. It looked like they would be willing to give him anything in exchange for his cooperation. But what about Lucky? If he helped the police, his relationship with his brother would be frayed. But he also had to get the fuck out of jail. He wasn't built to do time in a cell. "How soon can I be released?"

The men looked at one another before Brian spoke. "As soon as we can bring charges on one or both of them. We have others willing to cooperate, but we believe that you have knowledge that would give us our best chance at actually getting a conviction."

Desmond frowned. "What are you talking about?"

The men shared another look before Mitchell spoke. "We know that you were a 'hitman' of sorts for Polo. You were implicated in the murder of Made Mario as a favor for Polo. Give us the details of the murder as well as anything incriminating against Polo and Wacco, and we'll begin the process of setting you free."

Desmond paused again to look at both men. Their eagerness to get the deal done showed on their faces and leaked out the pores of their skin. And something about their desperation unnerved Desmond. "I need to talk to my lawyer first."

Mitchell's demeanor went from eager to worried. "C'mon, Desmond. We need to get this done as fast as we can. We're offering you a great opportunity to help your community and your country. We looked into your background and from what we were allowed to see, you are a decorated soldier. Help us help you. Work with us."

They were too eager to use him and for that reason, Desmond declined. "I need to talk to my lawyer before I agree to anything."

Defeat shone on the state attorneys' faces. "Okay. We'll be in touch," Mitchell said, pulling out a card. "Here is my number. Make sure you call me after you contact your lawyer."

"I will," he said as thoughts of the CO that locked him in the cell flashed in his head. "I need your help with something. I had a situation with the guard this morning and he won't let me use the phone. Can you help me out with that? I need to make this call."

Brian looked eager to help. "What unit are you on?"

"6B."

"I'll take care of it while you're on the way up. By the time you get to the unit, everything will be taken care of."

◆◆◆

When Desmond got back to the unit, the first thing he noticed was the CO standing behind the desk. There was a fiery anger in his eyes.

"Harrison, approach the desk."

Desmond walked slowly towards the officer's station, anticipating a heated argument. When the men were face to face, the CO's demeanor remained hostile but his voice came out in a humble whisper. "I want to apologize for the misunderstanding this morning. You are not on room confinement and there is a phone waiting for you."

Desmond couldn't hide the surprise at the CO's forced contrition, but he loved the sight of the cowering correctional officer. "Thank you, Officer. I appreciate the apology."

The CO nodded. "And if you need anything, let me know. You can go use the phone now."

Desmond walked away from the officer's desk smiling. When he got to the phone, he dialed Lasonya's number.

"Hey, baby," she answered quickly. "I was waiting on you to call."

"Hey. I just came from a meeting with the DA. They want me to work with them and they gonna let me go."

"Are you serious? When are they letting you out?" she yelled, sounding like she wanted to jump up and down.

"I don't know. I didn't agree to work with them. I don't trust them."

Her voice instantly changed to disappointment. "Why not? What did your lawyer say?"

"I haven't talked to him yet. I'm calling you first. But when I mentioned calling my lawyer, they didn't want me to. That didn't make sense to me."

Lasonya took a moment to consider what he said. "That doesn't make sense to me either. But I think you should do it so you can come home. I miss you so much."

Desmond let out a heavy sigh, his heart yearning to be with his girl. "I miss you, too. I wanna be with you so bad. I don't know how much longer I can stand being in here. This shit is driving me crazy."

"That's why you have to - "

"Is that Desmond?" Lucky asked in the background.

"Yeah. They talking about letting him out."

"Lemme see the phone. What they talkin' 'bout, Des?"

"The DA want me to work with them. Same shit Perry was talking about."

"Fuck that shit, brah. They don't got shit on you. That's why Perry didn't try to charge you. Take that shit to trial and you gon' beat it. Guaranteed. Don't fuck with them snakes."

"I hear you, brah. But you ain't the one doing this time. I'ma talk to Brandon when I finish this call and see what he think. But I can't do this time, brah. This shit fucking with my head. I need to get out."

"Listen, Desmond. We Harrison's, nigga. We built to overcome any obstacle. When I got locked up, I felt the same way. But I did that shit. And you can do it to. Don't fold, my nigga. You got it. And I got yo' back."

"I hear you, man. I'ma talk to Brandon first. Let me holla back at Lasonya."

"A'ight. Hold yo' head. Its gon' get greater later."

"Yep."

"I think you should do it," Lasonya said as soon as she got back on the phone. "We need you back out here. It's crazy. Yo' brother…"

"What was you about to say?"

She became emotional. "I don't want to say. We just need you to hurry up and come home."

"Lasonya, what's going on? You gotta tell me. Don't leave me hanging like that."

"I don't want to stress you out."

"Not telling me what's going on is stressing me out even more. Tell me."

"I can't, Des. Just get back out here. We need you."

Desmond lowered his head as the anger and frustration coursed through his body. "Okay. I'ma call Brandon and see what he think. I'ma call you back."

"Okay. I love you. Make sure you call me back."

"I am. I love you too."

After hanging up, Desmond called Brandon, but didn't get an answer. He left a message on the voicemail and instead of calling Lasonya, he headed to the gym to work out and blow off some steam. Worry for his woman's and brother's safety weighed heavily upon his mind. He had to get the fuck out of jail, but he didn't want to work with the police. He didn't trust Mitchell or Brian. They were trying to fuck him over and he could feel it. But what other choice did he have? Could he really go to trial and beat the case? He walked laps around the gym and did push-ups while trying to sort out his thoughts.

About thirty minutes into the workout, the gym door opened and JP walked in followed by two men. They didn't try to mask their intentions. They walked directly towards Desmond.

"I told yo' bitch ass I was gon' get in yo' ass if I caught you in the gym." JP mugged him, violence emanating from his being as he clenched his fists. His henchmen smiled, ready to back up the big man.

Desmond stopped walking, hands resting at his side as he waited. He needed a way to release the anger and frustration that built inside of him and the street punks would be his outlet.

When JP was close enough, he cocked his arm back and threw a slow motion punch. Desmond dodged the wild swing, grabbing hold of his arm and using the momentum to pull the big man to the ground. He rolled on top of JP, locking his arm in an arm bar and pulling until his bone snapped at the elbow.

"Aahhhhh!" the big man screamed as his arm snapped in half.

Without missing a beat, Desmond lifted his foot and brought the heel down, crushing the big man's throat. One of the goons intervened and kicked Desmond in the head. Instead of hurting Desmond, the kick only succeeded in pissing him off. He rolled off JP and directed his fury towards the man that kicked him. A leg whip at the knee made him buckle. An elbow to the face made him stumble backward, and the spinning back elbow made famous by the MMA fighter Jon "Bones" Jones took out several teeth as consciousness escaped the wannabe attacker. After dispatching the goons with quick work, Desmond turned to the final victim, an angry fire lighting his eyes. The man saw the fighting skills of Desmond and made the wise decision to flee. He spun towards the door and booked it. Desmond gave chase. He was in destroy mode and wanted to see more blood spill and break more bones. A sweeping leg kick made the man trip and take a nasty face slide. Desmond leapt high in the air and brought both knees crashing down on the man's spine. Bones shattered as vertebrae snapped.

"Aahhhhh!" The man cried as the worst pain he'd ever felt seized his body.

The painful cry snapped Desmond from his zone, bringing him back to reality. Three bodies lay on the floor in different stages of trauma. The gym door opened and the correctional officer stepped in. His eyes popped when he saw the carnage and for a moment he didn't know how to react.

"They started it," Desmond mumbled.

The CO lifted his hands up, palms out. "Please, man. You proved your point. I don't want any trouble. I need you to lay on the ground until back-up comes."

Chapter 7

Everything is different now.
That's what Lucky thought as he cruised the Mustang through the intersection. A joke he heard in church while in prison came to mind. "If you want to make God laugh, tell him your plans." How true. While locked up waiting to be released, he pictured a much different way of life when he got free again. Getting married and living a good clean life with Melissa and the kids had been his plans. Making the *New York Times* bestsellers list. Maybe having one of his books turned into a movie and starting a business. Now he was on the run from his parole officer, looking over his shoulder for drama from Wacco and Polo, and he had killed several men. He felt different. He had changed and he didn't know when or have the words to explain how it happened. And he was also unsure of the future. A few months ago, he thought he had the future figured out. Now everything appeared to be up in the air.

The vibrating of his phone pulled him from his thoughts. Lasonya's name shone on the screen. A vision of her fuck face flashed in his head as guilt and shame gripped his heart.

"What up, sis?" he answered.

"Hey, have you talked to Desmond lately?"

"Nah. Not since yesterday. Why? He good?"

"I don't know. He didn't call me back yesterday or today."

Lucky's guilty conscience began whispering about his indecent act with Lasonya. "You didn't tell Desmond about what happened, did you?"

Lasonya's voice went low with anger. "You know I'm not going to tell him about that. Why would I? We was high and you were tripping. That's it."

Lucky nodded as another vision of him fucking her from behind flashed in his mind. "Yeah. We was tripping. You right. What about Laronda or me being on the run from my P.O?"

"Nah. I'm not going to tell him anything that would stress him out. He got enough on his plate. I don't want to add to it. I'm just worried about him. It's not like him not to call. I had a visit set up, but he missed it."

"Yeah, that ain't like him. Call the county jail and see if they can tell you his status. And make sure you keep this shit out here to yo'self. He don't need to be worried about us."

"I know. Alright. I'ma call the jail."

"A'ight. Text me or call me to let me know what's up."

"I will."

The conversation with Lasonya brought back memories of their escapade. He didn't want to think about her, but couldn't help it. Lasonya was bad with some bomb-ass pussy. But that was his brother's girl. He forced himself to push the memory from his head and forget about it.

A few minutes later, he pulled up to Sharday's sister's house and climbed from the car. After climbing he steps, he rang the doorbell.

"Who is it?" a woman called.

"Lucky."

Locks clicked and the door swung open. In the doorway was April, Sharday's sister. She looked like she lived a rough life. Dark blotchy skin, a bad perm with lots of new growth, and her stomach stuck out like she was six months pregnant.

"Hey, Lucky." She smiled, looking him from head to toe like he was a snack.

"'Sup, April? Where Laronda?"

"She in the room. C'mon in here with yo' fine ass," she flirted, barely stepping to the side to allow him to pass.

Lucky tried to pass without touching her, but she pushed her stomach into his pelvis and reached for his dick.

"Ay, chill!" he admonished, grabbing her hand.

She smiled like she had been caught doing something wrong. "You need to come up off that dick, nigga. I remember how you used to look at my ass back in the day. We grown now. You can get it."

Lucky pictured her naked body in his mind and almost threw up. "I'm good on that," he said before going to look for Laronda.

He found her in the back room with her face glued to her phone. "Hey, baby girl."

The sound of his voice made her smile and she threw the phone, jumping up from the bed to wrap him in a hug. "Hey, Lucky! Took you long enough to come. Damn."

"I was tryna find somewhere to live. I can't just be sleeping on people couches. You ready to go?"

"Yeah. I been ready."

"Wait." Lucky paused, digging into his pocket and pulling out his mother's necklace. "I wanna give you this. Again."

Laronda smiled, turning around and lifting her ponytail. "Put it on."

Lucky put the chain around her neck and she spun around. "How it look?"

"Priceless. Let's go."

From April's house, Lucky drove to Bungalow, a soul food restaurant, where they had dinner and kicked it.

"You ever think about going to school and finishing your education?" Lucky asked.

Laronda looked up from the food like he asked a stupid question. "For what? School ain't finna pay no bills."

Lucky laughed, knowing the impatience of being young. "What about getting a diploma? Graduating? School isn't about the right now. It prepares you for the future. When I was yo' age, I thought the same way. I couldn't see how learning all that bullshit in school would translate into helping me in the real world. Niggas needed money now. My mama was a cluck and spent her money on dope. Me and my brother had to hit the streets at an early age. We was out there robbing, stealing, and hustling to eat. We thought that was our only option but looking back, we coulda made other choices. Better choices. Coulda saved me from doing fourteen years in a box. High school prepares you for college, and college equips you for the real world. It ain't no easy way to get it. Real success is a precious jewel that takes time to make. It takes time, sacrifice, and patience to create something precious."

A light shone in Laronda's eyes for a brief moment. "I like what you said. It makes sense. If I woulda heard it when I was younger, it might've helped me. But it's like you said. My mama on dope and would rather get high than buy me school clothes. I had to do what I had to do."

"You make it seem like you an old lady. You only fifteen. Got yo' whole life ahead of you. If you want, you could flip the script right now and get in school and change yo' life. You young enough that none of the stuff you doing now won't matter in ten or twenty years."

She stopped eating for a moment to give his words some thought. "You make everything sound so easy. Like tomorrow I could be a different person. But it don't work like that, Lucky. If I don't play these niggas, they gon' play me. If I don't get what I got coming, the next bitch gon' take it. Everybody don't need to go to school to be successful. School ain't for er'body. Plus, I don't wanna hear them gossiping-ass bitches talking about what I did or what kinda clothes I got on or who my mama is. I'm good on all that. I would rather do me. Have my own coins and live my own life."

Lucky paused to stare at his daughter. He saw so much of himself in her. He had probably used those same words back in the day when someone told him to go to school or get a job. But he wasn't going to let her stubborn ignorance stop him from trying to reach her. "I think I said that same shit." He laughed. "Let me ask you this. How much money do you got right now?"

She rolled her eyes, not understanding the relevance of the question. "I don't got no money. I'm broke."

"How much money you want?"

She thought for a moment. "You mean right now?"

"Yeah. Right now. If you could have one wish for some money from a genie, how much you want?"

"I wanna million dollars!"

"What would you do with the money?"

"Then I could buy my mama a house and move her from Milwaukee and try to help her get off drugs. And I could stunt on these bitches and niggas. Benzes and lady Rolex." She laughed.

Lucky felt his daughter's words like he spoke them. Despite Sharday's neglect, Laronda still loved and wanted to help her mama. Just like Lucky wanted to do with Cookie. "Damn, you sound just like me. No matter what Cookie did, I still wanted to help her. Don't ever lose that. And also, don't say no stupid shit like you only want a million dollars and you gon' spend it on cars and jewelry. A mil ain't no money in the real world."

Laronda smiled at the compliment, but twisted up her face at the admonishment.

"That's what people that ain't never had shit say. A million dollars is not a lot of money. And the better question is, what you gon' do with the mil? Buy a bunch of bullshit and be broke again? The worst thing you can do is give a fool some money. You know why? 'Cause all they gon' do is give it away and fuck it off. This is why school is important. The education gon' give you an ideas of what you can do. Knowledge opens the mind to possibility. You thinkin' like every nigga in the hood right now because that's all you know. But the world is way bigger than yo' zip code."

Laronda rolled her eyes at Lucky, crossing her arms over her chest.

Lucky cocked his head. "What happened? I say something wrong?"

She smacked her lips, catching an attitude. "Nah. I'm good. Can we leave now?"

Lucky continued to stare at her. "For real? We doing this?"

Her eyes became watery like she wanted to cry. "You ain't finna be making me feel stupid. I'm good on all that. You don't know me. Nigga, I just met you, and now you tryna play daddy and talk to me like I'm stupid. Ricky don't talk to me like that and you ain't either."

Lucky nodded and sat with her in silence for a moment. "You know the difference between me and Ricky? He told you he loved you, but I showed you. I risked everything for you. That nigga probably ain't even capable of expressing that kind of love. And you can be mad at me all you want, but one thing you gotta learn is that the people who really love you gon' tell you the truth. Even if it hurts. The Bible says 'faithful are the wounds of a friend.' Because they love you, they ain't gon' sugarcoat it. I'ma tell you a lot of shit you never heard before, and some of it might piss you off. But when you understand what I'm tryna do, you gon' thank me. Let's go. I'ma drop you back off with yo' aunty."

The ride back to April's house was mostly quiet. Lucky decided to break it with his news. "I think I'ma turn myself in when the night is over with."

This got Laronda's attention. "Why?"

"'Cause I gotta put this shit behind me. I told you I can't be on the run forever. Plus, I gotta get back to my career. I'm a writer. I need to travel and do business. I can't do that if I'm running from the police."

Laronda looked sad, but simply shrugged her shoulders. "Okay."

Lucky expected more. "That's it?"

"What more can I say? You gotta do what you gotta do."

"What about you writing and coming to visit? Don't tell me you about to let telling the truth affect how you treat me. It's my responsibility to tell you the truth. Getting to know you is important to me. I missed yo' whole life, and I want as much of you as I can get."

Laronda smiled, liking the affection in his words. "We good, Lucky. I'ma visit and write. I promise."

"That's what I'm talking about." Lucky smiled. "And one more thing. I don't know if anybody ever told you this before, but your smile is more beautiful than anything you can wear. Matter of fact, it's the best thing you can wear. These niggas out here that don't know you or love you gon' only see yo' ass and titties, but the people that really love you gon' notice yo' smile. So smile. Because you're beautiful."

When Lucky pulled up to April's house, Sharday was walking up on the front porch. He blew the born and waved. When she noticed her baby daddy, she turned and headed for the car.

"Uh oh. Here come trouble," Laronda joked as she climbed from the car.

"We good." Lucky laughed. "I'ma call you as soon as I can."

"Okay. Bye."

"Hey, baby," Sharday spoke to her daughter before hopping in the passenger seat. "Hey, baby daddy."

"What's good, baby mama?" Lucky laughed at the exchange. "That shit gon' take some getting used to."

"I know, right? But she already love you and only knew you for a couple weeks. You might be what she need to get her life together."

Lucky turned to look at her. "What about you? She need her mother, too."

Sharday shook her head. "Nah. I already did what I could and you see how that worked out. I can't teach her what you can. She needs to see what a responsible man looks like so she can find one. She need to see what real success looks like cause all she know is what's out in the streets. You saved her life, so she respects and looks up to you way more than she ever did me."

The car became silent as Lucky digested her words. Sharday was right. "Did you find a house yet?"

"Nah. I'm still looking. Why don't you just give me the money and let me pay for it."

Lucky looked at her like her face was falling off. "Stop playing. You ain't finna buy no dope with the rent money. But I really need you to get on that. I'm turning myself in soon and I wanted to get y'all straight before I go."

She looked surprised. "You turning yo'self in? Why?"

"Cause I gotta put this shit behind me so I can get back on the grind. I'm not finna live my life on the run. I got shit I need to accomplish, money to get the right way, and I can't do that with the police chasing me and constantly having to look over my shoulder."

Sharday nodded. "Yeah. I understand. You is an author and all that. Damn." Then something flashed in her eyes. "You wanna kick it with yo' baby mama one last time before you turn yo'self in? Remember what I said. Any time you want it, you can get it."

Lucky glanced over, giving her a head to toe. She wore jeans, a T-shirt, and sneakers, her hair in long braids. Her figure was slim and sexy. She wasn't fine, but she wasn't ugly either. And then he remembered the head she gave. Her shot was fiya! He put the car in drive and headed for the hotel, stopping along the way to grab a box of condoms. When they got to the hotel, they didn't waste time with foreplay. They both dropped their cell phones on the table and stripped naked. Lucky lay on the bed, the box of Magnums next to him, his dick pointing in the air like it was a flagpole.

"Mmmm! This what I'm talking about." Sharday smiled as she crawled on the bed. She wrapped a hand around his chocolate stick and sucked the tip between her lips while her tongue licked circles around the head.

"Aw shit!" Lucky moaned, tensing up from the oral pleasure.

Spittle dripped from the side of Sharday's mouth as she went to work, taking a little more of him in her mouth every few moments while her hand worked up and down his shaft.

"Damn, Sharday. What the fuck?" Lucky groaned, fighting off the urge to bust a nut.

Sharday used a free hand to grab his hand and put it on the back of her head so he could control her pace. Loving the rhythm of her head game, Lucky pushed her head down some more. She gagged a little, but continued taking more of him down her throat until all of him had disappeared down her esophagus. Then she touched her lips to his pelvis and held it there a few moments so she could flex her deep throating skills. She brought her head up slowly until only the tip was between her lips then went all the way down again.

"Aw shit! Fuck!" Lucky groaned, grabbing a fist full of her braids.

Sharday loved his reaction to her pleasure. Hearing his moans and feeling him squirm made her pussy wet, so she reached a hand between her legs to stroke her kitty. She continued sucking him hard and fast, driving Lucky crazy with her super head.

"Damn, Sharday. I'm finna bust!" Lucky warned as his dick spasmed.

Sharday continued sucking, swallowing everything until he was drained. When his dick went limp, she sucked him until he was fully hard again. Then she removed her mouth and smiled at the job well done. "Don't move. I got this," she said, reaching for the box of

Magnums. After slipping a condom on him, she spun around reverse cowgirl. She spread her legs and dipped her head down so that her ass opened, exposing her sphincter and pussy hole. Then she reached between her legs and grabbed hold of his dick and guided her pussy down slowly.

"Oh shit, Lucky!" she moaned while slowly taking him inch by inch until they were pelvis to pelvis. She paused a few moments to adjust to him. "Damn, baby daddy. Yo' dick fill me up so good. I'ma take it all too, baby."

Lucky reached his hands up to grip and rub her cheeks. Although she was slim, she had a nice ass and it jiggled under his caress. He was also loving the feel of her pussy. Sharday's box was tight, hot, and wet as fuck. If her fuck game was anything like her head game, he knew he was in for a treat. "Yo' pussy still feel good as a muthafucka. Now bounce that shit on my dick," he said, slapping her ass.

"Mm-hmm. That's what you want?" she purred.

"Yeah," he said aggressively before slapping her ass again. "Now get it!"

"Ahh!" she cried, loving the pleasure of pain. "Slap my ass again."

Slap!

"Ahhhh! Yeah, baby. I'ma do whatever you want," she moaned as she began to move her hips. She lifted up until only the head of his dick was in her pussy and then went back down slowly. She kept at it until she worked up a steady rhythm. When her pussy was ready, she sat all the way up, her head facing the ceiling, and rode him hard. "Damn, Lucky! You feel so good, baby. Oh my God!"

"Yeah, baby. Ride that muthafucka! Ride it, bitch!" Lucky cheered, slapping her ass some more. Sharday's pussy clenched every time he slapped her booty and Lucky loved it.

"Pull my hair, nigga," she demanded, leaning back and bouncing on his dick like she was jumping on a pogo stick.

Lucky reached his long arms out and took hold of her braids like he was grabbing a horse's mane.

"Yeah, nigga! Oh my God, yo' dick feel so good, Lucky. Oh shit!" Sharday cried as she continued to ride him and get her hair pulled.

Sharday got lost in the zone and rode him hard, wanting more of him inside her guts. "Oh, shit, Lucky! I'm about to cum, nigga. Oh shit!" Sharday cried before sitting down and creaming all over his dick. After taking a few moments to catch her breath, she looked back over her shoulder. "Damn, baby daddy. You 'bout to make me fall in love with yo' ass again."

"Fuck love, baby. Let's fuck."

Sharday purred, licking her lips. "I love to fuck, nigga. I need my ass fucked good," she said before climbing off him and laying on her back. She opened her legs and began playing with her pussy. Her lips were fat and glistening with a fresh coat of cum.

Lucky knelt between her legs and watched.

"You like that?" she asked, giving seductive eye contact.

"Yeah. I wanna watch you cum."

"Don't watch me, nigga. Help me. Get my ass loose."

Lucky stuck a finger deep in her pussy.

"Oh yeah!" Sharday moaned.

After a few pokes, he brought the slippery digit out and used it to coat her ass with pussy juice. Then he pushed it in.

"Oh yeah!" Sharday moaned, closing her eyes and kneading her clit harder while Lucky rammed the finger in and out of her ass. He went from one finger to two, then two to three.

"Gimme that dick, nigga. Fuck my ass, baby."

Lucky lifted her legs onto her shoulders and slipped his dick slowly into her anus. She was still tight, so he didn't go too deep.

"Oh, baby! Fuck my ass, nigga. Quit playin'," Sharday demanded.

Lucky went deep into her ass until he had everything inside her but his balls. Then he squatted so that he was hovering over her and gave her what she wanted. He beat her ass up like it was her pussy, going all the way in and coming all the way out with hard-hitting long strokes.

"Oh, gawd! Oh my gawd! Oh, shit, Lucky," she cried fingering her clit while he beat up her anal walls. They were sweating and moaning and caught up in the fuck session of a life time. "Oh shit, Lucky. I think I'm finna cum, but it ain't never felt like this before. Oh shit!"

Then she did something he had never seen before. She let out a wail and clenched her ass as her body went stiff. Clear liquid shot out of her pussy, splashing his torso. Watching her squirt and feeling her ass clench was enough to take Lucky over the edge. He dropped all of his weight on top of her, diving deep into her ass while filling the Magnum with his seed.

"Damn!" Lucky panted as he rolled off her. "I ain't never seen nobody squirt. That shit was the truth."

"I ain't never squirted before. That shit felt different. That was the best orgasm I ever had. I need a cigarette and a nap. That dick is the truth," she cracked.

"Shit, you ain't the only one. Damn, baby mama," Lucky mumbled before closing his eyes.

"I'ma wash my ass real quick," Sharday said, climbing out of bed. She went to the bathroom to take a quick wash up. When she came back into the room, Lucky was asleep. Seeing the opportunity to get a few dollars to buy some dog food, she grabbed his pants and began searching the pockets. She had just found the money when a phone began ringing.

Lucky's eyes opened and the first thing he noticed was Sharday standing in the middle of the room, frozen like a statue. The guilty look in her wide eyes made him look around. That's when he saw the pants laying at her feet. Anger surged through him when he realized what was going on. "That's how you do me? Gon' steal from a nigga while I'm asleep!"

"Nah, baby. It wasn't like that." She cowered, not knowing what else to say.

Lucky jumped up from the bed and got in her face, rage in his eyes. "Fuck you think I'm stupid, bitch? Why my pants right here?"

"I was just... Uh…"

Lucky's hand became a blur. Smack! Sharday fell to the floor holding the side of her face. "Bitch, how the fuck you gon' try to steal from me and I'm finna pay yo' rent for you to move in a new house? Yo' stupid ass got the game fucked up."

"I'm sorry, Lucky. I didn't mean to. I'm sorry."

Lucky was so mad that he thought about stomping a hole in her ass, but he didn't. His phone kept ringing and it grabbed his attention. He picked it up from the table and checked the screen. It was Brandon, Melissa's son. He didn't feel like talking to the kid, so he ended the call and set the phone back down, about to get in Sharday's ass some more. The phone rang again. It was a text from Brandon.

Help. Smbody in the house.

A cold terror shot through Lucky's bones while a worst case scenario played in his mind. Polo had gone to the house looking for him. Damn.

He called Brandon's phone, but didn't get an answer.

"Fuck," he cursed, grabbing his pants from the floor.

"What happened?" Sharday asked.

"Stay the fuck out my bidness, you shiesty-ass bitch," he snapped, grabbing the rest of his belonging and hitting the door.

Chapter 8

Polo was pissed off. Every move he tried to make as of late had gone wrong. Bad luck seemed to follow him like a shadow. His team was turning on him, he had lost several shooters, he had a beef with Wacco, and his niece was dead. And it all started when he ran into Lucky. Helping him kill Draco turned out to be one of the worst decisions he'd ever made. Now he needed to make things right and put an end to all the drama.

When the gray Blazer pulled to a stop in front of the black and white house, all four doors opened and armed goons piled out. Behind the Blazer was another SUV and more armed goons piled out as well. Polo led the way, the group of killers emanating violence as they moved towards the house. When they got to the front door, the squad paused long enough for two men to step forward with a battering ram. One swing of the heavy metal device broke the locks and smashed the door open.

Annie was standing in the kitchen, rinsing a plate in the sink, when the loud noise boomed through the house. "Ahhhh!" She screamed as two goons ran into the kitchen. Terror filled her body at the sight of the men holding guns. When she saw they weren't the police, the fear was replaced by anger.

"What the fuck y'all doing? What y'all want?"

"Shut up, bitch. Where Trevor?" one of them asked.

Automatic gunfire coming from the front of the house made everyone in the kitchen pause. The men took their eyes off Annie to look in the living room. Polo and his niggas were surrounding a bedroom, firing blindly into the door. The sound of a drawer opening made the men spin back to the woman just as she grabbed a pistol from the kitchen drawer.

Pop, pop, pop, pop, pop, pop!

One of the goons went down in a heap from a bullet to the face while the other went for Annie, trying to take the pistol. A struggle ensued and he overpowered her, body slamming her to the floor and taking the pistol.

"Get up, bitch, before I kill yo' stupid ass," he threatened, pointing a gun in her face.

"Fuck you! Do what you gotta do," she mugged, refusing to cooperate.

The goon reached down and grabbed her by the hair, forcing her to her feet. "Get'cho punk ass up, bitch. You ain't tough."

Annie tried to put up a fight, but a slap across the face from the hard steel made her stop resisting. The goon dragged her to the living room, where the shooting was still going on at the bedroom door. He saw Polo crouched low near the door.

"I got his bitch."

Polo lifted a hand to stop his niggas from engaging. "Trevor, can you hear me? I got yo' girl. C'mon out here, my nigga. Let's talk."

"Fuck you, pussy. Come in here and get these slugs," Trevor said before firing more shots.

Polo motioned for his goon to bring the woman closer. "C'mon, Trev. I'ma knock this bitch shit back. You can save her if you come out the room."

"Fuck them, baby!" Annie yelled. "Kill all these mutherfuckers."

Polo slapped her in the face with the butt of his gun.

"That's my bitch!" Trevor laughed before firing more rounds.

"This yo' last chance to save her." Polo said, pointing the gun at Annie's stomach.

"Quit talking and come in this room so I can fuck you up," Trevor laughed.

Pop!

"Ahhhh!" Annie yelled, doubling over in pain and grabbing her leg.

"Baby, you good?" Trevor called from behind the door, fear rising in his voice.

"No. He shot me in the leg," she whined.

"C'mon out here, Trev. Save yo' girl," Polo taunted.

Brrrrreaaaaatttt! Trevor fired again. "Fuck you, Polo. Yo' bitch ass. I'ma kill you, fuck boy."

Polo moved the gun towards Annie arm and fired again. Pop!

"Ahhhh!" she screamed.

"She bleeding real bad, Trevor. C'mon out here. I'ma give y'all a pass so you can take her to the hospital. Put the gun down and come holla at me."

The house was silent for a few heartbeats.

"Let her go outside right now," Trevor called.

Polo nodded to one of his men. "I got one of my niggas helping her outside right now."

"No, Trevor. Don't trust him," Annie fought. "Don't come out the room."

"Make sure she get to the hospital," Trevor called.

"You can make sure of that when you come out. I'm giving y'all a pass. I just wanna talk," Polo said.

There was another moment of silence before the splintered door moved. It opened slowly. Trevor held an assault rifle. "Tell yo' boys to put they guns down."

Polo motioned to his men. "It's good, y'all. Put 'em down."

The men lowered their weapons, but Trevor didn't. He kept it pointed at Polo. "Fuck y'all run in my house for if you giving passes?"

"I'm lookin' for Lucky. Tell me where he at and we gon' leave right now."

"I don't know where he at. After he got his daughter, we went our separate ways."

"C'mon, Trevor. Tell me somethin', my nigga. Where he say he was going? Who he with?"

"I don't know. I ain't talked to him."

Polo let out a frustrated breath. "Okay. A deal is a deal. We gone. Let's go," he said, waving to his niggas. The goons wore confused looks as they headed for the door.

Trevor went to his girl to check her injuries.

Right before he got to the door, Polo spun around quickly, his pistol high, catching Trevor off guard. "You don't make deals with the devil, stupid ass nigga."

Pop, pop, pop, pop, pop, pop, pop, pop, pop, pop!

Trevor and his woman fell to the ground, their bodies riddled with bullets. Just to make sure they were dead, Polo walked up on them and gave them each five bullets in the head.

"A'ight, let's get the fuck outta here."

Polo and his team of hitters climbed in their SUV's and smashed out. They were headed back to the trap when his phone rang. "What up, Reg? Tell me something good."

"The bitch just came home with her kids."

Polo perked up a bit. "Is Lucky with 'em?"

"Nah. Just her and the kids."

"You did good, nigga. I'm on my way," he said before hanging up the phone and signaling the driver. "Smurf, hit the East Side. We gotta anotha move to make."

Twenty minutes later, the caravan of killers pulled up to a big yellow townhouse on the upper East Side. Polo had a flashback of his last appearance at the house. He had barely escaped with his life. Desmond and Lucky got the ups on him and his niggas. Now Desmond was in jail and he was about to get one up on Lucky. The smile that crept into his face was that of an evil villain.

"We don't need er'body for this one. Smurf, wait in the car. Damo and Von, y'all wit' me. And bring the door banger so we can get in and out," Polo said before climbing from the truck. He walked towards the driver's side of a Ford Fusion parked a few houses away.

Reg climbed from the car and trotted over. "They still in there. Only them three."

"A'ight. You coming in with us. We killin' er'body."

Surprise lit Reg's eyes. "Even the kids?"

Polo nodded and smiled. "Even the kids."

The four killers moved quickly through the darkness. When they got to the door, Polo gave instructions. "Damo and Von, y'all find them kids. Reg, we got the bitch. Let's get it."

They used the battering ram to smash the door and the killers ran inside. Melissa rushed into the living room with two large knives in her hand. When she saw the killers with the guns, she began screaming. "Brandon, call the police! Somebody in the house!"

Clap, clap, clap, clap!"

Four bullets to the chest sent the mother crashing to the floor. "Find them kids!" Polo yelled.

Von, Damo, and Reg took off through the house to follow the order. Several more gunshots echoed through the house. A few moments later Von and Damo came back to the living room wearing sick grins. "We got they ass."

◆◆◆

Lasonya felt like she was about to have a heart attack.

Missing Desmond caused her physical pain. Heartache. In the short time they reconnected, he had become the most important person in her life, besides Quaysha. And not talking to him for two days felt like a lifetime. She missed him more than she'd ever missed a significant other. His sacrifice for her and Quaysha spoke of the love and devotion he had for them. He went to war to prove his love. For Lasonya, that act spoke more than any gift or word. Love was a sacrifice, and Desmond made it. And knowing how true his love was made her feel like shit because she couldn't give it back to him. A vision of her unholy deed with Lucky flashed into her mind, causing her heart to ache even more.

"What the fuck was I thinking?" she questioned for the millionth time.

If Desmond ever found out, he would be devastated. Their relationship would surely be over. She had finally found the man of her dreams, but one stupid action could ruin everything. Thoughts of getting pregnant by him filled her mind. If she had his baby, Desmond wouldn't leave. He couldn't. Duty and devotion to their child would keep him with her no matter how deep the betrayal. But he was in jail facing forever. It was impossible for her to get pregnant by him. Unless…

Vibrations from her phone made her look over. It was a text from an unknown number.

Come outside.

She texted back: who is this?

Wacco.

81

A burning fire lit in her chest when she read his name.

Fuck you.

Her phone vibrated again.

If you don't come out, I'm coming in. I'm not playing.

Lasonya glanced down at Quaysha. The child slept peacefully, ignorant to the issues facing her mother. Wacco probably wanted to see her. But Lasonya couldn't allow that. She swore that Wacco would never be allowed in her life. Plus, Marcy was in the other room and if she found out that Wacco was outside, the police would be called to investigate another homicide.

She texted back: I don't want to see you. Leave before my mother find out.

Wacco texted back: I'm walking on the porch. Answer the door.

"Shit!" she cursed and took off from the room. She couldn't let her mother see Wacco. She opened the front door just as Wacco was opening the screen door.

"I knew you was smart." He smiled, blue eyes shining in the dark.

"What do you want?" she asked angrily.

"I told you I wanted to talk. You coming outside, or should I come in?"

Lasonya stepped on the porch and closed the door. "My mother would kill you if she see you in her house."

Wacco laughed. "You never told me why Marcy hates me." Then his stare got serious. "You told her the same lie you been telling yo'self?"

Lasonya got angrier. "Fuck you, Tony. You ain't shit and I hate you."

He was unfazed by her outburst. "I know. But you didn't answer my question. What you tell Marcy that made her hate me?"

Lasonya rolled her eyes and gave him an angry stare. "What do you think? I told her you let your friends rape me."

Wacco shook his head and chuckled. "You still puttin' dirt on my name, huh?"

82

"What the fuck is that supposed to mean? I trusted you and you let them do that to me. Fuck you."

"I'm 'bout tired of you playing the muthafuckin victim." Wacco mugged, pointing a finger in her face. "Stop acting like you don't know what the fuck happened. You wanted to get fucked. You wanted my niggas to fuck you and you wanted me to watch. You loved that shit. You was drunk and the real you came out. You a freak, so stop playing like I did something wrong. Only reason you mad is 'cause I cut yo' ass off. I ain't finna be walking round wit' a buss down on my arm. You did all that shit."

Lasonya pushed Wacco in the chest, making him stumble backwards. "Fuck you, nigga! I didn't want that. You let them rape me. Get the fuck away from my mama house before I tell her you out here and she shoot yo' bitch ass."

The ex-lovers had an angry staring contest. It was broken when one of Wacco's shooters stepped from the Audi truck parked at the curb.

"Wacco, you good?"

"Yeah." He nodded before turning back to Lasonya. "Listen, shorty. I didn't come over here to fight you. I came to help. I heard Polo looking for Quaysha and I want y'all to stay with me until I take care of it."

Lasonya crossed her arms over her chest and became defiant. "We good."

"If you so good, why you hiding at yo' mama's house? Why Desmond ain't came out here and fucked me up? Oh, that's right. He locked up. Stop being stupid and stay with me before you or Quaysha get hurt."

"I said we good. You shouldn't have killed his niece. What did you think he was gon' do?"

"I didn't give that order. You know me good enough to know I don't fuck wit' kids. That was a mistake. But ain't nothing I can do. Go grab Quaysha and c'mon."

"I said no. We good. I'm staying with my mama."

Wacco shook his head in frustration. "A'ight. Since you acting stupid, I'ma keep some niggas watchin' the house. Where is Lucky?"

She shrugged her shoulders. "I don't know."

He laughed. "Yes, you do. I need to holla at him. Call him."

"I don't know his number."

Wacco stared at her for a moment. "Did you know he had something to do with my nephew getting killed?"

"That wasn't Lucky. It was Polo."

"How you know? Did he tell you?"

"No, but Desmond did. Polo did it so he could set up Lucky and have leverage over Desmond. He wanted to use Desmond as his hitman or some shit because he is a Navy SEAL."

Wacco studied her for another moment, trying to see if she was telling the truth. "Desmond really a Navy SEAL, huh? I seen it on jsonline. I still wanna holla at Lucky. Whenever you wanna stop playing games, give him my number and tell him to call me. I'ma leave some shooters to look out for y'all. And one day I'ma need you to stop bullshitting and let me see my daughter. I'm running out of patience."

When Wacco left, Lasonya went back in the house and called Lucky.

"Yeah," he answered, sounding depressed.

"Hey. Tony just came by my house. Are you okay?"

He let out a long breath and sniffled like he was trying to fight tears. "Nah. Polo killed Melissa and the kids," he mumbled before getting choked up.

"Oh, my God!" Lasonya cried. "Are you serious? Everybody dead?"

"Yeah. I need to get off this phone. I can't talk right now. I'ma call you later."

"Wait! Where are you going? I don't want you to get in trouble."

"To my hotel room. I need to think about my next move. I'ma call you later," he said before hanging up.

Lasonya's heart was crushed by Lucky's pain. She didn't want him to be alone, so she grabbed Quaysha and went to her mother's room. Marcy was sitting up in bed watching *Real Housewives* marathons.

"I need to use your car, Mom," she said, laying Quaysha across the bed.

"What's going on?" Marcy asked, ready to get her gun and shoot somebody.

"Lucky's girlfriend got killed."

Marcy grabbed her chest, eyes growing sad. "Oh Lord! What happened?"

"I don't know. He staying at a hotel and just found out."

"The keys is on my dresser. You want me to come with you?"

"Nah. I'm good. I just want to make sure he okay."

"Okay. Be careful out there. And take a gun just in case," Marcy said, handing her a small revolver.

After leaving the house, Lasonya stopped at a twenty-four hour grocery store to get a liter of vodka before heading to Lucky's room. He answered the door with red-rimmed eyes. Lasonya wrapped him in a hug.

"Hey, sis. What you doing here?" he asked, surprised to see her.

"I came to see how you were doing. Let me in."

Lucky stepped aside and allowed her in before locking the door. "This shit fucked me up. I didn't think that nigga would do no shit like this. Melissa didn't have nothing to do with our beef. When Brandon texted me, I tried to get there in time, but I couldn't make it. Police was already there."

"How do you know they dead? Did you see them?"

"Nah. I'm on the run, so I knew I couldn't talk to the police or go to the house. I talked to her mother. She devastated," Lucky breathed before collapsing on the bed.

Lasonya pulled the bottle of liquor from the bag and passed it to him. "Here. Drink some so you can relax a little. What do you wanna do?"

He cracked the bottle and took a long drink. When he looked at Lasonya again, his face was hard, eyes blazing hatred and murder. "I'm killin' that bitch-ass nigga. He violated me too many times. He got away when he took Laronda, but I'm not letting him get away again."

The pain and rage on his face was so intense that Lasonya had to look away for a moment. "What about your parole? You not gonna turn yo'self in?"

"I'm not doing nothing until I kill that nigga," Lucky said, taking another drink from the bottle before holding it out for Lasonya.

"I'm good," she declined. "I bought that for you."

Lucky tipped the bottle again and guzzled half. "They killed Trevor and Annie, too."

Devastation washed across Lasonya's face. "No, they didn't. Don't say that."

Lucky nodded. "I called Tyler. Him and Miguel fucked up about it. Them crazy-ass niggas looking for Polo too."

Lasonya covered her mouth with her hand, unable to speak for a few moments. "Damn. This got so outta hand. I wish Desmond was here."

"So do I. That nigga would kill er'body and make all this shit way easier. But I got it. Mark my word, I'ma kill that bitch-ass nigga."

Lasonya sat with Lucky until he had downed most of the bottle and passed out. He lay on the bed, still fully dressed, holding the bottle, in a drunken slumber. She took the bottle and set it on the table before taking off his clothes. When he was fully naked, she stopped to stare at him. He was a good-looking man with a nice body and package. She wasn't attracted to him, but he had something that she needed so she stripped naked and climbed in bed next to him. She grabbed the pillowcase off the pillow and folded it in half, using it as a blindfold to cover Lucky's eyes. When she was sure he couldn't see, she took his limp flesh in her hand and stroked it a few times. When it didn't get hard, she took him in her mouth and sucked him until he grew fully erect. Even though she didn't like what she was doing, she knew she couldn't stop. To avoid seeing his face, she climbed on top in reverse cowgirl and slid down his pole slowly. Since this wasn't for pleasure, she controlled her noise, sticking to business and riding him.

"Mmmhhh, shit!" Lucky moaned, coming to life.

Lasonya looked over her shoulder as she rode him. One of his hands found her ass and the other pulled up the blindfold. He blinked a couple of times like he couldn't believe what he was seeing. "Lasonya, what you doing?"

"Shhh," she whispered, reaching a hand over his face and pulling down the blindfold. "Close your eyes."

Lucky relaxed, a smile as big as the ocean covering his face. "Okay, Lasonya."

Not wanting him to remember the moment, she used his drunkenness against him. "My name not Lasonya. I'm Melissa."

His body went stiff. "Melissa? You came back?"

She reached a hand back and rubbed his chest. "Yeah, baby. It's me. Melissa. I'm here."

Lucky relaxed again. "I knew you wasn't dead. I knew you was gon' come back."

Tears filled Lasonya's eyes as she continued to ride him. She felt terrible on so many levels. Not only was she was cheating on her man with his brother, but she was doing it to get pregnant. And she convinced him that he was sleeping with his dead girlfriend. Damn. If hell was a real place, she knew this deed would probably get her a front row seat. But she was committed and continued riding until she could feel his dick spasming inside her walls.

When she looked back over her shoulder, Lucky wasn't moving. She climbed off him and watched him while she dressed. He still didn't move. After covering him with a sheet, Lasonya grabbed the almost empty bottle of vodka and went home.

Chapter 9

Being in the hole was cruel and unusual punishment. It was loud all day and all night. Twenty-four hours of metal doors opening and closing, niggas yelling about nothing, toilets flushing, and loud-ass ventilation systems turning on and off. However, Desmond found comfort in the constant noise. He could listen to niggas talk shit for hours about nothing and be entertained. Or he could count how many times toilets flushed and how often. And when he was really bored, he could stand in the doorway and watch the big booty guards make rounds and listen to niggas yell obscenities. Desmond was cool with the noise in the hole. What he didn't like was the silence. That's when his mind wandered. And that was dangerous for his sanity. He was starting to see things that weren't real and hear things that weren't there. As long as it was noisy, like it was now, he was good. He lay on his bed reading *The Alchemist*, liking the story of destiny and how it is attainable to those that follow the right path.

A tap on the door grabbed his attention. It was Mrs. Johnson, a pretty brown-skinned woman in her early thirties. She wore the sheriff's uniform tight, showing her curves and driving the incarcerated men crazy.

"Harrison, you got an attorney visit."

He climbed from under the thin sheets, slipping on the red smock and matching pants before stepping into a pair of rubber shower shoes and walking to the door. Mrs. Johnson unlocked a trap for him to stick his hands out and put on a pair of handcuffs. He backed away and the door opened.

"C'mon out here and let me put this belt on. How you doing today?"

"Fine, and you?" he asked, stepping onto the tier as cat calls and obscenities rained down on Mrs. Johnson.

"The day just started. Talk to me about two o'clock," she joked while sliding a secure belt around his waist and locking the handcuffs in front.

"Ay, my nigga," the man in the cell next door called.

Desmond looked over and saw a short young nigga with lots of gaps in his teeth. "What up?"

"Do me a favor and grab that ass for me and tell me if it's soft. I think Mrs. Johnson got ass shots." He laughed.

"Boy, shut the fuck up, Lewis! Yo' punk ass just mad 'cause you got a li'l dick. Probably ain't even got no pussy yet, virgin-ass nigga."

Desmond and all the other niggas in earshot of the comments busted out laughing.

After being escorted from the hole, Desmond was led to a small holding room, where Mitchell Sellers was waiting with Brian Schick. There were no pleasantries, and Desmond could feel hostility emanating from the men.

"You never called," Mitchell began after Desmond was seated.

"I don't want the deal. My lawyer said he would talk to you."

"Let me tell you something about Brandon," Brian spoke up, disdain in his voice. "He's a Boy Scout, and he's in over his head. The deal we offered is as good as it gets. And because you said fuck us, we're about to fuck you. You know those guys you beat up in the gymnasium? One of them is paralyzed, one of them is eating through a straw, and the other has a cast from his shoulder to wrist. Medical expenses are in the hundred thousands. And you know who's footing the bill?"

Desmond stared blankly, already knowing the answer, but refusing to give them the satisfaction of hearing him say it.

"You are, in the form of restitution. And we're charging you with two counts of felony battery and one count of attempted murder for your actions," Brian said smugly.

This got a rise from Desmond. "C'mon, man. This is bullshit. They tried to jump me. It was self-defense. Look at the camera."

"We did," Mitchell spoke up. "We seen everything. And we seen you chase Dramon Hudson down and jump on his back and paralyze him. You are trained to kill, and it looks like you tried to kill him. Now, I want to help you. I really do. But I can't. Only you can help you."

Silence filled the room as the men gave Desmond time to consider his folly. They had him right where they wanted. He was in a jam, and the pressure to work with them was starting to build. He was becoming frustrated and angry at their bogus attempts. "Man, why y'all playing with my life like this? Y'all took oaths to uphold the law, and y'all taking advantage of my situation for y'all own gain. This is bullshit."

"You wanna talk about bullshit?" Brian asked, raising his ire. "What's bullshit is you going around Milwaukee killing people like you're in a foreign country with no laws. What's bullshit is you killing a police officer and getting away with it. What's bullshit is you coming in here acting all high and mighty when you ain't nothing but a street thug trained by the government!"

Desmond shot to his feet, closing the distance between him and Brian in the blink of an eye. He grabbed the district attorney by the collar and shoved him against the wall, bringing his face inches from his. "Better watch who the fuck you talking to like that, fuck boy! I killed to protect your freedom so you can walk around wearing expensive suits and drink expensive coffee from Starbucks. Don't ever disrespect my service again."

"Okay, Desmond! That's enough!" Mitchell yelled, unsuccessfully trying to pull Desmond away from Brian.

The fear of God shone on Brian's face when he felt Desmond's strength and saw his rage.

"Desmond, let him go right now or I'll call the guards!" Mitchell yelled again.

Desmond released the frightened man, backing away slowly, anger, hatred, and the desire to spill blood showing in his eyes. "Y'all can take that deal and shove it up y'all asses. Take me back to my cell."

◆◆◆

Desmond paced the cell for more than an hour while thinking about the meeting with the district attorneys. He hated them and their tactics. They used the law to pursue their own interests. And since they didn't have a solid case, they continued to trump up charges, hoping he folded. Because of the fight, they got more ammo against him and now had his balls in a vice, squeezing it tighter. And they also knew he killed Detective Perry. The good thing was they couldn't prove it. But how long before they brought charges against him for it anyway? It didn't matter if they could prove it or not, based on everything they did. They wanted him to work with them or go to prison. That was all. He wanted to stick to his guns and say fuck them, but the additional charges were making it hard.

A knock on the door interrupted his pacing. It was Mrs. Johnson again. "You got another visit, Harrison."

He stopped pacing, his face going hard. "Is it those white boys again? If it is, I'm good."

"Nah, it's not them. But I can see that you made them just as mad as they made you." She laughed. "These are people from the Army. You ready?"

"The Army?" Desmond frowned.

"Yeah. A man and a woman. They got on uniforms and looking all serious. If you come on, you can see."

During the walk to the room, Desmond tried to think of who had come from the military to visit and why. Was it a court martial? But why? He didn't break any military law – not that he knew. Or maybe it was a military lawyer coming to represent him? That made more sense. But would the military really use government resources to help him fight state criminal charges? His mind continued to wonder all the way to the room.

When the door opened, Lieutenant Colonel Jones and First Mate Amber Maldonado sat at the small table. Seeing them dressed in their crisp white uniforms triggered something inside of Desmond, making him feel ashamed to be wearing the red segregation clothes.

"Oh, my God! Desmond, look at you," Amber cried, shooting to her feet, eyeing him like he had come back from the dead.

"Dammit, Harrison. I knew you were having a rough time, but I wasn't expecting this," the colonel mumbled, turning his nose up at Desmond's wrinkled jail clothes.

Desmond looked himself over self-consciously. He hadn't shaved or brushed his hair in a while and felt inadequate in their presence. "It's okay." He attempted a fake smile. "I've been through worse. What are you doing here?"

"We need to talk. Have a seat, Desmond." The colonel gestured. "I should've come sooner, but it's hard to get away right now with everything that happened with your team and what's going on right now in Iran."

Hearing about his team got Desmond's attention. "Did you find Slayer?"

"I'll get to that. For now, let's talk about you. Why won't you work with the district attorney and get yourself out of this hell hole?"

"With all due respect, sir, I don't trust them. I think they're trying to use my skills and then railroad me. They keep bringing more charges, trying to force my cooperation. That doesn't seem right. If you want to work with someone, you don't treat them like shit and then ask for their help."

The colonel nodded. "I see your point. It is a touchy situation. But what happens if you can't beat all the charges? They told me you were facing over one hundred years in prison. Are you prepared to throw away everything you've worked for and spend a significant part of your life in a cell?"

Desmond thought about how rough the week in jail had been and knew that it would probably get worse before it got better. "I don't know, sir. Honestly, I don't think so."

"Then you need to come up with a good exit strategy. And don't be surprised if someone shows up soon with an offer that you can't refuse."

"What's that's supposed to mean?" Desmond frowned.

"You will find out in due time," the colonel said, remaining cryptic. "And to answer your other question, we haven't found Marshall Sanchez, but we have good intel that he set your team up to be executed."

Desmond felt like he had been punched in the chest. "What? No way. I don't believe it. Slayer was a decorated SEAL. What proof do you have?"

"Most of the information is classified, but I'll tell you a little since it affects you personally. We recovered text messages from Slayer's phone. He was going back and forth with Grenandish Muhammad's top general, Azwalla Brescia, hours before your team went on the mission. He set you guys up, but we don't know why. Maybe the court martial for the rape drove him to betray us. Maybe it was money. We don't know. But we have all our resources stretched thin looking for him, and are continuing to run special ops. Without your team, we're a bit behind the curve. Your team was one of the best squads I've ever seen. You were the best of your group. Based on everything I've been briefed on since I arrived concerning you, it sounds like you haven't lost a beat. If you can manage to get your way out of this, I'll pull all the strings I can to get you back on base and back in combat. Like I said, you were one of the best and I don't want to see your talents go to waste in a prison cell."

The colonel's comments made Desmond pause to reflect. He thought the injuries took his military career and now the colonel was giving him a second chance. The information was a game changer. It was the best news he heard in a long time. "Okay. I'm going to figure something out."

The colonel stood and extended a hand. "Okay. That's all I got. The first mate wants a few words alone." He winked. "Take care of yourself, Harrison."

When the colonel left the room, Amber went to Desmond and hugged him. "Oh my God, Desmond! I was so worried about you!"

"I'm good. I'm still alive."

She grabbed his face in the palms of her hands to look him in the eyes. "What's going on with you? Do you know what they're saying about you? That you're a vigilante, killing everybody. They even think you killed a detective."

He didn't respond to the accusations. Just stared at her blankly.

Her eyes grew wide when she realized the truth. "Holy shit, Desmond! What the hell is wrong with you? Are you crazy?"

He looked away for a moment. "Honestly, I don't know. It feels like I'm going crazy. Everything is just happening and I'm reacting. I keep getting pulled deeper into this shit. It feels like I'm being chained to the streets. Every time I try to put an end to one issue, something else comes along."

Amber nodded, understanding perfectly well the power the streets had on those that come from the environment. "You can't let the streets suck you in, Desmond. You're better than that. You have to get out of here and leave. Forget this city. You can come to my hometown and we can start over new. Just me and you."

Hearing the warmth in her voice and seeing the compassion in her eyes made Desmond's insides grow warm. It was the most emotion she had ever shown. It made him wish he could be with her. Then Lasonya flashed in his head. He had already made a commitment. And he loved her.

"What is it?" Amber asked, picking up the change in his emotions.

He stared at the beautiful Latina woman for a moment, trying to find the words to say. "I can't go home with you, Amber."

She searched his face for the true meaning behind his words. "Why not? What happened?"

He reached a cuffed hand up and took her hand in his palm. "I met somebody. Well, not really met her, but ran into her again. My childhood girlfriend. We've kinda gotten serious."

Amber pulled her hand away and took a step back. True emotions played on her face. Hurt and disappointment. She looked blindsided by the omission. She tried blinking away the emotions but couldn't hold her bearing. "Wow. I wasn't expecting to hear that," she mumbled.

Desmond stood. "I know. And I didn't know this was going to happen, but when I came home to heal, things just took off."

She nodded, steeling her appearance. "It's okay. You don't have to explain anything. We weren't serious. We're just friends."

Desmond watched the words leave her lips and knew she was lying. They were more than friends, but agreed to focus on their careers. Now Desmond had gotten serious with someone else. No words would comfort her so he didn't even try. "Okay. Right. Just friends."

They continued to stare at one another, both of them having so much to say but neither speaking. After a long and uncomfortable silence, Amber broke it.

"Okay, Desmond." She nodded. "Take care of yourself. And get the hell out of jail. You're better than this."

◆◆◆

Desmond made up his mind. He needed to get out of jail. The colonel offered him an opportunity that he couldn't turn down. His entire adult life was spent in the military. It was all he wanted, all he'd known since he turned eighteen. And now the opportunity had arrived for him to get back in and maybe finish out his career. He hoped he hadn't ruined the deal offered by Mitchell Sellers because first thing in the morning, he was going to reach out and take the offer. Even if it meant being used, he had to get the fuck out of jail.

And then there was Amber. He didn't mean to hurt her. The pain he'd seen in her eyes cut him deep. She had come to confess her love and try to help him, and he spit in her face. Damn. And Lasonya. His woman. The one he risked his freedom to protect. What would she do if he went back to the military? Would she agree to come along? Polo was still searching for her daughter and he wouldn't be able to protect them when he was on assignment. Then there was his and Lucky's beef with Wacco. Could he really just up and leave everybody to their own demise? There were so many questions and not enough answers. He fell asleep with the questions still playing through his mind.

The next morning he was awakened by a knock on the door. It was breakfast. He scrambled out of bed to get the tray from the slat in the door. Today's meal was a peanut butter and jelly sandwich, a small portion of bran cereal, and an apple. He scarfed the meager meal and thought about how well he slept. For the first time since he'd been locked up, he didn't have a nightmare. As a matter of fact, he didn't even remember falling asleep or even remember the dream. He figured it must've been because he was emotionally exhausted from the meetings with Amber, the colonel, and his looking forward to getting in contact with Mitchell Sellers. After using the bathroom, he stripped down to his underwear and hit the floor for the morning workout. He went hard for thirty minutes. He had just finished completing a set of upside-down push-ups when there was a knock on the door. It was Mrs. Johnson.

"Harrison, you got a - " she was saying but stopped. Her eyes traveled down his sweaty muscular physique, stopping at the bulge in his underwear.

"What's up, Mrs. Johnson?" he asked.

She tore her eyes away from his package and locked eyes with him. "Uh, you have someone. You ready?"

He cocked an eyebrow. Her words didn't make sense. "What you say?"

She laughed nervously, trying hard to maintain eye contact and not look at his body again. "I'm sorry. You got me all flustered. I said you have a visitor. You ready?"

Thoughts of freedom flashed in his head. "Yeah. Let me get dressed. Who is it?" he asked, hoping Mitchell Sellers showed up for one more attempt to get him on their team.

"I don't know and I don't think you want me putting your business over the tier. But this is important."

Desmond rushed into the clothes and hurried to the door. "I don't give a fuck about what these niggas think. Is it the D.A. again?"

She shook her head. "Nah, baby. It's the Feds."

Desmond flinched a little. "The Feds?"

She nodded. "Yeah. Stick your hands out the trap so I can put the cuffs on."

During the walk to the meeting, Desmond racked his brain trying to think of what the Feds could want. He couldn't come up with any answers except the murder of Detective Perry. The situation was serious and he hoped that somehow he could get the military involved on his behalf because the federal government didn't play.

When he got to the room, there were two people inside sitting at a small table. A black man and white woman. Both wore black suits. When he stepped into the room, they stood to greet him.

"Good morning, Desmond," the man spoke. "I'm Agent Wright and this is my partner, Agent Johanson. We want to talk."

Desmond nodded warily. "Okay. Do I need my lawyer?"

"That's up to you, soldier," the woman spoke. "If you want to leave with us, I suggest you leave your lawyer wherever he is because he will only slow down this process. So, what do you want? You wanna call Brandon Williams?"

Desmond studied the Feds for a moment. The woman name dropped his lawyer like they had been watching him and knew all there was to know. They didn't seem hostile and they spoke of letting him leave. But so did Mitchell and Brian. It was probably too good to be true. "When you say leave with y'all, what exactly are you talking about?"

Agent Johanson nodded to Mrs. Johnson. "Uncuff him."

"I'm sorry but I can't uncuff a prisoner while they are in segregation status," she refused.

Agent Wright intervened. "Listen, deputy. I have strict orders from the Defense Secretary to remove this prisoner from your custody and into mine. This is a matter of national security and you are hampering the process. I've already talked to your supervisors. Uncuff him."

Mrs. Johnson didn't ask any more questions.

"And after you uncuff him, you can leave the room and radio Sheriff Clark and tell him to meet us at the sally port door," Johanson added.

When Mrs. Johnson left, the Feds got down to business.

"Listen, Desmond, we don't have much time. We need your services and we are about to make you a deal that you can't refuse. Whatever you have going on with the state will be taken care of. No charges. You can leave with us right now. What do you say?" Agent Wright asked.

The situation was like a whirlwind. He was expecting to meet with Mitchell Sellers and now the Feds were offering him a deal of a lifetime. He didn't know what to do or think. "I'm sorry if I seem skeptical, but I am. I've been going back and forth with the district attorney about working with them and they were supposed to bring more charges against me. You guys are telling me that all that will disappear?"

"That's exactly what we're saying." Wright nodded. "Whatever you had with Mitchell Sellers is over. We've taken a look at everything concerning you, and you are our man. The secretary advised us to do whatever necessary to secure you. If you agree to work with us, your slate will be clean. I'm going to tell you right now, the job isn't easy, but we believe you're the only one that can complete the mission."

Damn. It seemed too good to be true, but Desmond knew he couldn't turn down the opportunity. But there was one more thing nagging at him. He couldn't leave Lasonya and Quaysha behind. Polo would kill them. Lucky was another story. If he found out Desmond was about to work with the Feds, it would start a world war. "Okay. I'm in. But I have some family members that are in danger that need my help."

The Feds looked to one another. "What would you like us to do?"

"Can they come with me? It's my girlfriend and her daughter."

Chapter 10

Lasonya lay in bed being tortured by guilty thoughts. She had gone too far. To keep her man, she traded in the morals and principles she stood for as a woman and did the unthinkable. She had slept with her man's brother. Twice. Now she hoped his seed would fertilize the egg to bring a baby and guarantee Desmond's love and devotion. More lies. More deceit. But it was too late to turn back. She would have to live with the pain and guilt. She had gone too far. And once a good girl goes bad, she's gone forever.

"Mommy, Granny want you," Quaysha said, appearing at the bedroom door and interrupting her mother's thoughts.

"Okay. Tell her I'm coming."

"Hurry up, sleepy head." Quaysha laughed as she bounced from the room.

Lasonya climbed out of bed slowly, dragging herself to the kitchen. Marcy was standing near the stove cooking breakfast.

"Good morning," Marcy said. "Why do you look like you had a rough night? You okay?"

Lasonya wasn't aware that she wore her mood so openly. She couldn't tell her mother the truth that the shame of her deeds was eating at her mind, so she added to the lies she had become accustomed to telling. "Desmond still ain't called and I'm worried about him."

"Aw, my baby is love sick," Marcy teased. "He still in the hole?"

"Yeah, I guess. They said he gets a phone call once a week. I'm hoping he calls today."

"I'm sure he'll call. I gotta make a few runs and go to the doctor. You want me to pick up anything while I'm out?" she asked as the doorbell rang.

"No. We're okay," Lasonya said before spinning and heading for the front door. "Who is it?"

"It's me," a man called.

"Me who?" Lasonya asked as she looked out the window. When she saw Desmond standing on the front porch, her knees went weak and she almost fainted. "AHHHH! OH MY GOD!" she screamed, her hands shaking as she fumbled with the locks. When she finally got the door opened, she launched herself into Desmond's arms, holding him tight, her body trembling and tears streaming down her face.

"Hey, baby," he groaned.

"Oh my God, Desmond. I can't believe it's you!" Lasonya cried.

"I told you I was coming back."

"Lasonya! You okay?" Marcy screamed, showing up at the door with a big black revolver, ready to let bullets fly. When she saw Desmond, elation lit the matriarch's face and she joined in the embrace. "Desmond! Aw shit, nigga, how you get out?"

"They dropped the charges about an hour ago. I need y'all to let me go so we can go inside and talk. I don't got that much time."

Lasonya stepped away from him, anger filling her tear stained eyes. "Nuh-uh. Where you think you going?"

Desmond looked over his shoulder at the black sedan waiting at the curb than back at Lasonya. "I got a ride."

"Who is that?"

"They got me out of jail. Let's go inside and talk."

When they stepped in the house, Quaysha ran at Desmond and hugged his knees. "Desmond! Hi, Desmond! Mommy was crying for you."

He reached down and picked up the toddler. "I know. Did you give her hugs and kisses for me like I told you?"

"Yes. Lots of 'em." She smiled. "And now I got one for you. Mwah."

"What's going on, Desmond? Where are you going? How did you get out?" Lasonya asked impatiently.

"I'm about to work with the ATF. They dropped everything. All the charges are gone. I'm good. I came for you and Quaysha. I want y'all to come with me."

Lasonya was speechless.

"Hold on a minute, Desmond," Marcy spoke, waving the gun to get his attention. "What do you mean you want my daughter and grandbaby to come with you? Where the hell is you going?"

"To Detroit. But you can't tell anyone. My brother doesn't even know. I want to take them with me to get them away from Polo. I'm the only one that can protect them. We'll all be in protective custody while I work the mission. Once it's done, we can go wherever we want and live our life."

"All the way to Detroit! Oh hell nah!" Marcy spat. "Ain't no way you taking my babies away. I won't never be able to see them."

"Listen, Marcy. Polo ain't gon' stop looking for Quaysha. I can protect them. The only way Polo will get to them is if he kills me first. And I don't think there are many people alive that can kill me. Trust me. I'll take care of them. And when the time is right, I will buy you a plane ticket for you to come see us."

Marcy wasn't going for it. "No, Desmond. I ain't met a nigga that can stop a .357 bullet. I can protect my family just fine."

Lasonya turned to her mother. "I'm going with him."

Marcy gave her daughter an evil look like she had just raised a hand to fight her. "I said you staying here. You not taking my grand-baby nowhere."

Lasonya kept her voice calm but firm. "Mama, I'm going with Desmond. He is my man. I love him and I'm going where he goes. And my daughter is coming with me."

The mother and daughter had a long staring contest. Lasonya stood firm, refusing to back down under the intimidating motherly stare. Then Marcy turned to Desmond. "Well, Desmond you betta go out there and tell them muthafuckas I'm coming too."

♦♦♦

Lucky's bladder woke him from the liquor-induced slumber. When he opened his eyes, the pounding headache made him wish he could go back to sleep. But he couldn't. The throbbing inside his head and full bladder demanded attention. He sat up in bed, rubbing his temples and trying to remember the previous evening. And that's when he discovered he was naked. He climbed out of bed and headed for the bathroom, trying to remember last night. He didn't even remember taking off his clothes. As he stood over the toilet and drained the snake, he tried to put the pieces together. Pain touched his heart when he remembered the conversation he had with Melissa's mother about the murder of the family. He had come back to the hotel to grieve in silence and plot his next move. Then Lasonya showed up with a bottle of vodka. They talked and drank. Everything after that was gone. How the fuck did I get naked? He wondered as he shook the dribbles of urine from his tool. And that's when he noticed the white dried stains on his dick.

"What the fuck?" he mumbled, trying to recall if he fucked Lasonya again. There were cum stains on his dick, but he couldn't remember how they got there. He walked back into the room and tried to find a signs of a woman. There was nothing. Not even a liquor bottle.

"What the fuck?" he mumbled again, lost for a moment.

He plopped down on the bed and thought, hoping to retrieve something. After a few minutes of nothing, he gave up, realizing the power of alcohol to dull the mind was too much.

He grabbed the phone to check messages and seen a text and voicemail from his literary agent. He had been ghosting her ever since the drama started. He couldn't get focused on writing and being a public figure while trying to stay alive. He would get in contact with her when he had time. When the phone rang he checked the screen. It was Lasonya. Just who he needed to talk to.

"Hey, sis," he answered groggily. "What happened last night?"

"Hey. You don't sound good. You okay?"

"Nah. I'm hung over. I can't even remember last night. Did we
- "

"I talked to Desmond," she interrupted.

Hearing his brother's name made him push thoughts of sex with Lasonya to the back burner. "What did he say? How's he doing?"

"He's good. They're transferring him to a military prison in Texas. I guess the army is taking over his case or something."

"What?" Lucky frowned. "That don't even make sense. How can the military charge him if he didn't commit a military crime?"

"I don't know. He said he's going to call you soon. I'm leaving town today with my mama and daughter. Milwaukee is too crazy right now and I'm getting away with my family."

The sudden departure of the people he was closest too unnerved him. "Damn. You leaving just like that? Where you going?"

"We have family in California. Polo won't stop until he gets my daughter. I can't let him do that. I'm heading to the airport right now."

"Okay. I guess I understand," he said, giving pause. "Hey, about last night. What happened?"

"I don't know what you're talking about," she answered quickly.

"After you came over, I remember drinking and kicking it, then everything went blank. I woke up nak-"

"I'm sorry, Lucky, but I gotta go. My plane is about to leave. I'ma tell Desmond you're waiting for his call. Take care."

She hung up before he could say another word. Lucky stared at the phone for a moment. Lasonya was acting weird. Something wasn't right. But he couldn't be too focused on her. He had too many other problems to deal with. Maybe he went out and found a night walker. Women of the night didn't stay until the next day. He pushed thoughts of sex from his mind and thought about Desmond. The military had taken over. He made a mental note to call Brandon and get the scoop. The most important issue facing him was killing Polo. He had an idea how to get to the snake, but he needed to find some allies. He picked up the phone and called Miguel.

"'Sup, Lucky?"

"Any word on Polo?"

"No. But I'm gonna find that son of a bitch and paint the ground with all the blood in his body," the certified killer promised.

"I think I might know how to find him. I'ma make a couple of moves and get with you and Tyler later. Let me know if y'all catch anything on y'all end."

◆◆◆

Thirsty Thursdays in Exotica was for the average working nigga that didn't have a lot of money to blow. The admission fee was only five dollars, shots of top shelf liquor were five dollars, and bottom shelf only one dollar. The women that entertained weren't the best of the flock, but they looked good enough in the dim light for a nigga with a good buzz to think they were dimes.

Lucky sat at a booth in the VIP watching the strippers shake what their mama's gave em. Most of his attention was paid to one dancer in particular: Black Barbie. The brown-skinned beauty was currently giving another patron a sexy lap dance while giving Lucky seductive eye contact from across the room. They had been playing this game for over an hour. She would come to his booth to say a couple words and then hit the floor to keep getting her coins. When the song was over, she kept to her ways and sashayed back to his booth.

"I think that was my last one for the night. I'm tired of these niggas," she breathed, sitting down heavily. "How is that hangover?"

"Better." Lucky nodded, taking a drink from the bottle of Budweiser. "You should be a doctor."

She grabbed the bottle of Remy Martin from the table and poured a shot. "I thought about being a doctor when I was little. I think I woulda been good at it too. My daddy told me he wanted me to be a doctor or lawyer. My rotten ass fell far from that apple tree." She laughed before slamming the shot.

"I don't think it's too late for you to be a doctor. When you want something bad enough, you won't let nobody or nothing stop you from getting it. That's what a go-getter is."

"Yeah. You're right." She nodded in agreement. "But being a doctor ain't in my plans. I'm just tryna live and do my own thang. That was my daddy plans, but he been gone out my life since I was fifteen. It's on me now."

"What happened to yo' pop? Where he at?"

"He in Waupun. Got life 'cause his supposed-to-be nigga told on him."

"I was in Waupun. I did seven years. What's yo' pop name?"

"Big Mike."

Lucky's eyes popped. "Get the fuck outta here! OG Big Mike is yo' pops?"

She smiled. "Yeah, that's my old man. You know him, for real?"

"Everybody in Waupun know OG Big Mike. Nigga a legend. Well-respected by er'body. Police and prisoners. Damn. It's a small world. Next time you holla at him, tell him I said what up. He should remember my step back jumper."

She looked confused. "What that mean?"

"Some basketball shit. Just say it to him and he gon' know. Yo' pops is one of the realest niggas I ever met. And he stay in that law library. I think he gon' get another chance out here. He working hard to get back to you and one thing I know is that hard work always pay off. I think that's a universal law because I never seen a nigga that work hard not get what he working for."

She smiled again, the admiration for him growing in her eyes. "Whatever happened with you and that woman you said held you down for five years? You still doing that?"

Thoughts of Melissa brought instant pain to Lucky's chest, his demeanor growing a little dim. "Nah," he mumbled, growing quiet and looking away so she wouldn't see the pain in his eyes.

Barbie noticed the mood change. She grabbed his chin and turned his face back to her. "Hey, what's going on? Why you flip on me like that?"

Lucky could see compassion in her eyes, but wasn't sure if she was being sincere. Good strippers were great actresses, and he didn't want to have his emotions toyed with. "Maybe some other time. "

She stared into his face for a moment, trying to solve the puzzle he'd become. When she noticed the pain in his eyes disappear and his resolve steel up, she nodded. "The truth hurt, don't it?"

"More than you can imagine," he said, taking a sip of beer to quench the fire of emotions that had welled up in his chest.

For the first time since he entered the club, silence stood in the way of getting to know Barbie.

"I'm just about done for the night and thirsty Thursdays is always slow. You wanna go get something to eat?" she asked.

"Yeah. Let's modulate."

After Black Barbie changed into a pair of jeans and T-shirt, they left the club and headed to Harold's. The conversation flowed effortlessly over their soul food platters and during the exchange Lucky earned a great deal of respect for the exotic dancer. She was in the middle of telling him what separated her from other strippers, and he found her explanation interesting.

"See, these other dancers let money rule them and they will do anything for it. But I know that money is not everything. It's not a god, but a tool. Anything that you let rule you becomes your God. When you sell your soul for money, you become a slave to it. I like money, but I'm not about to give some nasty dick-ass nigga my precious pearl for one hundred dollars. I'm worth more than that."

"So you've never turned a trick?"

She stared at him for a moment, contemplating her answer. "Not in the sense of here go some money, now give me some pussy. I won't give my body to a nigga just because he offers me money. But I do have a sponsor."

"So if a nigga offered you ten thousand for a shot, would you turn it down?"

She frowned, looking like she was getting ready to curse him out. "What the fuck kind of question is that? Nigga, I'm not stupid. Of course I would give him the kitty for ten thousand dollars. How often you think that's gon' happen? I believe in everything I just said about money and gods and all that, but I gotta do what I gotta do for ten stickers. Would you?"

Lucky thought for a moment. "To be real, if I need the money, I would probably go for a couple hunnit."

"Damn, baby. You a cheap hoe." Barbie laughed.

"I'm just being real." He laughed. "So, this sponsor. What's that about?"

She looked off in the distance to gather her thoughts. "He's not my man, but he's more than a friend."

"It's just one? Is it Polo?"

Her face went flat. "You tryna call me a hoe?"

"Nah, nah. I wouldn't do that. I just wanna know what I'm getting into."

She smiled. "Oh, so you think you getting into something?"

"C'mon, now. You know what I mean."

She crossed her arms over her breasts, looking amused. "I don't know what you mean. Explain."

Lucky laughed. "You serious?"

"As cancer."

"Okay," he said, taking a moment to gather his thoughts. "I came to see you because you left an impression on me. I had a feeling that you wasn't the average stripper that would do anything for money, and I liked that about you. Now here we are."

She laughed. "Your game is terrible."

"That's because it wasn't game. The reason people believe lies is because they sound good. The truth is always dull, but it's still the truth."

She nodded in respect. "Now that was good game."

"I just told you I don't got game."

"Relax, man. Damn. I was just playing. Jeesh."

He shook his head and chuckled.

"What?" she asked, curious to know his thoughts.

"You crazy, but I like it."

"You gotta have a little crazy in your life. It keeps it spicy."

He nodded. "I try to stay away from crazy. I'm on parole and I seen that crazy shit get niggas cooked. But you... It's something about you."

She squinted her eyes low. "Thank you. I think. That was a compliment, right?" she asked sarcastically.

"Yeah. Something like that," he said and then paused.

She could see there was something on his mind. "What you gotta say?"

He looked away, wondering if he should speak his mind. "This sponsor of yours. I gotta know if it's Polo."

She smiled, mischief lighting her eyes. "Why? You wanna take his place and be my new sponsor?"

He became serious. "Nah. I don't pay for pussy. I come from an era where it was something special to have the ability to talk a girl out the draws. Anything that I pay for I possess or own. And one thing that I learned is you can't keep nothing that don't belong to you or want to be kept. And I also don't like sharing with niggas I broke bread with."

She recognized the go-getter in his eyes and got serious as well. "And how you know I'ma share anything with you? You getting ahead of yo'self, ain't you?"

He returned a confident stare. "Nah, I'm not getting ahead. We right where we supposed to be. And you've already shared more than enough to let me know that I can have it all. I see you and you see me. What's real can't be faked or denied. This is real. Tell me I'm lying."

A smile crept slowly onto her face. "You feeling yo'self way too much."

"I accept you not answering the question as the truth. So, is Polo yo' sponsor or what?"

Mischief lit her eyes again. "Wouldn't you like to know?"

Chapter 11

Lucky awoke at a little after 11 a.m. to the sound of his phone ringing. The caller was unknown.

"Hello?"

"What's going on, brah?"

Lucky perked up when he heard his brother's voice. "Des, what up, nigga? Where you at?"

"I'm in Texas at a military prison. I'm being court martialed for some bullshit that happened overseas. They say I knew about Slayer betraying the team. It's bullshit."

"Damn. That sound like some bitch-ass shit. You lost yo' eye and got fucked up and this how they do?"

"Yeah. The state dropped all those charges and handed me over. I guess they felt like they couldn't convict me, but the military could. Just bullshit."

"Do you need a lawyer? What Brandon say?"

"Military court is different. I got an attorney. She pretty good. But enough about me. How you doing? Lasonya told me what happened to Melissa and her kids."

A dark cloud came and hovered over Lucky's mood, instantly turning him dark. "Shit is fucking with my head, man. That shit was uncalled for. It was a violation."

"Polo?"

"Who else? I'ma take care of it. I promise that."

"C'mon, Lucky. You gotta be smart about this. You got too much to lose. What the police say?"

"The police?" Lucky scoffed. "You still screaming that police shit after what they did to you? Fuck the police. I got it."

"C'mon, Lucky. I know you mad, but you still on parole. Think about this. I know you don't want to be in a cell again. I hate this shit."

"I thought about it, brah. Ain't no talking me out of it. You just wasting yo' breath."

The phone went silent for a few beats. "Damn, Lucky. I get it. Just be careful."

After talking with Desmond, Lucky lay in bed and let his thoughts roam. It was fucked up what they were doing to his brother. He didn't deserve what was happening. Desmond spent almost fifteen years in the army fighting for this country, and now America was treating him like a redheaded stepchild. He liked that Desmond was taking the charges like a man and not trying to blame other people, because not many people would. He just hoped that his little brother would make it out.

He jumped out of bed and hit the shower. When he came back into the hotel room, his phone showed two missed text messages. One was from Laronda. She wanted some money. The other was from his agent.

Since you haven't returned any of my calls I'm going to void the contract. Hope everything is okay. Call me if you need help. Take care.

He sat and thought about how to react. There was really nothing he could do. He couldn't think about writing and selling books with everything that was going on in his life. When he got back focused, he would give her a call. For now, he was most concerned about finding and killing Polo. And he wasn't going to let anything stand in the way. Not even his writing career. After getting fresh, he made a call to Barbie.

"Hey, Lucky."

"What's good, Barbie?"

"Why you still calling me that? You know my real name."

"I know. I like Barbie."

"I don't. Especially after you talked about you seeing me for who I am. Niggas that pay for my time call me Black Barbie. People that I chose to spend time with call me Rachel. So, you got some money for me, Lucky?"

"Nah, Rachel," he laughed. "I see you."

"You crazy, man. So, what's up? How you doing?"

"I'm good. I would he doing a lot better if I could see you."

"Look at you tryna step your game up. Tell me what you got in mind."

"I'm a spontaneous nigga. How about I pull up and you just get in the car and leave the rest up to me. Clear yo' schedule for the day. You with me."

"Okay, baby!" She laughed. "Talk that shit. Gimme some time to get ready."

"I'ma be there in an hour."

"Can't wait to see you, baby."

After hanging up, Lucky threw on some clothes and hit the mall. He copped a Rockstar fit and Giuseppe sneakers then went to change in the dressing room. He stood in front of the mirror checking his appearance, doing a few poses. When he was satisfied with his look, he paid for it with his credit card and jumped in the ride, heading for a rental car agency. Driving the Mustang was no longer an option. He wasn't going to turn himself in any time soon and since the car was registered to him, it would have to go in storage. After roaming the lot, he settled on a black 600 Benz.

He pulled up to Rachel's house twenty minutes later. She answered the door wearing a strapless red dress and red bottoms. Her auburn and black hair was long and curly with a wet look.

"Damn!" Lucky mumbled, grabbing her arm and giving her a twirl. "You look good enough to eat."

"If you play your cards right, I might let you." She smiled seductively.

"Only card game I play is strip poker. And I always win. All in on the first hand. Call or fold." He grinned.

"I don't know what all that means, but it sound slick," she said, giving him an approving head to look. "And I like those shoes."

He struck a pose. "Gotta stay fly. You ready?"

"Yeah. Where we going?"

He gave her a serious stare. "I told you, I'm a spontaneous nigga. Just sit back and enjoy the ride. I got this."

The first destination on their all-day date was Victoria's Secret. She tried on lingerie and modeled it for Lucky before he paid for several of the sexy outfits. Next they went to Devin's Steak and

Seafood and pigged out on surf and turf meals. They ended the night at Replay, an upscale bar on the East Side known for having great local entertainment. Tonight was open mic night, and Lucky had a surprise.

"I don't say this too often, Lucky, but you that nigga." Rachel nodded, looking at him with admiration and lust in her eyes.

"So I take it you enjoying yo'self?"

She nodded. "I had fun with you all day. And this bar is a good setting. It's intimate and got a good vibe. You have good taste."

"I'm glad you enjoying yourself. But don't think we done yet. I got one more surprise."

Her eyes lit up. "What is it?"

"In due time, li'l one," he teased.

"You ain't no good." She frowned.

"I know. I'm better than good. I'm great."

She rolled her eyes. "That ain't what my daddy said."

"You talked to OG Mike?"

She nodded and took a sip of her drink. "This morning after you called. He remembers you. He said you could play a little ball and write books."

"A little ball?" Lucky scoffed. "I used to fuck yo' pops up. Did you ask him about that step back?"

"Nah, I forgot. But what about those books? Did you get any published?"

He nodded. "Yeah. Five star reviews on Amazon. Check me out."

Her eyes lit up in surprise. "Oh my God! That's so cool. I can't believe I'm talking to a real author. What kind of books do you write?"

"Mostly urban novels. I was working on a biography, but I had to put it on the back burner."

"Why?" She frowned. "Why don't you finish it?"

Thinking on the reasons for him no longer pursuing his writing career took some of the air out of their good vibes. "It's just been hard for me lately," he said vaguely.

She waited, expecting more. "That's all? Tell me what happened."

He shook his head and looked away. "I don't wanna ruin the good vibes. We can talk about it some other time."

She gave him a long look, concern in her eyes. "Okay. But just make sure you get back to it. And I wanna read some of your work."

He nodded again, standing to his feet. "I got one better for you. Remember that surprise I told you about? Here it is," he said before walking towards the small stage next to the bar. He had a couple words with the Emcee before walking upon stage and grabbing the mic.

"How's everybody doing tonight?" he asked.

He got a warm reception from the small crowd.

"That's good. If I can, I want to share a poem that I wrote. I'm here with a really special lady, and I wanna dedicate it to her. It's called SHE.

"A delicate vision. Spirit wrapped in earth, Eve's likeness.

Aura decorated by fire. Wings from heaven. Flightless.

Seasons change in her brown irises. Spring to summer. Fall to winter.

Seductive language wasting my will to be strong. The temptress tempting the tempter.

A siren. Her voice a liquid song. Erotically enticing.

The promise of infinite pleasure whispered across ancient writings.

Communicator to the senses. Hear. Smell. Sight. Taste. Touch.

Deeply engraved principles efface rapidly at the precipice of lust.

Dangerous desires. Adventurous illusions. Spiritual communion.

The fourth dimension of fantasy brought to life within our union.

My muse is a masterpiece. Framed in mythology. Blessed by Rah.

Painted across silk canvases with brushes forged by gods.

She dove into my deeper self. Lifted me high. Up and above.

We wrote manuscripts on tantric eroticism. Spoke the five languages of love.

She was. She is. She will always be.

My earth. My stars. My universe. SHE."

When Lucky finished reciting the poem, the crowd gave him a standing ovation. He walked back to the table and was greeted by Rachel with a long and passionate French kiss.

"I'm ready to go." She smiled, lust lighting her eyes.

Lucky didn't waste time getting her out of the bar and back to the Benz. The ride to her house was filled with foreplay. By the time they walked in her house, both of them were practically naked. She didn't think twice about the pistol he placed on the table because they were too busy making out. And he didn't think twice about grabbing a condom because he didn't want to ruin the mood.

They didn't make it to the bedroom, instead falling on the couch, kissing, touching, and tugging at each other's clothes until they were fully nude. She pulled him between her legs and yanked on Lucky's hardness, trying to pull him into her hot box. He resisted, leaning back on his haunches to stare at her body. Rachel was banging. Big perky breasts. A small waist. Thick thighs. Pussy clean shaved. Artful tattoos covering her soft brown skin. A six inch cross in the middle of her chest. A rose and a tulip on each arm. On her thighs were two black Barbie Dolls. Lucky lifted her right leg and kissed his way from her ankle to inner thigh.

"Ssss! Oh my God, Lucky!" she moaned, cupping her own breasts as shivers went through her body.

He continued kissing his way to her labia, taking his time and licking his tongue from the top to the bottom of each swollen pussy lip.

"Damn, Lucky. Oooh, baby, you killin' me, nigga," she whined, rubbing his head, encouraging him to eat.

He pressed both thumbs into the top of her slit, making her clitoris pop out. Then he flicked his tongue across the tender ball of flesh, making her yelp.

"Oh, shit! Yeah, Lucky. Don't stop. Please, don't stop!"

His tongue became a blur as he flicked it across her pearl tongue rapidly. Rachel pulled her nipples and screamed in pleasure at the top of her lungs. After a few moments of licking, he sucked the ball of flesh between his lips and began sucking while slipping a finger deep into her wetness.

"Oh, my God! Ohh! Ohh! Ohh my God!"

He continued sucking her clitoris and fingering her pussy, eventually slipping three fingers inside and fucking her good. When she began bucking her hips, he knew she was close to orgasm and kept his lips and fingers moving.

"Oh shit! Oh, shit! Ohh!" she screamed as her body locked up and the orgasm ran through her body in waves.

When Lucky climbed on top of her, she wrapped her arms around his neck and pulled him in for a long and wet tongue kiss. During the smooch, he slipped deep inside her love canal. Her pussy was wet as the ocean and warm as a preheated oven. After giving her a few moments to adjust to him being inside, he started fucking her with short slow strokes.

"Mmmhhh!" she moaned, gripping his shoulders and biting his lips.

"Damn, Rachel. Yo' pussy feel so good," he groaned, struggling to control himself. He really wanted to unleash his inner animal and beat the pussy up. But he didn't. He used control and went slow, paying attention to her body and giving her what she yearned for.

"Oh, Lucky! Oh damn, nigga!" she moaned, loving the feel of him deep in her guts.

He moved his lips to her ear and began whispering the poem he had recited at the open mic while giving her more of the D. "A delicate vision. Spirit wrapped in earth. Eve's likeness…"

Rachel went mad. Never had she experienced the mental and physical stimulation that she was experiencing with Lucky. Her body tingled and explosions ignited all across her skin. She called his name over and over while crying out to God. Her second orgasm was the most pleasurable feeling she'd ever experienced in her life.

It took all the strength from her body and all she could do is lay there until Lucky busted.

"Damn," Lucky groaned as he collapsed on top of her.

Rachel's body vibrated and shivered like she was cold. "Damn, Lucky. What the fuck you just do to me?" she questioned, her speech slurred like she was high on some kind of super drug.

"Made you speak the five languages of love," he cracked.

"Fuck you, nigga." She slapped him on the shoulder. "But I do need you to do me a favor and grab the blanket from my bed, because I don't think I can walk."

◆◆◆

Lucky was asleep on the couch when he heard the unmistakable sound of a key being inserted into the lock on the front door. Rachel lay on top of him, her head on his chest, in a deep slumber. He kept his eye on the door as he shook her.

"Rachel, wake up. Somebody at the door."

She lifted her head slowly. "What?"

"Somebody at the door," he repeated as the door began to open. The chain on the door kept it from opening all the way.

"Rachel! You in there?" a man called.

Rachel became instantly alert at the sound of the voice. "Oh shit!" she cried, leaping off Lucky, her eyes wide with fear. She stood naked in the middle of the living room, frozen like a statue.

"Who the fuck is that?" Lucky questioned, reaching for the pistol on the table.

"My sponsor!"

A vision of Polo's face flashed in Lucky's head as an angry fire burned throughout his being. He had been waiting for this moment. Praying for it. And God had delivered. He leapt from the couch, flipping the safety off the pistol, not caring that he was naked or that Rachel was about to witness the killing.

"What the fuck are you doing?" Rachel screamed.

"I'm killin' this nigga!" Lucky barked, shoving the door closed and going for the chain.

"Rachel, you good?" the man called again.

"No, Lucky!" Rachel screamed, running over and trying to stop him from opening the door. "What are you doing? Stop!"

Lucky shoved her to the side. "Fuck that! He killed my people. He gotta go!" he roared, snatching the chain off and yanking the door open. He lifted the gun, applying pressure to the trigger.

And that's when he noticed it wasn't Polo. The man before him looked to be in his early forties, had light brown skin and a short Afro with a receding hairline. He stood about six foot with a slim build and wore designer clothes with a watch that looked like it cost as much as a car.

"Ay, nigga! What the fuck?" the man yelled.

"Lucky, what the fuck are you doing?" Rachel yelled.

Lucky stood there for a moment unsure of what to do next. "I thought... I thought it was Polo."

The man looked from Lucky to Rachel, growing angrier by the moment. "Rachel, what the fuck is this shit?" he asked. Then he turned back to Lucky. "If you don't stop pointing that gun at me, nigga, we gon' have a serious problem."

Lucky stared the man in the eyes for a moment, reading no fear. Only anger. An air of importance swelled around the newcomer and somehow Lucky knew he was in the presence of a boss. "My bad," he apologized, lowering the gun. "I thought you was somebody else."

"Rachel, what the fuck kinda shit is this? This the type of trifling shit you be on when I'm not around?"

"No, Donny. It's not like that. Lucky is my friend."

Lucky knew the sight of a domestic situation when he saw one and went for his clothes. He wanted to get the fuck out of there before the bullets started flying or the police got called.

"Friend my ass! Why this nigga answering the door naked and pointing a gun in my fucking face?" Donny asked, stepping into the house.

"I don't know why he got the gun," she tried to explain. "We went out last night. I didn't know you was coming to town. Why didn't you call?"

"'Cause I don't gotta call. You know who the fuck I am. I do what the fuck I want. And don't you ever fix yo' mouth to ask me some shit like that ever again. This ain't about me. This about you," he said, pulling a pistol from his waist. "Now ain't nobody leaving this house til I find out what the fuck is going on." Then he turned and yelled outside. "Fifty! Scooby! Get y'all asses in here! It's a nigga in here with a gun."

Lucky was halfway dressed, holding the gun in his hand, when two niggas that looked like linebackers for the Green Bay Packers ran into the house clutching heat. When they saw Lucky with the gun, they covered Donny and pointed their pistols.

"Put that gun down, nigga!" one of them yelled.

"Hell nah. You put yo' gun down," Lucky refused, keeping the gun at his side.

"Put that shit down before I fan you down, nigga," the other bodyguard threatened.

Lucky continued to stand his ground. "Do what you gotta do, but I ain't dropping shit."

"Lucky, put the gun down," Rachel pleaded, covering herself with the blanket.

He looked at her like she was stupid. "Tell them niggas to drop they shit. It's three of them and one of me."

"Move out the way," Donny told his security as he stepped forward, still holding the pistol. "Why the fuck you pointing a muthafuckin' gun in my face, nigga."

"I thought you was somebody else?"

"You gon' have to say more than that, my nigga, if you wanna walk out this house alive. You just pointed a gun in my face, and that was a violation to the highest degree. I killed muthafuckas for less," Donny said, meaning every word.

Lucky looked from Donny to his henchmen. They all wore serious looks, leaving no doubt that not cooperating would cause bullets to fly. The odds were stacked against him, death almost certain. "I thought you was this nigga, Polo. He killed some of my people."

"Why did you think I was Polo?" Donny asked before turning to Rachel. "You fucking Polo?"

"Nah," she frowned.

"You sure? He seems to think you is?"

"I never fucked with Polo. Ever."

Donny turned his attention back to Lucky, awaiting an explanation.

"When I first met her at the club, Polo introduced us. He used to be my nigga, and now we beefing. A couple nights ago she made it seem like he was her sponsor."

"I didn't make it seem like nothing," Rachel said. "If I woulda knew you was trying to kill him, I woulda told you."

"Shut up, Rachel. Go put some clothes on," Donny ordered.

She left the room without another word.

Donny tucked his pistol in the waist of his pants and sat down, eyeing Lucky. "Put the gun up and have a seat. You making my boys nervous and I don't want you to get hurt."

Lucky tucked the pistol and had a seat, trying to read Donny. He had never been in a situation like this and didn't know how to react.

"I been in the streets a long time, Lucky. Seen it all and done it all. Learned to read people as well as any psychologist or body language expert and I can see that you telling the truth. I can also read between the lines and see that you used Rachel to get to Polo without ever revealing your intentions. You coulda killed her and Polo and nobody woulda seen it coming. That takes some skill and cunning. As an employer, I can recognize talent when I see it. And you have the potential to go far." Donny smiled, eyeing Lucky like he was proud of him. "I seen the Benz outside. What do you do to make money?"

He wondered where the conversation was going. "I'm a writer."

Donny's eyes lit up. "A professional, huh? I didn't expect that. I thought you was a d-boy. So, you an author that can handle heat," he said, running a hand across his mustache, eyeing Lucky, trying to read more about him. And then his eyes lit up again. "You learned how to write in the joint, didn't you? How long you been out?"

Lucky was surprised at the way the man's mind worked. The way he put together situations and profiled people was uncanny. "A couple of months."

He nodded. "And whatever Polo did got you ready to trade your freedom for revenge. Who did he kill?"

"My ex-girlfriend and her kids."

"So this is personal."

Nobody spoke for a few moments. Rachel walked back into the living room, surprised to see the men sitting down talking.

"Rachel, baby, give us a few more minutes," Donny said. When she left the room, he addressed Lucky again. "I like you, my nigga. You gotta loyal spirit surrounding you. And you smarter than the average street nigga. What if I told you that I could make all of yo' problems disappear. Would you believe me?"

Lucky shook his head. "Anything that's too good to be true probably is."

Donny found that funny. "Yeah. You are a rare gem, Lucky. I'm going to make you an offer. I'm a powerful man with unlimited reach. I will take care of all of your problems if you agree to work for me."

Lucky paused to think about the offer. Donny exuded power and confidence. Sitting on the couch, he seemed almost godlike. And Lucky knew that jumping into bed with him would probably reap great rewards along with huge problems. "I'm sorry, but I have to decline the offer."

Donny smiled. "I expected you to say that. You not the kinda nigga that jumps into shit. Had you agreed right away, I would have lost respect for you. But the offer will remain if you change your mind," he said and stood. "Rachel is a good woman. A rare breed of street smarts and loyalty. Comes from good stock. It'll do you some good to keep her around. This is the last time I'll come to visit.

This situation has taught me that everyone is susceptible to tempta-tion. Whatever you did to her was good enough for her to defy me. I think she's more yours than mine. She knows how to get in contact with me if you change your mind."

Chapter 12

Rich Red carried himself like a boss. He stood at 5'11" and 180 pounds with light red freckles covering his face, and a short, natural, bronze-colored afro. He stepped from the driver's seat of the burnt orange Porsche Cayenne, sauce dripping from his swag. He wore Balmain from head to toe. When he noticed the handmade 24 carat gold lace in the left shoe come undone, he bent low to tie the custom shoelace. Whenever he made an appearance anywhere in Detroit, he made sure to flex hard so the world knew the young boss was on deck. Today's "I'm so icy" displays were the shoestrings. They cost 19,000 dollars and were so exclusive that the company only made one hundred pair a year. Rich Red was in a rare class and the shoestrings let the world know what he had known since he was a pup: that Rich Red was a boss!

"Rich Red!"

He turned at the sound of his name being called. A short, chubby nigga walked quickly in his direction. "Nut, what's good, slime?"

"Shit. Out here posted. I see you lighting up the block. Fuck you got in them shoes?" he asked, studying the laces.

Rich Red struck a pose. "Twenty G's for the shoelaces, nigga. 24 carat. I'm fucking the city up, on what?"

Nut's eyes popped. "On what, you just spent twenty bands on them?"

"What kinda question is that? When you used to doing this shit, it come natural. I get money and I spend money. Shit go hand in hand like Percs and lean."

"I hear you, slime." Nut laughed.

"What's goin' on out here? The block shaking?"

"Not really. It's still early. You know niggas don't start stepping out til the afternoon."

Rich Red checked the time on his Audemar. It was 10:47 a.m. "Yeah. That's why these niggas still broke. Early bird get the first worm. I'm out here. Let's go grab somethin' to eat. You can whip the Porsche."

Glee lit Nut's eyes when Rich Red tossed him the keys. From the block they rode the luxury whip to Starlet's and ordered rib platters. They were sitting in the parking lot grubbing when Rich Red noticed a black Challenger with dark tint pull into the lot. Through the windshield, he could see two clean cut white men. In the ghetto, the Caucasians stuck out like niggas at a Klan rally.

"There go the Feds, pull off," Rich Red said shakily as he watched the car drive slowly past the Porsche.

Nut looked up too late and couldn't see who drove the car because of the tint. "Where they at?"

"In the Challenger! Pull off, nigga!"

The alarm in Rich Red's voice made Nut snap into action. He dropped the Styrofoam tray in his lap and whipped the sports car from the lot. The Challenger pulled out right behind them.

"Shit! They coming!" Rich panicked. He opened the console and pulled out fifty grams of dog food and a Glock. "I need you to hop out and run. Take this shit wit'chu."

Nut glanced at the contraband like it was a deadly poison. "Hell nah! Nigga, I got my own shit," he said before checking the rearview mirror. The black car was still behind them.

"C'mon, my nigga. Speed up and hit some corners and jump out. Take my shit with you, since you gotta run. Ain't no sense in both of us getting knocked. I'ma pay yo' bail if they catch you."

"If they catch me?" Nut said incredulously as he whipped the car around a corner. "Nigga, I'm fat. You know they gon' catch me. You should run and take my shit with you!"

"Bitch-ass shit!" Rich Red cursed, watching the car in the side mirror.

Nut put a little distance between them when he turned onto a one way and Rich Red saw his opportunity to run. "A'ight. Turn left up here and let me out."

"You gon' take my shit?" Nut asked.

"Hell nah! You wouldn't take my shit! Turn right here and let me out!"

Nut hit the corner hard and brought the Porsche to a screeching stop. Rich Red fled from the passenger seat, trying hard to imitate

Usain Bolt as he ran through a yard. Tires screeched as the Porsche sped away. When Rich Red looked behind him, he saw the black Challenger stopping and the white men hopping out to chase him. He kept on running through a yard, an alley, and another yard on the opposite side of the block. He was running across the street when he saw a blue Infiniti speeding towards him. At the last second, the tires screeched and the car slid. All Rich could do was close his eyes and prepare for impact because he knew the car was about to fuck him up. When it seemed like it was too late, the car came to a complete stop, so close to Rich that he was able to touch it. The nigga behind the wheel wore a big chain with diamonds and Cartier glasses. Rich knew a hustler when he saw one.

"Ay, brah! I need a ride," he said, running to the passenger door.

The driver looked from Rich to the two white men that emerged from the yard across the street. "Get in, nigga!"

Rich jumped in the passenger seat as the car sped away. "Good looking, fam."

"You got it, my nigga. What the fuck was that?" the driver asked.

Rich Red turned to look out the back window to see if they were being followed. "I think them was the alphabet boys. Damn. Good looking, my nigga. You saved my ass."

"Damn. We gotta get the fuck off these streets. Where you going, brah?"

"Take me to my bitch's crib. I can pay you. What's yo name?" he asked, taking a long look at his savior. He was big, about 6'4", and in good shape, like he worked out regularly. The fitted T-shirt showed big arms and good definition. The distinguishing mark was the scar on his left eye.

"They call me D-Money. You gon' have to direct me to where yo' bitch live 'cause I'm from Flint and I don't really know my way around Detroit."

Ten minutes later the car stopped in front of a blue and green duplex. Rich pulled the bag of dope from his pocket along with a stack of cash. He counted off fifteen hundred dollars. "This for helping me get out that jam."

D-Money looked at the cash than the drugs. "Man, I really don't want yo' money, fam. I appreciate it, but I really need a good plug on that dog food."

Opportunity lit Rich Red's eyes. "Say less, my nigga. I gotta get the fuck off these streets and see what the fuck up with 12. But gimme yo' number. Soon as I get straight, I'ma get wit'chu. Good lookin' on that ride."

After a handshake, Rich Red climbed from the car and double-timed it into the house. His girlfriend, Teona, was sitting on the couch doing another woman's makeup. Teona was super bad. Light, thick, with a banging body.

"Hey baby. Why you looking like that?" she asked, noticing the distressed look on his face.

"I think the Feds on me. They just chased me and Nut," he said, pulling out his phone and dialing Nut's number.

Teona stopped doing the woman's makeup and turned to her man. "What happened? You okay? Where is Nut?"

"He in my car still. Damn, and he ain't answering the phone. They probably got him."

"What you gon' do, baby?"

Rich Red thought for a moment. He wasn't sure what to do other than lay low. When the Feds were after somebody, they usually got 'em. The federal government had too much money, resources, and firepower. And their reach was limitless. "Shit, ain't nothin I really can do but fall back."

"I think that's a good idea. Stay out the streets for a li'l while and see what happen. Can I have some money so I can buy a new bag? I seen a Louis Vuitton bag that I need."

Rich Red gave her a look that could kill. "I just told you the Feds after me and you worried about a mu'fuckin' bag?"

Teona shrugged, not understanding his anger. "Ain't nothing you can do about it. Why I can't get a bag because the police chased you? What that got to do with me?"

Rich Red pulled all the money from his pocket and threw it in Teona's face as hard as he could. Then he left out the back door, walking two blocks over to his side bitch's house.

"Who is it?" a female called after he rang the doorbell.

"Rich."

A tall dark-skinned woman with big lips, big breasts, and a huge booty answered the door wearing next to nothing for clothing. A pink half T-shirt and ripped miniskirt barely covered her body. "Oh, so now you know a bitch! You didn't know a hoe when I seen you out wit' Teona's bitch ass," she sassed, eyeing him angrily.

"C'mon, Shandrika," Rich Red breathed. "Now ain't the right time. Let me in."

She swung the door open, mugging him and barely moving to let him in. "What happened? What the bitch do now?"

"She just talkin' shit and I don't need that shit right now. I got too much on my plate," he mumbled, flopping down on the couch.

Shandrika locked the door and rushed to his side. "What happened, baby?"

"I just got chased by the Feds. I barely got away and this bitch worried about a Louis bag."

Shandrika shook her head like she had heard the most ridiculous thing ever. "That's fucked up, baby. What the Feds do?"

"They chased us, but I got away. I think they got my nigga Nut."

"Damn. I'm tripping on some jealous bullshit and you almost went to prison. I'm sorry, baby," she apologized in a whiny voice, reaching out to hug and kiss him.

Rich Red loved the affection given by his side chick. She loved him and cared about his freedom. This was the reaction he wanted from Teona, but she was too concerned about a purse. "We good, baby. I know you got me. I got you, too. I ain't going nowhere. Fuck the Feds. They can't fuck wit' Rich Red. I ain't the average goofy."

"That's right, baby. Fuck them bitch-ass Feds."

Rich Red nodded, feeling himself way too much, so much so that he pulled out his phone and went live on Facebook. "Yeah. Rich Red reporting live from the D. Bitch-ass alphabet boys tried to flag me down, but I got too many moves. Tell the bitches to come with the helicopters next time, 'cause my Porsche too fast for they weak-ass Challengers!" He laughed. "Yeah, I'm sittin' here wit' my side bitch like a boss. Tell them how much of a boss Rich Red is, baby," he said, turning the phone to Shandrika.

"Rich Red is the boss of all bosses." She grinned.

"Yeah, baby. Tell 'em how much money Rich Red got."

"Rich Red is ballin'. Chasing a bag. We got bags, and diamonds, and foreigns."

"Yeah, baby. Tell them how Rich Red make you feel."

"Rich Red make me feel priceless."

"Okay, world. Rich Red signing out. My bitch 'bout to use them lips to make Rich Red bust a nut. You gon' swallow it all, baby?"

She moved her hands towards his zipper. "I'ma swallow it all, baby. I ain't gon' waste a drop."

"Rich Red out."

By the time he ended the post, Shandrika's head was bobbing up and down in his lap. She sucked him like a champ, her deep throat crucial. She had learned how to use her big pillow soft lips a long time ago to bring a man pleasure. Rich put a hand on the back of her head to guide her and closed his eyes. It didn't take long for the chocolate vixen to slay the dragon.

"Aw, shit!" Rich Red moaned as nut erupted from his dick right down her throat. Shandrika did as promised and swallowed every drop and continued sucking to make sure he stayed hard.

"Damn, baby. My pussy so fucking wet. You gon' fuck me?" she begged.

"I'm a boss, baby. I ain't gon' fuck you. You gon' fuck me," he said, putting his hands behind his head and chilling.

Shandrika dropped to her knees and took off his shoes, pants, and underwear. Then she stood and helped him out of his shirt. All the while, Rich Red barely moved. After he was naked, she stood to undress, revealing a body that looked like it was made to be fucked. Big DD breasts, a flat stomach, wide hips, and an ass that needed to be on the cover of *Straight Stuntin* magazine. She spun around and sat down on him reverse cowgirl and did what she did best: pleased her nigga.

After a round of sex on the couch, Shandrika went to make him some food while Rich Red lay on the couch, staring up and the ceiling, collecting his thoughts. A federal holding cell flashed in his mind. Although he acted like he didn't care, he was worried about his freedom. The Feds were real. And in real life, he was unsure about his next move. So he did what he always did when he wasn't sure: picked up the phone and made a call.

"What up, li'l nigga?" Royce answered.

"Where my uncle?"

"He taking care of some business right now. What's going on?"

"I just need to holla at my uncle. How long he gon' been busy?"

"I don't know. Thirty minutes, maybe. After we finish what we doing, we headed back to The Ranch."

"A'ight. I'ma meet y'all at The Ranch."

After eating a corned beef sandwich and potato wedges, Rich Red borrowed Shandrika's Camry and headed for The Ranch. Thirty minutes later, he parked in the circular driveway of a mansion in the suburbs. The Ranch was an impressive two point three million dollar structure. He climbed up the fifteen step white granite staircase and rang the doorbell.

"Who is it?" a female called.

"Rich."

Locks clicked and a fine Puerto Rican woman wearing a French maid outfit answered the door. "Hey, Richie. C'mon in."

"What up, Jenny. Where my uncle?" he asked, stepping into the plush pad.

"He's upstairs in the study."

Rich Red climbed the impressive blue and green marble spiraled staircase to the second level of the house and walked down the hall towards the study. His uncle sat behind the desk going over paperwork. He wore a tailored blue suit with onyx cufflinks. On his feet were hand sewn Tom Ford loafers. Donny was a major player in the state of Michigan. Heroin, coke, weed, pills - you name it, the old school hustler sold it. After more than twenty years in the game, he had amassed a nice fortune and bought real estate and a few business to wash the drug money.

"What's going on, nephew? Royce said you called."

Rich Red moped into the office and slunk down in the chair.

Donny noticed the body language. "What's going on, Richie? What happened?"

"I think I got chased by the Feds."

Donny pulled the glasses from his face and gave his nephew a serious stare. "I beg your pardon?"

Rich didn't want to say it again, but he did. "I think I got chased by the Feds earlier."

"How you know it was the Feds?"

"I don't know for sure, but two white people in a Challenger chased me in my Porsche. I jumped out and ran and they chased me on foot, but I got away."

Donny studied Rich for a long moment, gathering his thoughts. When he spoke again, his voice was firm and serious. "So, you think you got chased by the Feds and you call my lieutenant and come by my house? What the fuck is wrong with you, li'l nigga?"

"I didn't know what else to do," he mumbled.

"You shouldn't have brought yo ass to my house!" Donny exploded. "You s'posed to get yo' ass off the streets and lay low, boy! The Feds is serious. I can go to jail for just talking to you, li'l nigga. You done lost yo' rabbit-ass mind showing up at my house with the Feds chasing yo' ass! If you wasn't my brother's son, I'd have Scooby or Fifty fuck you in the ass and throw you over a bridge, li'l nigga."

Rich Red hung his head in shame and anger, not saying another word. Trying to argue with his uncle or defend his actions would only lead to more trouble. He had fucked up, and now he had to accept the consequences.

Donny continued to stare at his nephew in disgust. The youngster showed promise in the world of hustling and knew how to get money. But he was also reckless and stupid, like most twenty-one-year-olds. "Get yo ass outta my house and go hide under a rock until I tell you to come outside. I'ma make some calls and try to figure out what the hell is going on. Don't bring yo' ass out of the house until I tell you to."

Chapter 13

"Oh, God! Oh, Desmond. Damn, baby!" Lasonya moaned before collapsing on top of her man's chest.

The lovers lay still for a moment, catching their breath.

"I missed yo' ass so much," Desmond groaned, running a hand through her hair.

Lasonya sat up and stared into his face for a moment. She looked like she wanted to say something, but averted her eyes and looked away. Desmond had noticed a change in Lasonya since he'd been home. She'd become quiet, a little distant, and a lot more serious.

"What's going on, baby?"

When she looked at him again, there was real emotion in her eyes. "Do you want kids?"

"What kinda question is that?" he asked, a little uncomfortable by the question.

"When you were in jail, I wanted a piece of you out here with me. And you live a dangerous life. I've been thinking about what happens if you don't come back to me one day. Don't you want to have a piece of you in the world just in case?"

Desmond thought on the question. He never had to consider another person's feelings before. When he went out on missions, it was all about him. He didn't have any responsibilities. And now everything was different. He and Lasonya were getting serious. "I never thought about it like that before. I've been responsible for only me for so long. I hear what you're saying and it makes sense. But I don't think I'm ready to have a kid. It's a lot of responsibility."

"Do you love me?"

"You know I do. I already proved that. And I brought you with me on a mission with the federal government so I could protect you."

"Well, if you love me, have a family with me."

"C'mon, baby. Don't try to use my love for you against me like that. We not ready for a kid. We live in a federal safe house and we're under federal protection. Anything could happen and force us to have to run. We don't have anything of our own. I still have to figure out what to do with my career. When we have a kid, I want to be there to raise it. It won't be fair if you have to do everything and I'm always on missions."

She rolled off of him, wrapping a sheet around her body and crossing her arms over her chest. "I know what I want. You're the one that's unsure."

"I know. That's what I just said. And you can't be mad at me for not being sure. You knew what I wanted to do with my life before we got together. You can't expect my plans to change because yours did."

She smacked her lips and rolled her eyes. Silence filled the room.

"What's going on, Lasonya? This is our first time talking about kids. How are you going to get mad about something we've just started talking about?"

She didn't answer right away. When she responded, the words came out in a mumble. "I stopped taking my pills two days ago."

Desmond's expression went from understanding boyfriend to pissed-off soldier in an instant. "What the fuck you just say?"

She turned up her anger a notch. "I stopped taking my pills! I want a family."

Desmond ran a hand across his face in frustration. "How the fuck you gon' make a decision for us without telling me? You can't be doing stuff like that. We both in this relationship."

"It's my body. I can do what I want."

"No you can't. Not when it concerns me. I feel like you tryna trap me, and this ain't like you. What's going on?"

Desmond's words were like salt on an open wound. Lasonya coiled back like a snake, her face twisted in an angry mask. The truth was devastating. "Trap you!" she yelled, standing and pointing her fingers and rolling her neck. "I don't need to trap a man. I can get any nigga I want. I love you and want a family with you and you in here calling me a sack chasing thot. Fuck you, Desmond," she said before storming from the room.

Desmond sat in bed and stared at the door, wondering what the hell just happened. Nothing made sense. They went from making love to arguing over a baby that he wasn't ready to have.

The ringing of his phone pulled him from the puzzle that Lasonya had become. He grabbed it and saw Rich's name on the screen.

"What's up, boss man?"

"D-Money, what's good?"

"Hoping you shook them Jakes and you about to tell me some good news."

"Yeah. Everything is good on my end. You ready to hit the mall and go shopping?"

"Fa'sho."

"Okay. You remember the house you dropped me off at?"

"Yeah."

"Come through and pick me up. Let's get it."

After hanging up, Desmond called Agent Johanson.

"Hey, Desmond. What's going on?"

"Rich just called me. He wanna meet for a buy."

"Oh, that's great. We're going to track your phone and listen to everything. Just make sure you don't turn the phone off. Good luck."

◆◆◆

During the drive to Detroit, Desmond couldn't stop thinking about Lasonya. He had left the house not on speaking terms with her. That wasn't like them. Their love was fresh and new. The sex was great. They were still getting to know each other. But something about Lasonya was different. It made him wonder if something had happened while he was locked up. But he was only gone for a week. How much could she and their relationship have changed in such a short amount of time? Apparently a lot.

And then there was Lucky. Lasonya had filled him in on Laronda's kidnapping, the high speed shootout, and Lucky hooking up with Trevor and his guys to get his daughter back. And then Trevor ended up dead the same day as Melissa and her kids. Things in

Milwaukee were crazy and he wished he could be there to help his brother out of the jam. But Desmond had his own set of problems. Mainly staying free. Plus, he couldn't let Lucky know that he was out of jail and working with the Feds because that would be another problem.

When he pulled up in front of Rich Red's woman's house, he pushed his problems to the back of his mind and focused on the mission. He needed to keep his wits about him because one false move could blow his cover and put him in a grave.

He climbed from the blue Infiniti, checking his clothes as he strolled upon the porch. He wore a Giuseppe 'fit, a gold chain, and Cartier glasses, embodying the dope boy persona. When he was satisfied with his appearance, he rang the doorbell.

"Who is it?" a woman called from inside the house a few moments later.

"D-Money. Is Rich Red here?"

When the door opened, Desmond stood face to face with a good-looking petite woman with green hair. She looked him over from head to toe and smiled. "C'mon in. He waiting for you in the back room."

He stepped into the house and saw hair and makeup strewn across the couch and tables in the living room. Two young women sat on the couch in different stages of getting their hair and makeup done. One of them looked good enough to be a popular Instagram girl. The other looked like she needed more than hair and makeup to look better than a pig in a wig.

"Damn. Who is you, baby?" the ugly one asked.

"I'm D-Money." He smiled.

She looked him from head to toe and smacked her lips. "Dayum, you fine, D-Money. What it's gon' take for me to be yo' bitch?"

"I'm good. I got a complicated situation on my hands."

"Shit, I'll be yo' side bitch then. She can have Monday through Friday. Just gimme the weekend."

Desmond cracked up. "It's more complicated than that."

"Chante, leave him alone," the woman that had answered the door intervened. "Rich is in the back room."

The smell of stank weed hit Desmond in the face as soon as he walked in the kitchen. He followed the scent towards a room at the back of the house. Rich sat in a recliner chair smoking a blunt and posting on Facebook.

"D-Money, what it do, fool?" He smiled, setting the phone down to shake hands.

"You got it, Rich. Ready to get to it. What you got for me?"

"Damn. You don't waste time."

"Niggas wit' time ain't got no money and niggas wit' money ain't got no time."

"That was some real shit." Rich Red nodded, passing him the blunt.

"I'm good on the strong, my nigga. I don't smoke," Desmond declined.

Rich gave him a funny look. "On what?"

"Real language. Shit be having niggas slipping. I might pop a bottle every now and then, but I try to stay away from bad habits. I work out and take care of my temple. I'm focused on getting a bag. I ain't gon' hustle forever."

"That sound good. All I know is yayo. I think I'ma hustle forever."

"I ain't knockin' it, my nigga. Gotta get that paper by any means."

Rich Red nodded. "So, what you tryna cop? Since this our first time doing business, I'ma hit you with the specials. You buy a hunnit grits or more and it's sixty a pop. Less than a hunnit is eighty a move. I don't fuck with that fentanyl shit 'cause too many mu'fuckas is dying. So what you looking for?"

Desmond took a moment to consider the deals. "I like that hunnit piece for six G's. And I'm loving how you keep it uncut. That's what my people want."

"A'ight. Wait right here." Rich said before leaving the room. He came back a few moments later with four baggies half-filled with off white powder. "How that look?"

Desmond had never handled heroin before so as far as he knew, everything was the way it was supposed to be. "Shit look A-1," he said before going into his pocket and pulling out a dope boy wad of cash filled with blue face hundreds. He counted off six thousand and gave it to Rich Red.

"That's what I'm talkin' 'bout, D-Money. You niggas in Flint eating, huh?"

"We do a'ight. But niggas could always do better."

"Say less, my nigga. What you movin' and how often you shop?"

"I can do a hunnit every couple days. But my niggas talkin' 'bout a power move that could put us in the big leagues."

Rich's eyes grew wide with greed. "Oh yeah? What it look like?"

Desmond smiled, keeping up the suspense. "Don't trip, my nigga. When it happen, you gon' know because I'm coming with some real money."

Rich Red nodded. "Alright, my nigga. I hope shit work out for you, 'cause I love money and I need more of it."

"Shit, I can't never have enough." Desmond laughed. "Let me get back in traffic. I'ma be at you in a minute."

"Fa'sho. Lemme walk you to the door," Rich said as he stood. "My bitch's friends feeling you too. They was askin' me 'bout you when I grabbed that work. Chante ain't shit, but Pebbles might be worth taking a look at."

"That's the baddy, huh?"

"Yeah. And she come from a family of niggas wit' money, so she know how to do a nigga that's getting to it. I tried to slide in, but she ain't goin'. She choosy. Matter fact, she grew up in Flint. You might know her people."

Desmond filed Pebbles in the back of his mind. If another opportunity presented itself, he would look into the woman. For now, he stayed focused on the current mission. "I got a few baddys on my line, but a nigga can never have too many. Lemme shoot a shot real quick."

When they stepped into the living room, Chante noticed immediately. "There he go. You realized you needed a bad bitch in yo' life and came to yo' senses, didn't you?"

"Somethin' like that." Desmond laughed before turning to Pebbles. "I heard you from Flint?"

138

"I grew up there, but we moved to Detroit and was raised here. That's where you from?"

He nodded. "My name D-Money. Pebbles, right?"

"Yeah."

"Look, I don't got that much time because I'm in between making a move, but I wanna holla at you some time. Let's exchange info and I'ma get at you later."

"No, he didn't!" Chante smacked her lips.

"Sorry, Chante. I normally don't break the girl code, but you see him," Pebbles said before turning back to Desmond. "I thought you said you had a girl."

"Nah, you heard wrong. I never said I had a girl. I said I was in a complicated situation. And that's because I'm married to getting a bag."

Pebbles looked impressed by the reply. "Oh. Well, in that case we got a lot in common, because a bitch is definitely about her coins. Make sure you hit me up."

After exchanging information, Desmond hopped in the Infiniti and pulled the phone from his pocket. "Johanson, you there?"

"Yeah. We heard everything. Good job. You're in. Keep going and see how far you can work yourself up the ladder. We don't want the small guys. Look for the big dogs. And don't worry about anything. We have your back."

Chapter 14

The mood in Exotica was charged with sexuality. It was Sunday, and the premier dancers were in the club and the ballers came out to show them love. Money rained down like confetti, no one seeming to care about financial problems. Mixed in the crowd were Lucky, Miguel, and Tyler. They met up to discuss their next move and a way to find Polo.

"So, what happened to the plan you had to find him?" Tyler asked.

Lucky forced his eyes away from Black Barbie, who was busy giving a lap dance, to address the question. "It didn't turn out the way I wanted. I thought I knew someone that knew him, but it didn't work out," he said, craning his neck to find the stripper again. She had been avoiding him since he stepped in the club.

"That's all?" Miguel asked, waving a hand to get his attention. "Tell us more. Where are his family members? Do you know anybody else that might know something about him?"

"Nah. I only had one lead. All I knew was they used to be on Florist, but we drove through several times and y'all seen it. They ghost. I don't know what else to do," he said before locating Black Barbie again. She glanced in his direction, then turned up her nose when they made eye contact.

"What's up with her?" Miguel asked.

"Who?"

"The stripper you've been eyeing since we walked in the fucking place," Tyler said. "You want a dance, tell her to come over. Stop acting like a fucking virgin and man up."

Lucky mugged the big white man. "Shut up, fool. I know her. And I fucked her already, so beat it with the virgin shit."

"Oh, so you stalking her?" Tyler laughed. "You see this shit, Miguel. Fucker got us in here thinking we're meeting about killing Polo and he's stalking a fucking stripper."

Miguel shook his head. "So, that T-Pain song about loving a stripper is real, huh?"

"Fuck both of you niggas. I thought she knew Polo. When I first met her, I was with him. I thought he tricked off with her, but he didn't. I almost killed her real trick thinking it was Polo."

Miguel and Tyler looked at each other.

"Why you just now telling us this?" Miguel asked.

"Because I wasn't sure if she knew him. And it was a blank mission."

"You sure she ain't fucking Polo and just didn't tell you?" Tyler asked.

"Yeah, I'm sure," Lucky said, watching as Black Barbie walked to the bar. "I'ma be right back. I gotta get another bottle."

Lucky Left the table quickly, not giving his boys the opportunity to say another word. He approached Black Barbie from behind, sliding close enough so that he didn't have to talk loudly. "So, I guess that game of strip poker ain't gon' happen."

She spun around with an angry look on her pretty face. "What do you want, Lucky?"

"I wanna talk. Yo' ghost game is cold."

"Because I don't got nothing to say to you. You used me. I thought we was better than that, but we obviously ain't."

Lucky could see the hurt in her eyes and wanted to fix it. "We is better than that. Gimme the chance to explain."

"I don't got time to listen to yo' lies or hear you run game," she said, ready to walk away, but stopping like she remembered something. "I said you didn't have no game, but I was wrong. I never met a nigga wit' more game than you because I believed all that shit. I'm good, Lucky. Do you and I'ma do me. I'm at work right now so I would appreciate it if you left me alone. Excuse me."

Lucky's eyes followed her as she walked into the back room. He wanted to follow her, but two huge bodyguards blocked the door. He stood at the bar thinking on her words. They cut him deeper than he thought they would. The hurt in her eyes tugged at his heart. He wanted to explain himself. Then he remembered Donny's words. She was smart, loyal, and worth having on his side. He looked towards the table and seen Miguel and Tyler watching him. Their meeting was important. They needed to find Polo and get him out of the way. But he also wanted to make things right with Rachel and that might be the easier mission to complete. He moved towards the dressing room, but was stopped by one of the big men.

"Hold on, boss. Nobody but the girls go in here."

"I just need to have a couple words with Black Barbie real quick."

"Wait til she comes back on the floor. I can't let you pass."

"I got money," Lucky said, pulling out cash. "How much you want?"

"Listen, man. Just wait til she come back out. I'm not losing my job because you can't control yo'self. Move around."

Lucky eyed the huge bouncer. Fighting the man was out of the question, but if he could find the right words or the right price...

"Listen, big guy. I ain't one of these perverts that come in here and try to buy or take pussy. I know Rachel personally. I need to talk to her in private and I'm willing to pay whatever. I ain't no rapist or no crazy nigga. This shit is important. So important that I'm willing to let you hold my watch until I come out and give y'all both a hunnit dollars," he said, flashing the forty thousand dollar Patek watch that was a gift from Polo.

Both bouncers eyed the iced-out time piece. "That ain't real, nigga."

Lucky took it off and handed it to him. "Look at how those diamonds shine in this dim light. That's forty stacks you holding."

The big man held the watch up and watched rainbows light in the ice. "Check it out. Give us two hunnit apiece and I'ma let you pass. If you get on any bullshit back there, I'ma beat cho ass and I'm keepin' the watch."

Lucky counted off four blue bills and handed them over.

The big man stepped aside. "Hurry up."

The back room looked like a plush locker room. All the women were out on the floor hustling, so it was empty. Lucky looked around for a moment when he heard movement from a closed door. It was the bathroom. He walked over just as the door opened.

"Ahh shit!" Rachel screamed. "What the fuck you doing in here?"

Lucky pushed her in the bathroom and closed the door. "I need to talk to you. This shit just cost me four hunnit dollars and maybe my forty thousand dollar watch."

She tried to push past him. "I don't care about none of that. Get out. I don't got nothing to say to you."

He shoved her onto the toilet. "Good. Because all I need you to do is listen."

When she realized he wasn't going to let her go, she stopped resisting, crossing her arms over her chest and staring up at him.

"I didn't run game on you. Everything I said to you, I meant. But I did try to use you to get close to Polo. He violated me and I needed to get back at him and I thought you could help me."

"You didn't ask for my help, Lucky. You used me. Told me lies to get close to me because you thought he was my sponsor. Stop acting like you didn't lie. You didn't think about my feelings. You thought about you."

"He killed my ex-girlfriend and her kids, Rachel. I did what I had to do to try and get back at him. He the reason my brother in jail. I had to do everything possible to get this nigga. What would you do if you was me? You telling me you wouldn't try everything to get him too?"

The information surprised Rachel. Even in her anger, she had to sympathize with him. "Damn. I didn't know all that. He really killed your girlfriend and her kids?"

Lucky nodded. "Yeah. And my li'l brother locked up for killing his people. This shit is real."

"Why didn't you tell me instead of lying?"

"Because I didn't know you like I do now. I couldn't come to you and tell you I was trying to kill him and ask for your help. You might've called the police."

She nodded. "I probably wouldn't have called the police, but I definitely wouldn't have fucked with you. But you still used me. I ain't cool with that shit."

"I know. And I'm sorry about that. For real."

A knock on the door interrupted them. "Black Barbie, you good in there?" Security called.

She looked at Lucky. "Yeah. I'm good. Give us some more time."

Lucky relaxed a little. "So, can I have my friend back? Can we stop the ghost games?"

She studied him for a long moment. "I don't know, man. You gave me a lot to think about. You got a lot going on. Plus, you made me lose Donny."

"Fuck Donny. You don't need him."

"Yes, I do. He paid my bills. You gon' pay my bills now?"

He laughed. "So, that's what it's all about? Gettin' them bills paid? I thought you said you wasn't like the rest of the strippers out there." He nodded towards the door.

She mugged him and stood. "Fuck you, nigga. I don't appreciate you tryna call me a hoe."

"I wasn't calling you a hoe. You the one tryna treat me like a trick."

She waved a hand and tried to push past him. "Whatever, nigga. I ain't finna argue with you. Move out the way. I got money to make."

Lucky didn't move. "So, this how we finna be? I open up and let you in and you just turn and walk away?"

She avoided his eyes and sighed like he was getting on her nerves. "I don't got time for this right now, nigga. I just need you to move."

Lucky wrapped a hand around her throat and pushed her against the sink. "Stop playing with me, Rachel, before I fuck you up!"

She stared up at him, fear and excitement lighting her eyes. "Stop. Let me go," she said weakly.

Something about the look in her eyes sent a spark through Lucky. The air became sexually charged. When he bent to kiss her, she opened her mouth readily and sucked his tongue. The kiss was aggressive. He continued choking her while sticking a hand in her thong and slipping a finger in her pussy.

"Mmmm!" she moaned, going for his belt. When his pants fell to the floor, she reached into his boxers, unleashing his meat and stroking it roughly. Then she realized they were about to fuck in the bathroom of her job. If they were caught, she might get fired. "Wait. We can't do this here," she said, letting go of his dick, breaking the kiss.

Lucky was baptized in the lust. He pulled off his shirt, unable to think past sticking his dick into her good-ass pussy and fucking her until he exploded. "You can't leave me like this." he said, lifting her onto the sink, sliding her thong to the side and diving in. "God damn!" he groaned, loving the feel of her love canal wrapped around his dick.

"Damn, Lucky!" Rachel whispered, wrapping her arms around his shoulders. "You gon' get me in trouble."

"We good, baby. I got you," he mumbled, thrusting his hips and going deeper into her guts.

She put a hand on his stomach to stop him from going all the way in. "Wait. Don't go. Too. Deep. I'ma make. Too much. Noise."

Her words sounded like music to his ears. He grabbed her hand out of the way and dug deeper.

"Oh shit, Lucky! You. Gotta. Stop. Stop!"

"I can't, baby. Aw shit. I can't stop," he groaned, fighting back the urge to bust while prying her legs apart so he could go deeper.

"Oh, shit! Oh, shit! I hate yo' ass, Lucky. I. Hate. You."

Her words were like adding fuel to a fire. They encouraged him to go deeper, hit it harder and faster. He fucked her like he really hated her pussy. All Rachel could do was hold on and cry out in pleasure.

"Tell me you hate me again," he demanded, pile driving his dick into her pussy.

"Oh shit! I! Hate! Yo'! Ass! Lucky!"

He smiled, feeling energized by the words as he continued to punish her womb. "This my pussy. I don't want you giving my pussy to nobody else. I don't care how much they offer. You bet' not give my pussy away. You hear me?"

Rachel was lost in a zone of pleasure and pain. At the moment she would've agreed to follow Lucky into hell to fight the devil. "Yeah. Yeah."

"Say it! Tell me this my pussy."

146

"This. Yo'. Pussy, baby. Ahh, shit!"

"Say you ain't gon' give my pussy away. Say it!"

"I. Won't. Give. Yo'. Pussy. To. Nobody."

Sweat poured down Lucky's face and his clothes were drenched, but he didn't care. All he cared about was busting a nut. And he was getting close. He grabbed her face. "Open yo' eyes and look at me." She did what he asked. Her eyes were lust glazed like she was high.

"Say 'fuck Donny'."

Her eyes seemed to gain focus when she heard the name. She stared into Lucky's eyes for a moment like she was weighing the seriousness of the statement. When she finally made up her mind, it reflected in her eyes. "Fuck Donny."

Lucky smiled again, the words seeming to bring him closer to busting. "Say it again. Say it again."

"Fuck Donny! Fuck Donny!" she screamed grabbing hold of Lucky's shoulders as her body went stiff. "Oh shit, Lucky! Ohh!"

When her pussy clenched around Lucky's dick, it was too much. He dove deep into her guts as the nut rushed out of his dick like a flood. The lovers remained glued together, looking into each other's eyes.

"I'm not playing," Lucky panted. "This my pussy."

A smile crept onto her face as she leaned forward to kiss him. "Okay. It's yours."

"Don't give my pussy to nobody. I don't care who they is or what they got."

She nodded. "Okay. You don't gotta repeat it. I know what loyalty means. This yo' pussy. That's it. You my nigga. I chose you."

He nodded, satisfied by the words.

"Now you gotta get the fuck outta here so I can freshen up and get back out on the floor."

He pulled out of her and got dressed again. "What time you leaving?"

"I'm staying until closing. At 2:30. You taking me home?"

"Wouldn't have it no other way." He grinned before leaving the bathroom.

147

When he stepped out of the bathroom, two women stood near a row of lockers ogling him. "How y'all doing?" he asked, wiping sweat from his brow as he headed for the door.

"Not as good as you," one of them cracked.

When he stepped back into the club, the bouncers gave him a look.

"You a'ight?" one of them asked.

"Yeah." Lucky smiled. "I'm good."

"That nigga just got some pussy." The other one laughed.

The guilty smile remained on Lucky's face. "C'mon, my nigga. Let me get that watch."

The bouncer hesitated. "You took a li'l longer than necessary."

Lucky shrugged. "Something came up."

"Give the nigga his watch back, Drew. I like him. Nigga got some flavor." The other bouncer nodded.

After getting his watch, Desmond headed back to the table with his boys. Tyler and Miguel mugged him.

"Damn, bro! How you gonna leave us out here?" Tyler gruffed.

Lucky continued to wear the "I just got some pussy" smile. "Something came up."

Miguel knew the look. "Oh shit! He went in there and fucked her!"

Tyler studied Lucky for a moment. "No you didn't. Did you?"

Lucky was about to answer when a face in the crowd caught his eyes. "When he come in?"

Tyler and Miguel turned to see who he was looking at. The man was light skinned with blue eyes. He wore an all-white suit and was surrounded by an entourage.

"Who is he?" Tyler asked.

"Wacco. And if he see me, it might get ugly."

As if on cue, as soon as Lucky finished speaking, Wacco looked in his direction. When the men locked eyes, the truth spoke across the room. The crime boss spoke to a few of his goons and a sea of men moved towards Lucky's table.

"Shit. Do y'all got heat?" Lucky asked.

"In the car. These mutherfuckers pat search like TSA," Tyler rumbled.

"I haven't had a good bar fight in a long time." Miguel smiled. Lucky, Miguel, and Tyler, grabbed liquor bottles, ready to go to war, as their table was surrounded by eight members of CSG. Wacco stepped forward with the air of a made man. He looked at the bottles in Lucky and his boys hands and smirked. "If I came for a problem, we wouldn't even be this close. Me and my niggas don't get searched."

Lucky heard the threat of violence in his voice and seen it on his goons' faces. They were all packing heat.

"So, are they supposed to be a part of a welcoming party?" Tyler asked.

Everyone looked at the white man like he had spoken out of turn.

"I heard you had something to do with my nephew getting killed," Wacco said.

"You heard wrong. I didn't have no problem with yo' people."

"Even though he killed yo mama?"

"You saying he did it?" Lucky countered.

Wacco gave him a stare. "It was an accident. Wrong place wrong time. My condolences. I had love for yo' moms. She let us get away with murder when we was growing up."

Lucky nodded. He didn't speak for fear of saying the wrong thing.

"The streets talking a lot about you and yo' brother. Where is he at anyways? I got some holla for him, too."

"He not here."

Wacco nodded, noticing the icy reception. "Damn, so we enemies now? Why the serious face and the mug? You used to be my dawg."

"It's whatever you want it to be. You the one that got a green light on my brother. Is it a green light on me too?"

"He spilled CSG blood and gotta be held accountable."

"Yo' nephew spilled my mama's blood and had to be held accountable too," Lucky mugged.

Wacco's lips twitched as his face twisted into a mug. "You lucky they got cameras in here or I'd have one of my niggas stretch you out right now."

Lucky had no comeback for the threat. The last thing he wanted to do was talk himself into being shot, so he continued to match Wacco's stare and hold his ground.

"That green light starting to get bigger, Lucky. Be careful," Wacco taunted before he and his team walked away.

"Man, I wanted to crash those mutherfuckers!" Miguel breathed, clenching the liquor bottles tightly.

"We can't bring bottles to a gun fight. Let's get the fuck outta here," Lucky said.

"You read my mind, brother," Tyler said, moving for the door. "I got a Glock in the car with a drum on it. Betcha my shit stand strong in a gun fight."

The trio left the club in a hurry and moved towards their vehicles. Tyler and Miguel went for Tyler's truck while Lucky went for the rented Benz. As soon as they clicked their alarms, the club door opened and four CSG members walked outside.

"Look up!" Lucky alerted.

"Oh, hell yeah!" Miguel smiled as he opened the passenger door of the truck and pulled a .45 Desert Eagle from under the seat. He didn't wait for the CSG niggas to make an aggressive move. As soon as he pulled the Desert Eagle, he started shooting.

Boom, boom, boom, boom, boom!

One of the CSG members went down in a heap. The others pulled guns and returned fire. When Tyler pulled his Glock with the drum on it, the parking lot turned into a small war zone. Lucky grabbed his own weapon and joined the gunfight. He couldn't get a good aim at anyone because they were ducked behind cars. The club door opened again and more armed CSG members poured into the parking lot. All of their gunfire was trained on Tyler's truck, riddling the SUV with bullets. Lucky knew they were outmanned and out gunned and took cover behind the Benz.

"Tyler! Miguel! Let's get the fuck outta here!" he called over the gunfire.

Neither man answered. Lucky poked his head up to take a look when a bullet whizzed by his head and exploded the Benz's rear window.

"Shit!" he cursed, ducking low again. He didn't want to leave his niggas, but he also didn't want to die. The gunfire remained rapid like every CSG member had extra ammo. He couldn't hop in the Benz because they would fill it with bullets like they were doing Tyler's truck. Lucky did the only thing he could do and put his feet to the pavement and got the hell out of the parking lot.

Chapter 15

"The dog went into the dog house and got a bone. Then the doggy put the bone in the ground and covered it up," Quaysha said before turning the page. She sat on Desmond's lap going through a kids' picture book, describing the stories shown on the page.

"Then the rain came and made the grounds wet and another doggy came and took his bone. Ain't that stealing?"

"It's two ways you can look at the situation. It can be looked at as stealing. But it can also be looked at as finders keepers."

She frowned, giving it some thought. "What is finders keepers?"

"It's like if you find some money on the ground. You didn't steal it; you found it. Stealing is when you take something that belongs to somebody else."

"But wasn't the money somebody else's first?"

"Yep. But they lost it. When you lose something and somebody else finds it, it becomes finders keepers."

Understanding lit her eyes. "Oh. Okay. Can we go look for some money, Desmond?"

He laughed. "Not right now. Maybe later on."

"Okay. I'ma go tell my granny that we going to find some money!" she sang, jumping off the couch and running towards the back of the house.

Desmond flipped a couple more pages in the book and thought about what it would be like to have a kid of his own. Before meeting back up with Lasonya and being around Quaysha, he'd never given thought to having a kid. Now that Lasonya had planted the thought, every time he interacted with Quaysha, he thought about having a kid. And the more he was around Quaysha, the more he fell in love with her. She was a beautiful, smart, and inquisitive child. Her innocence and energy made people fall in love with her.

"What are you doing?" Lasonya asked when she walked into the living room and seen him with the book.

"Quaysha was telling me the story in this book. She just ran off to find Marcy and tell her about finders keepers."

Lasonya scrunched up her face. "Say what now?"

"In the book, one dog finds another dog's bone. Finders keepers. Now she wants to go outside and see if she can find some money."

Lasonya laughed. "You just started something that you gon have to finish."

"I know. Baby girl is something else."

"You already know," Lasonya said, turning to walk away.

Desmond grabbed her wrist. "Hey, where you going? Come here," he said, pulling her onto the couch.

"Wait, baby. I gotta get back to cleaning out that closet. This house still needs a lot of work."

"Forget that closet. Hopefully we ain't gonna be here too long. Kick it with yo' man for a minute. How are you doing today?"

"I'm okay. I wanna finish making this house a home. What's on your mind?"

"I was thinking about what you said a couple days ago about a baby."

The light atmosphere was instantly changed to serious. "We don't have to go there, Desmond. I don't want you to think I'm trying to trap you."

"That's not what I was about to say. Can I tell you what was on my mind now, or are you going to continue to play fortune teller?"

She slapped him on the chest. "Don't talk to me like that."

"Well stop trying to read my mind and let me talk."

She rolled her eyes. "Well, talk then."

He looked into her eyes for a few beats before speaking. "I think I'm ready to have a baby."

Lasonya searched his face, trying to gauge his sincerity. "You don't have to do it if you don't want to."

"I know. I'm a man capable of making my own decisions. And I'm deciding that I want you to have my baby. After Quaysha finished telling me the story, I thought about what it would be like for us to have a son. I've thought about it almost every time I interacted with Quaysha since we talked about it. And like you said, I live a dangerous life. I don't want to go and not leave behind somebody to keep my bloodline going. I'm ready."

Lasonya leapt on top of him, straddling his lap and sticking her tongue down his throat.

"Get a room!" Marcy lectured. "Me and the baby are coming in the living room. Go to y'all own room."

Lasonya climbed off Desmond, glee lighting her eyes. "We about to have a baby!"

The same excitement in Lasonya's eyes was transferred to her mother. "You pregnant?"

"No. Not yet. But we about to get a lot of practice."

◆◆◆

Rich Red loved to shine. And when it came to showing off, there weren't many that did it like the young rich nigga from Detroit. Today's "I'm so icy" display was a black velour Balmain bomber jacket with a tiger embroidered across the front. The price tag was 9,200 dollars. He completed the 'fit with an 800 dollar sweater, 600 dollar jeans, and a 900 dollar pair of high top Balmain shoes. He pulled the Cartier frames from his face and eyed the thick woman that walked past the front of his Lotus. She was caramel-skinned with hair cut close to her scalp and dyed blonde. She wore a pair of pussy-cutting jean shorts and a half tank top that showed the bottom of her DD breasts. She had the kind of sex appeal that made a nigga's dick get hard from just looking at her. He blew the born to get her attention.

"Ay, shawty! Ay!"

She turned to look over her shoulder and kept walking.

"Oh, you wanna play hard to get? Okay." He laughed, pulling the car over and hopping out to follow. "You too good to holla back at a nigga?"

She looked over her shoulder again. "I don't respond to a nigga blowing his horn and calling me shawty. I gotta name. I'm tired of niggas calling me saying the same shit."

Normally Rich Red would cut a female down with words for talking to him in such a way, but something about her made him want to step his game up. He caught up to her and walked alongside her. "You know what? I like that you strong enough to put a nigga in his place when he wrong. If it's cool with you, I wanna start over. My name is Rich. You mind if I take up a li'l bit of yo' time?"

She looked over at him and smiled, happy with the new approach. "You gon' leave yo' car back there?"

"It's material. I can get another one. It's only one of you and I don't wanna pass up this opportunity."

"That was good, Rich." She smiled again. "But why you wanna talk to me? I'm sure you got something else more important to do."

"Why I wanna talk to you?" he cracked. "Have you seen you? Anybody with a heartbeat should wanna talk to you. If you want, I can give you a ride to wherever you going," he offered as his phone rang. "D-Money" shone on the screen.

"Is that your girlfriend?" she asked.

"What is that?"

She laughed. "You funny, Rich."

"This is an important call and I gotta make a move. So, can I get yo' name and number and hit you up some time?"

"My name is Gayle. And I don't give out my number, but I'll take yours."

"That don't sound like a fair exchange, but I guess I gotta do what I gotta do. Make sure you gimme a call because I wanna make sure you don't have to walk nowhere else. Ain't no way a precious jewel like you should be hurting yo' feet on this concrete."

After giving Gayle his number, Rich Red hopped in the Lotus and called D-Money. "D-Money, what's good, fam? I missed yo' call."

"I was just about to hit you back. I need to get in yo' face, my dude. Finish that conversation we had last time I seen you."

Rich Red thought for a moment, trying to remember the last conversation they had. "I don't remember the details. Refresh my memory."

"I'm talking about that power move, baby. I'm ready for the big leagues!"

Rich Red could hear the excitement in D-Money's voice and it got him excited. "Oh yeah! I remember that conversation well. Let's get together and talk. Where you at?"

"I'm walking out my front door right now. You say the word and I'ma hit the e-way and come to you. I got the credit card on me, ready to go shopping."

"Go head and hit the e-way, family. Let's hit the mall and fuck up some commas. Meet me at my bitch's house again."

"Say less, my dude. I'm on the way."

Rich Red drove to Teona's house with money on his mind. Between the call from D-Money and meeting Gayle, he felt like he was walking on clouds. He was so caught up in the wonderful feeling that he didn't notice the blue Lincoln Aviator trailing him from a distance.

Before going to his bitch's house, he stopped at the mall to buy a Birkin bag. When he got to Teona's house, he hid the bag behind his back and knocked on the door. She answered a few moments later.

"Aw, hell nah, nigga! Fuck you want?" she sassed.

"C'mon, baby. We don't do this. Lemme in."

"Nah, nigga. Take yo' ass by the bitch's house you was live on Facebook with. You ain't coming up in here. That shit over with."

"C'mon, Teona. That bitch wasn't shit to me. You know how it is out here. Hoes be chasing a nigga wit' a bag. But that wasn't nothing. You the only one that matters to me. And I bought this for you."

When he brought the bag from behind his back, Teona's eyes lit up like diamonds in the sunlight. "Oh my God! Is that a Birkin bag?"

"You know it! Only the best shit for my number one," he smiled. "So, can I come in, or you gonna leave me out here?"

Teona snatched the bag from his arm and pulled him in the house at the same time. "Oh, my God, Rich! I love it, baby! I love you!" she sang, modeling the bag on her arm and pulling out her phone to take pictures.

"You know I love to make you feel good, baby."

Excitement and mischief flashed in her eyes. "And when you make me feel good, I'ma make you feel good," she said, kissing him on the lips and dropping to her knees.

"Oh, yeah! Make yo' boss nigga feel good."

Teona unbuckled his pants and pulled out his piece, maintaining sexy eye contact as she took him in her mouth.

"Ssss! Yeah, baby! Suck that mu'fucka," Rich groaned.

A knock on the door interrupted the sex act.

"Damn, I know this nigga ain't here already. Get the door. That's D-Money," Rich sulked, buttoning his pants.

"We can finish later," Teona said, getting up and walking to the door. "Who is it?"

"I'm looking for Rich," a man called.

Teona opened the door and screamed when she saw two men standing on the porch with guns.

"Get back and shut the fuck up!" the men called as they rushed in the house.

Rich Red was caught off guard and all he could do was put his hands up. "C'mon, fam! What's this shit?" he asked, studying the men's bare faces. One of them looked familiar, but he couldn't put a name to the face.

"You know what it is, nigga! Gimme that shit 'fore I blaze yo' shit!" one of the niggas yelled, pointing a pistol in Rich's face.

"Breed?" Rich asked when he recognized the face. "This what it is, brah?"

"Shut yo' bitch ass up!" he snarled, slapping Rich across the face with the pistol.

"Ahhhh!" Teona screamed.

"Shut up, bitch!" the other man yelled, slapping her to the floor.

"Give that shit up, nigga! Where it at?" Breed demanded, pointing the pistol in Rich's face again.

Rich thought fast on his toes. He saw their faces, so there was no doubt in his mind that he would die as soon as he gave up the prize. "I don't got nothing in here."

Breed hit him across the head with the pistol. "Quit lying 'fore I off yo' bitch ass! Where it's at, nigga?"

"I don't got nothing in here! I swear to God!"

The men looked unsure of their next move. "What you wanna do?" the other jacker asked Breed.

"We gon' make this nigga take us to it. Get'cho bitch ass up," he mugged, snatching Rich off the ground.

The doorbell rang and scared everybody in the house.

"Who the fuck outside?" Breed demanded.

"I don't know," Rich lied.

Breed turned to Teona. "Ask who outside."

"Who is it?" she called.

"D-Money."

"Who the fuck is D-Money?" Breed asked.

"I don't know. This her house. Ask her," Rich deflected.

Teona stared at him in disbelief.

Breed pointed the gun in her face. "Who is D-Money?"

"It's his friend," she confessed.

Rich Red mugged her, mad that she told the truth.

"We getting his ass too. Take Rich back in the living room," Breed told his boy. Then he pointed the gun at Teona and hid behind the door. "Open the door."

She did as she was told.

"What's up, Teona? Rich here?" Desmond asked.

She nodded, but didn't step aside to let him in.

"You good?" Desmond asked, noticing her weird vibe.

"Let him in!" Breed whispered angrily from behind the door.

"Y-yeah. I'm okay. Come in," she stuttered, stepping aside.

Desmond stepped in the house warily, his battle senses on edge, muscles tensed and coiled, ready to strike like a cobra. He knew something was amiss and watched Teona's face, hoping she would give a tell. When her eyes darted to the right, he knew that someone was behind the door.

Breed slid from the hiding spot, pointing the pistol.

Desmond could feel the danger coming from behind like he had a sixth sense. His movements were fast, almost superhuman-like. He spun around quickly, grabbing the top slide and sliding it back. The gun cocked back, ejecting a bullet from the chamber. Before the shell could hit the ground, he punched Breed in the chin. The robber didn't even know what hit him. His legs went limp and eyes rolled to the back of his head as he collapsed to the ground like dead weight. Desmond kept the gun, spinning around and pointing it in Teona's face.

"Who else in here?" he demanded, ready to blow her brains out.

"He in the living room!" she yelled.

Desmond spun towards the living room with the gun ready as jack boy number two came into view holding a gun.

Pop!

The single gunshot sent a bullet through his forehead. He died with the pistol in his fist, never getting get off a shot.

"How many more?" he demanded, pointing the gun at Teona again.

She lifted her hands in the air. "That was it! Ain't no more."

Desmond pushed her in front of him, using her as a shield as he moved towards the living room. Rich Red lay on his stomach holding his bruised face. Desmond shoved Teona onto the ground and pointed the gun at Rich.

"Rich, what the fuck going on?"

He looked up at Desmond with the fear of God in his eyes. Then he looked at the robber on the floor leaking blood. "D-Money! That's you, fooly?"

"Yeah, nigga. What the fuck? That's how you try to set me up, nigga? I should smoke yo' punk ass!"

"What?" Rich yelled incredulously. "Them niggas just tried to rob me. You saved my ass."

Desmond looked to Teona, knowing she was a bad liar and would tell the truth. "He serious?"

She nodded.

"Damn, Rich. My bad. Look like I came just in time."

Movement near the front door made Desmond rush to check on Breed. He was gone.

"Damn. One of them got away. You knew them niggas?" he asked, closing the front door.

"The nigga that got away was Breed. Bitch-ass jack boy. I went to school with that nigga. I can't believe that fuck nigga tried to get down on me like that."

"What about the dead nigga on my floor?" Teona panicked. "What if somebody call the police?"

"Ain't nobody gon' do shit. Don't say shit to nobody. I'ma call my uncle. He gon' help us," Rich said as he pulled out the phone and dialed a number.

Desmond could feel eyes on him and turned to see Teona watching him. "You good?"

"Yeah." She nodded. "Where you learn how to do that?"

Desmond played stupid. "What you talking about?"

"What you did to Breed. That looked like some karate or something."

"Just some shit I picked up."

"My uncle Donny sending some niggas through to help us." Rich said as he hung up the phone. "She said you know karate? On what?"

Desmond shrugged, trying to think of an excuse to explain his fighting skills. "I did a little time in the military. Went to Iraq and Afghanistan."

Rich Red's eyes popped. "Damn, my nigga. You a soldier?"

"Used to be. Once my eye got fucked up, I hit the streets. But fuck that shit. We need to hide this body just in case somebody come over. Teona, grab some blankets so I can wrap him up. And if you got some bleach, bring that too."

Chapter 16

Lucky knew he was fucked in the game.

That's what flipped in his mind over and over as he rode in the backseat of the Uber. Drama with Polo and Wacco had eliminated his allies, and pressure from the police was starting to make him feel trapped. He was wanted for questioning concerning Melissa's murder, probation and parole wanted him for absconding, and he was certain that parking lot video from the strip club shooting two nights ago would make him a prime suspect in Tyler and Miguel's killings. As he rode in the car, he tried to figure where he went wrong. He got out of prison focused on pursuing the goals he'd set. He was in love, had a family, a home, and a career. And it only took a few months for everything to go up in smoke.

"How in the fuck did I get here?" he mumbled.

"You say something?" the female driver asked.

"Nah. I'm just talking to myself."

"Oh. Okay." She nodded before focusing back on the road.

Polo. All the problems began when he ran into him at the corner store. Polo was his downfall as a youngster and why he'd gone to prison. Now the once-close friend had become a sworn mortal enemy. Why couldn't he see it while he was in prison and make up in his mind to not ever fuck with him again? How could he have been so blind?

"Here you go. This is your stop," the driver interrupted his thoughts. "Have a nice day." She smiled.

"You too." He nodded before getting out of the car.

He stepped onto the sidewalk and took a look around. The city of Franklin was a small suburb just outside of Milwaukee. The small town was filled with upper class homeowners. Mansions and expensive condominiums were as common as trees. The house he walked towards was a mid-century townhouse that came fully furnished. After walking up on the porch of the white and blue two story abode, he used a key to let himself in.

Laronda sat on the couch talking on Facebook. When her father walked in, she ended the call and looked up from her phone.

"I hate it way out here."

"You told me that already," he said, sitting next to her. "But what about being alive and safe? That don't matter?"

"Yeah. But it's boring. I'm stuck all the way out here by myself."

"Where yo' mama?"

"I don't know. She ain't been home in a couple days. I only seen her twice since you got us the house. It's too far away."

"That's the point, Laronda. Polo is looking for us. You can't be walking around Milwaukee when people tryna kill you. I'm trying to take care of everything but its gon take some time."

"Why can't you just pay somebody to kill him and then let it be done?"

"It ain't that easy. For one, Polo is hard to find. And for two, you can't be trusting people to take care of problems like that. It's a different world out here. Niggas will kill for you and then tell on you. I'ma take care of it. I just gotta figure out a new plan because my old one didn't work."

"What happened? Why didn't it work?" she asked, giving all her attention.

"I'm not about to talk to you about it. You a shorty. I got it."

"Why not?" She smacked her lips, crossing arms over her chest. "He tryna kill me, too. And don't act like I don't know about the streets. I been runnin' in 'em since I was a ten."

"And that's over with now. I can take care of you so you don't have to be in the streets any more. Did yo' mama look into a school?"

She mugged him. "Nah. I ain't going to school with all these white people way out here."

"Why not? These good schools."

"Because Sharday didn't enroll me and I'm not going to school with all these white people. I'ma go back to school when we get back to Milwaukee. If you hurry up and kill Polo, then I can go to school. So, when you gon kill him."

He shook his head. "Stop asking me that. This ain't no game."

"I know it's not a game. I'm not playing, Lucky. I wanna go back where my family is. I don't wanna be in Franklin," she whined, tears filling her eyes.

164

"I'm trying, baby. I am. But things ain't going my way right now. The police looking for me and my niggas just got killed at the club the other night. And don't forget that Desmond is in jail. If he was out here, we could take on everybody in Milwaukee. But it's just me. I don't got a team. Honestly, I don't know what to do. I might be in over my head. I'm thinking about turning myself in, but I don't wanna leave you out here unprotected."

"Turning yo'self in won't make the problems go away though. You can't run from drama by going to jail. Polo got niggas everywhere."

He nodded. "I know. That's why I need a team. I can't take this nigga out on my own."

Laronda went silent for a moment. "Do you know any girls that you can have get close to him and set him up?"

"I tried that. It didn't work."

"Damn, Lucky. I don't know what else to say. Should we move outta town?"

He gave the option some thought. "I don't know. But the way things looking, that might be the only option."

◆◆◆

Lucky lay in bed running his fingers through Rachel's hair. They were at her house lying in bed. The mood was dark because of the shooting at the club. It was all they had talked about for two days. And since the club was closed down, she didn't have anything to do but lay around the house.

"I'm thinking about moving out of town," he blurted.

She looked up at him with sympathy in her eyes. "I'm not surprised. Where you talking about going?"

"I don't know. I'm too hot in Milwaukee. I got Polo chasing me on one side, Wacco on the other, and the police behind me. I can't take everybody on and I don't wanna go back to jail. I'm thinkin' about taking my daughter and leaving."

Rachel was silent for a moment. "Considering everything going on around you, that might not be a bad idea. Yo' friends got killed and you all on yo' own. I don't want to see you go, but I don't want you to get killed either."

"I just don't want to be looking over my shoulder for the police. I won't even be able to promote my books. I'ma have to go underground. This wasn't the life I pictured for myself when I got outta prison."

"That's the thing about life, baby. We can't really control what happens. We can only control how we react to what happens. You gotta change the plan you made and deal with right now."

"Right now the police want me locked up and niggas want me dead. Only way out is to run from these niggas or try to get on they level. And I don't got nobody to go at these niggas with me. So right now, the smartest thing for me to do is to get outta town."

They went silent for a moment.

"Didn't you say Donny said he would help you or something like that?"

"Yeah. He wants me to work for him, but he didn't say what I'd be doing. If I agree, I know that price tag is gon' be a big one."

She shrugged. "I don't know that much about what he do to make money, but Donny is a boss. And I think he's fair. I know how fucked up the streets is, but I think Donny is one of those rare real niggas. Like you. That's what I liked about both of y'all. It seems like you out of options. I think you should call him and see what he got to offer."

Donny couldn't wipe the smile from his face after hanging up the phone. The call with Lucky had brightened his mood. A great saying often quoted by psychologists popped into his head: "when a man is truly ready for a thing, it puts in its appearance."

"I am the master of my fate, the captain of my soul," he muttered to himself as he reclined in the office chair. His eyes searched the wall of his office until they landed on the pictures of Martin Luther King Jr. and Barack Obama. The two powerful black men were his idols. Both had come from the bottom and reached monumental status. Both were driven by dreams and didn't let anything or anyone stop them from pursuing what they wanted. That was Donny's mentality. Nothing would stop him from winning. The burning desire to win was deeply imbedded within his core. He was success conscious. Things always came together for him because he only thought about succeeding. Failure came to those that accepted it.

He picked up the cell phone from his desktop and sent a text. *Scooby, come to my office. It's important.*

A few moments later there was a knock on the door. A tall, muscular nigga with brushed waves stuck his head in. "What up, boss man?"

"Come in. Have a seat. We need to put our heads together and come up with a strategy to grow our operation westward."

Scooby smiled, greed showing in his eyes as he sat. "Where we talking? All the way west to Cali?"

"I like your ambition, but not that far west. Not yet. Just across Lake Michigan. Wisconsin. I got a call from Milwaukee. You remember the nigga that was at one of my nests?"

Scooby nodded. "Yeah. The dancer. Nigga wouldn't put down the gun."

"Yeah. His name is Lucky. He needs our assistance taking care of a problem. In exchange, he will join the team."

Scooby nodded again but the look on his face showed he wasn't fully on board with the plan.

Donny picked up on his demeanor. "Speak your mind. That's why I called you in here. I value your opinion."

"That's Wacco Tony's neck of the woods. Stepping on a nigga's toes can put a chink in the entire operation. You sure you want to risk fracturing the family over money?"

"I considered that. And I admit, this is a risky move. But two years ago, some Wisconsin niggas tried to move into Michigan. Remember that?"

Scooby nodded. "Yeah. I remember some shit popped off on 8 Mile."

"Those was Wacco's niggas. And now I have the opportunity to get back. He failed because he brought Milwaukee niggas to the D. Unlike him, I got a local nigga making our moves in Milwaukee. And, they are enemies. This is a perfect storm."

Scooby nodded again. "That sounds like a good plan. Almost fool proof. So what you want me to do, kill Wacco?"

"Nah, nah. I can't risk you getting caught up in the bullshit. You are too important. Plus, Wacco Tony knows you. Something happens to you, it gets back to me and the family gets involved. We don't need that. Lucky has two problems, Wacco and a nigga named Polo. What I want to do is give him some foot soldiers. Let's say, four shooters. You pick them and lead them to kill Polo. When that is done, leave the shooters and get yo' ass back home and let him take Wacco on his own. If he succeeds, we take over Wisconsin. If he fails, we don't lose anything. I think it's worth a roll of the dice."

Scooby shrugged indifferently. "I like it. How soon you wanna get to it?"

"As soon as possible."

Scooby got up to leave when he paused. "You remember what li'l Richie was saying about the army nigga from Flint that saved his ass from the jack boys?"

A light shone in Donny's eyes. "I like the way you think. I'ma call my nephew and see if we can track him down. You gather up some soldiers and I'ma check on the real soldier."

◆◆◆

Desmond sat at the head of the conference table listening to Special Agent Edmond Wright's briefing. He was updating the ATF superior on the status of the mission. Killing the jack boy and allowing Donny's team to dispose of the body caused a rift between the ATF brass. Some felt the mission was getting out of control and he had gone too far. Now they were meeting to discuss how much rope to give him Desmond.

"Mr. Harrison is exactly where he needs to be to infiltrate the organization. Rich Red trusts him. He can only get in deeper. It's messed up that people had to die but what did you expect him to do? He's a Navy SEAL and somebody pulled a gun on him."

"That doesn't give him a license to kill," the assistant director of the Alcohol Tobacco and Firearms Bureau, Mark Simeon, spoke up. "The media and local authorities are asking questions. There were witnesses."

"With all due respect, sir," Agent Johanson cut in, "We lie to the media all the time. We're on a secret mission to bring down a nationwide drug trafficking and crime family. Things will get ugly. People are going to die whether we have a guy on the inside or not. You have to know the rules in the streets. What Desmond did will get him stripes with the organization. This was the best situation we could hope for."

The assistant director looked at Desmond and then both agents. "I don't like the thought of giving an asset license to kill people. If he was a federal agent, things would be different. It would be easier to explain. Having a Navy SEAL going around destroying the city isn't what I want," he said and then addressed Desmond. "I read your file. You tore up Milwaukee and dropped bodies all over. They even think you killed a detective. This is all being swept under a rug because you're working with us. But I don't want you turning this into Milwaukee all over again. Tread carefully. Kill only when it's your last resort."

"I understand, director." Desmond nodded. "But they had guns. My only option was to neutralize the man. I kept my phone on so Johanson and Wright heard everything. I will use my own judgement when I'm forced to decide between me and them. And it will always be them."

The director nodded. "Spoken like a soldier. Just try to keep the casualties and damage to a minimum. I want to bring down the family just as bad as you all, but we can't get reckless. Okay?"

The agents and Desmond all nodded.

"And let's work on getting him a pair of glasses with a camera so we can have visual evidence of the mission. That cell phone recording is good, but video would be better."

When the director left the room, Desmond and the agents let out collective breaths.

"We dodged that bullet and might've gotten more leverage." Agent Wright spoke.

"I think we're good. He wants Donny and his people as bad as we do."

Desmond's phone rang, breaking up the party. "It's Rich."

The agents grew serious. "Answer it," Johanson encouraged.

"Rich Red! What's good, my nigga?"

"D-Money! You know you got the best hand, my nigga. I'm tryna see how you fairing over there in Flint."

"I could always be doing better. We couldn't go shopping last time I seen you, so the flow is at a standstill. Was yo' people able to take care of that situation?"

"Oh yeah. That's why I'm calling. Everything is good on all fronts. I'm heavy right now and can take care of whatever you need."

"Okay. Say less. Let me put some shit together and I'ma send you a text when I'm on the way."

"Meet me at Teona's house. Fuck wit' me, you know I got it."

After hanging up, Desmond turned to the agents. "I'ma go to Detroit. We good here?"

"Yep. Oh, and we had our tech guys create a fake army profile under Derrick Anderson. We've dotted the I's and crossed our T's. Take care." Wright winked.

Desmond left the federal building and drove home to get fifty thousand dollars and then jumped on the highway. When he pulled up to Teona's house, Rich Red was sitting on the hood of his Lotus. Desmond grabbed the bag of money and hopped out the car.

"What's good, my nigga?" Rich smiled, greeting Desmond with a hug like they had known each other for years.

"You got it. You don't think we should stop meeting here? Yo' girl's house is hot now, ain't it?"

"Nah, nah. We good. My uncle got people all over Michigan. Even got people in the federal building. That's how I found out the Feds wasn't after me. Hop in the whip with me and take a ride."

Desmond hopped in the luxury car and was taken on a short ride through Detroit. When the car stopped, they were in the back parking lot of Juan's Cleaning Service.

"What is this?"

Rich Red smiled. "I got somebody I want you to meet. Follow me."

The look on Rich's face told Desmond that whoever wanted to meet him was important. That meant it could only be one person: Uncle Donny.

The cleaning service was in a small storefront office building. They walked in through the back door and were greeted by members of Donny's team.

"Royce. Fifty. What up?" Rich greeted them.

"'Sup, li'l nigga," Royce greeted. "This the soldier?" he asked, looking Desmond over from head to toe.

Desmond remained silent.

"Yeah. This my nigga D-Money. Where Unc?"

"He in the office."

After exchanging another glance with the security, Desmond followed Rich Red through the small cleaning service building and into an office at the back. Donny sat behind a desk talking on the phone. When Desmond and Rich walked in, he lifted a finger for them to hold on. After ending the call, he turned an eye to Desmond.

"So you are the famous D-Money!" He smiled.

"I don't know about famous, but I'm D-Money."

Donny nodded, eyeing Desmond with admiration. "Humility is an attribute not often found in the hood. So, you really are a solider, huh?"

"Was," Desmond corrected.

"What happened? My nephew told me you had skills. Why did you leave the service?"

Desmond removed his glasses, showing the scar on his eye. "America don't give a fuck about a nigga that can't do nothing for them. They use niggas up and throw you away when you damaged. Bitch-ass shit," he cursed as if recalling a bitter memory.

171

"Unfortunately, that is the world we live in," Donny said as he got up from the desk and walked to stand in front of Desmond. He searched the soldier's face, looking from good eye to bad eye. "Some people can't see past exteriors. But I see in you an indomitable spirit. And someone with your skills will always have opportunity placed before them. The question is whether or not you are prepared to take hold of the opportunity before you."

Desmond met the searching stare of Donny with one of his own. "I'ma be real with you, Donny. I don't plan on hustling forever. This shit just kinda fell into my lap and I had to do what I had to do to eat. If you asking me to hustle for you, I'ma have to pass because I'm not in this for the long haul."

Donny nodded in agreement. "No, hustling ain't for everybody and you are too talented to be a pusher. I got bigger plans for someone like you. And if you let me use your talents, I will make you a very rich man."

Desmond smiled like he just heard the winning numbers to his lottery ticket. "I like the way you talking, my dude. Tell me more."

Donny walked back around the desk and sat down. He sat silently for a moment, letting the suspense build. "Have you ever been to Milwaukee, Wisconsin?"

Chapter 17

When it came to finding people, nobody was better than Jonathan Clemons. He was fifty-three years old, wore no facial hair, and his mixed race gave him very light skin, which enabled him to easily blend into any environment. Standing just 5'7" with a slim build, he looked unassuming and harmless. As a CIA agent, he made connections in all the right places: the DMV, police force, and different branches of the federal government. When he retired from being a Fed and began the P.I. service, it seemed like a natural transition. He had the connections to get any information he needed on almost anyone on earth. He could also work his own hours, charge according to his own scale, and he didn't have to answer to anyone but himself. Five years later, he'd become one of the best P.I.'s in Detroit and was highly recommended, so much so that he could choose his clientele. When he got the call from Donny, he readily accepted the mission, knowing he would be well-compensated for his work. The job seemed easy. Find a mark.

He'd been in Milwaukee, Wisconsin for four days and was close to earning his paycheck. After a little digging, he was able to come up with an address for a woman named Yolanda Steele. She lived in the Parklawn Housing Projects just off Sherman Boulevard. Finding the house was easy. Extracting the information might not be. The P.I clipped a fake name tag to his shirt before ringing the doorbell.

"Who is it?" a woman called.

"My name is Steven Ferris. I'm looking for Yolanda Steele."

The big metal door unlocked and a short, light-skinned woman appeared. "Who is you?"

"I'm Steven Ferris with the Child Support Agency. I'm looking for Yolanda Steele."

Mistrust shone in her eyes as she gave him a suspicious look. "Child support?"

"I have a checking issue that I need to clear up. There was a payment made, but we can't issue the check until we confirm the sender and recipient's current information," he explained, hoping the talk of money would soften her demeanor.

"A check?" she asked, her eyes growing wide with interest.

"Yes, ma'am. I have a payment for Yolanda. Is that you?"

"Yeah, yeah. C'mon in here," she said, opening the door wide.

"Thank you. This shouldn't take but a moment," he said after stepping into the modestly-furnished project apartment. "With all the scams and things happening now a days, we have to do these types of things in person and not on the phone or online."

"Yeah. I understand. Have a seat. How much is the check?" she asked, ready to receive her just due.

"Well, before we get to that, do you mind if I see some identification so I can make sure I'm talking to the right person? A state ID would be sufficient."

Yolanda ran from the living room and up the stairs like her hair was in fire. She came back a moment later breathing heavily. "Here you go."

After checking the ID, he gave it back and pulled out a laptop computer. "Okay. Now that we proved you're the right person, I have to ask some questions about the father and child. How many children do you have?"

"Three."

"And how many do you have by Sammy Dawkins?"

"Just one."

He nodded and typed on the computer. "Okay. What is the child's name?"

"April Dawkins. Is this about Sammy, for real?"

He nodded. "Yeah. Did you take a paternity test to prove he is the father?"

When she realized which one of her baby daddy's this was about, her mood seemed to get a little dark. "Yeah, we took a test. That no good muthafucka still don't wanna admit that she his or help me."

"Well, it appears those days are gone. I have a check for you for four hundred thirty-four dollars. All I need you to do is give me his

174

current address and I will go see him and confirm paternity and we will get you some financial help."

"I don't know where he lives," she said, almost in a panic.

The private investigator frowned. "Well, do you at least know the general area?"

She paused for a moment as if weighing options. "If you go to his house, he'll know I sent you and we might have some problems."

He nodded sympathetically. "Oh. So, you're not seeing eye to eye right now. Okay. Um, what if I could guarantee that he won't find out you gave me his address? Would that make it better?"

She looked skeptical. "Could you really do that? Because I don't want no problems with Polo. He can get really stupid."

He nodded. "Yeah. I swear I won't tell him that you sent me. I'm with the government, so I could get his address. It would just take longer."

She looked satisfied. "Okay. He lives in Brookfield. On North Avenue."

Jonathan typed on the lap top some more before standing and pulling out a check. "Okay, ma'am. I have everything I need. Here is your child support check for four hundred thirty-four dollars. I'll confirm paternity with Mr. Dawkins. And I won't mention that I talked to you. You have my word."

Yolanda showed him to the door. "Thank you so much. I really needed this money. Will the checks be regular from now on?"

"Hopefully. I'm going to talk to him and see if we can work out a regular payment. Have a nice day."

Jonathan left the low income apartment with a smile on his face and a little bit of guilt on his conscience. He hated lying to the single mother and fooling her with the fake check. But he had a job to do, and if he let every lie or false impression get to him, he would have drowned in guilt and blown his brains out a long time ago. Instead of focusing on Yolanda, he thought about the next task. Make sure Sammy still lived at the address. He hopped in the rented Toyota Highlander and used the GPS to get to the town of Brookfield.

◆◆◆

Lucky drove through the intersection, not giving much thought to the traffic laws. His mind was consumed by thoughts of the deal he made with Donny. For five days it was all he thought about. He felt like he'd made a deal with the devil. In exchange for his soul, Polo would die. Now that the ink had dried on the contract, he was second and third guessing his actions - not because he didn't want Polo dead, but because he didn't know what the exchange was. Donny never told what he wanted in exchange for the kill. It reminded him of the deal Desmond made with Polo. Desmond backed out when Polo wanted Quaysha. What if Donny's demands were too high? Could he survive telling a man as powerful as Donny no? If he had enough juice to find and kill Polo from Detroit when Lucky couldn't do it from Milwaukee, then Donny definitely wasn't to be fucked over. But what did he want from Lucky? That was the million dollar question, one he wouldn't be able to answer until Donny called.

A car closing in on the bumper made him look in the rearview mirror.

"Shit!" he cursed, body going stiff with fear. A black and white patrol car crept up behind him. He could see one officer inside. Panic flooded his body as thoughts of a cell filled his mind. He was wanted for parole violations and questioning in several shootings. Plus, there was a Glock on his waist. His days as a free man seemed to be over. He continued watching the rearview mirror while contemplating his next move. He didn't want to go back to jail. That was hell. Life in prison looked almost certain. He couldn't accept the slow torturous death. He would rather die than go back to prison for the rest of his life. He thought of his daughter and Desmond as he pulled the Glock from his pants. He hoped they would understand.

"Please, God. Don't let it end like this," he prayed.

Whoop-whoop!

Lucky's heart dropped when the sirens flashed. He checked the safety on the gun, making sure it was off as he pulled to the side of the road. To his surprise and relief, the police car zoomed down the street.

"Damn," he exhaled, his body shaking as his nerves went crazy. He continued to sit and think about what almost happened. He was about to kill a police officer. Damn. The vibrating of his phone brought him back to the now. When he saw Desmond's number, a mix of emotions flooded his body.

"What's going on, brah?" he answered, feeling and sounding emotionally drained.

"Damn, Lucky. You alright?"

A vision of shooting the cop flashed in his head. "Nah, brah. I'm not gon' even lie. I feel like I'm losing it, man."

"What's going on, my nigga. Talk to me."

"Its crazy out here, Des," Lucky breathed. "I don't know if I'ma make it. Every time I turn around, I got another problem that's worse than the one before it. I'm in so much shit that I don't know how to move. It's all bad."

"Talk to me, Lucky. What you talking 'bout?"

"I can't say on this phone, man. I didn't imagine my life turning out like this. I just want you to know that I tried to do the right thing. You knew that. But this world won't let you do the right thing. If you don't fuck somebody over when you have the opportunity, they will turn around and do it to you. It's crazy out here."

Desmond's voice came back full of understanding. "I know exactly what you talking about, man. That's how I got myself in this crazy situation I'm in. The streets will make you do things you never thought you would. Survival of the fittest."

Lucky went silent for a moment, thinking on how to say his next words. "Listen, Des. I just want you to know that I tried. Everything that happens from here on out, I was forced to do. I made a deal with somebody that I can't turn back from. I don't know where it's gonna take me, but I don't have a choice. I did it because I want to stay alive and keep my daughter safe."

"What deal, Lucky? What did you do?"

"I can't tell you right now. I just wanted to tell you that I tried to do the right thing. Now it's all about survival. My P.O is looking for me, the police looking for me, and Polo and Wacco keep making my life hell. I'm tired of running. I'm tired of playing fair. Like you said, its survival of the fittest and I survived too much to let them beat me. I'ma win, my nigga. Or die trying."

◆◆◆

During the flight to Milwaukee, Desmond couldn't stop thinking about the phone call with his brother last night. Lucky sounded stressed and close to the edge, like he was at his wits end. And the deal he made had Desmond's skin crawling. He wondered if his mission to kill Polo had something to do with the deal Lucky made. But how? Donny was in Michigan and Lucky was in Wisconsin. Did they somehow cross paths, or was it just a coincidence? Desmond had a hard time believing in coincidences. Everything inside him told him everything was connected. But how?

The flight landed at Mitchell International Airport at 10:15 p.m. Desmond, Scooby, and four shooters walked off the plane. There was a rented van waiting, and a suite at the Intercontinental Hotel had already been booked for three days. Since Desmond was familiar with the city, he drove. In the suite's living room they found a large suitcase. Inside was a cache of guns, several pistols, and two Dracos. There were also six Kevlar bulletproof vests.

"A'ight, y'all. Grab a pistol and let's go check these spots. We gotta check Polo's house and get up with this nigga Lucky," Scooby directed.

The sound of his brother's name snapped Desmond's attention. "Who the fuck is Lucky? I thought we was here to clap Polo and hit it."

"Info is on a need to know basis, brah," Scooby said.

Desmond couldn't allow the meet with his brother to happen. It could blow his cover and ruin everything. "I say we don't even meet Lucky. Ain't no need for us to meet a nigga that ain't going on the move. Plus, I don't want none of these Milwaukee niggas to see my face."

"Let me worry about how we moving, D-Money. I just need you to be ready when I say go."

178

Desmond didn't like being treated like a flunky. "Well I don't draw like that. I know I'm new to y'all squad, but I ain't new to making moves and going on missions. When I move, I don't like surprises. That shit can get a nigga killed. Anything else I should know about before we move?"

Scooby stopped and turned to face Desmond. The men had a stare off. "I normally don't explain myself to the shooters, but since you new and the boss took a liking to you, I'ma make this one exception. We expanding into Wisconsin and Lucky gon' lead the operation. Me and you leaving once we kill Polo. The shooters staying and they need to meet the nigga they runnin' under."

Desmond tried to act like the news didn't affect him, but couldn't. "Why do we need to be in Wisconsin? This don't make sense."

Scooby eyed him suspiciously. "Why you so worried about shit that don't concern you? You here for once reason," he mugged, pulling a pistol from his waist. "Either you with us or against us. Yo' choice."

The men had another staring contest. Desmond recognized the look in Scooby's eyes. If he said the wrong thing, he would die on the spot. And when he looked to the shooters, they wore the same looks as their leader. He would have to find another way to stop the meet with his brother. "I'm in, my nigga. I just don't like surprises."

After another stare down, Scooby tucked the pistol in his waist. "This the last time I'ma tell you not to go against what I say. We don't know you, brah. If you wanna stay down wit' us, do as I say. Grab y'all shit and let's ride. D-Money, you the driver."

The squad of killers left the hotel suite and took an elevator downstairs. Desmond led the way through the lobby. He was almost to the door when he felt someone watching him. After a quick search, he spotted his watchers by the front desk. There were two niggas standing with four women at the check in counter. One of them was tall and skinny with an uncombed afro, the other a few inches shorter with cornrows to the back. Kareem and Six. Both members of CSG. A flashback ran quickly through Desmond's head. He had crushed Kareem's throat when he killed Big Man. And Six shot Jamar in the back when he shot up the Cadillac truck. The men eyed Desmond and his squad as they walked out the front door. Desmond turned to Scooby and the shooters to see if they noticed the CSG niggas. Unfortunately, they were too busy sightseeing, enamored with the luxury hotel to notice the hostile looks.

Desmond was conflicted. He wasn't sure if he should alert his team of the danger or keep it moving and hope the CSG niggas didn't try anything stupid. If he told Scooby about them, he might have to explain how he knew them and that could open another can of worms. So he chose to stay silent.

The team of killers from Detroit walked out into the darkness and had just hopped into the Chrysler Pacifica when Kareem and Six followed them into the parking lot. Desmond kept an eye on them as he pulled the van out into traffic. The CSG niggas hopped into a Lexus crossover and tailed them.

"We going to Lucky first." Scooby spoke up from the passenger seat. "He live in Franklin. You know where that is?"

Desmond only heard bits and pieces of what Scooby said because he was too busy watching the Lexus in the rear view mirror. "What you say?"

"I said, we going to Lucky. He live in Franklin. What's wrong? You see something back there?" Scooby asked, looking out the back window.

"Nah. I'm just watching everything," Desmond recovered. "Yeah, I know Franklin. It ain't that far."

Scooby eyed Desmond for a moment. "What's going on with you, brah? What's yo' story?"

Desmond glanced over and seen the mistrust in Scooby's eyes. "What you mean? Shit, I'm out here tryna eat just like you."

Scooby smirked. "Where you from? You got people in Wisconsin?"

Desmond recalled the lie he'd practiced. He was about to tell it when headlights in the mirror got his attention. The Lexus had picked up speed and was coming along the passenger side. Scooby was so busy eyeing Desmond that he didn't see the Mac-11 hanging out the window.

Pop, pop, pop, pop, pop, pop, pop, pop, pop, pop, pop, pop, pop! Scooby's head exploded as the passenger window shattered. Desmond swerved into oncoming traffic, ducking low and trying to avoid being shot. Headlights from oncoming traffic made him whip back into the right lane behind the Lexus truck.

"What the fuck?" one of the shooters called from the back seat.

"Scooby! Scooby!" another called, checking on their fallen comrade.

"He dead!" Desmond screamed, mashing the gas and gaining on the Lexus. "Open that door and fuck them niggas up!"

The sliding doors on both sides of the van opened and shooters hung out and opened fire. The windows on the Lexus exploded as the high speed gun battle ensued and slugs tore into the crossover's frame. When the first two guns were empty, two more shooters took their spots and continued firing. The Lexus lost control and slid off the road, smashing into a parked car. Desmond brought the van to a skidding stop.

"Get out and make sure them niggas dead!" he ordered.

All four of the shooters hopped out of the van and fired so many rounds into the Lexus that a cloud of smoke hung in the air even after the Pacifica drove away.

Chapter 18

"What the fuck do you mean Scooby is dead?" Donny roared. Quincy winced at the phone like he was standing in the boss man's presence. "It came out of nowhere. We don't even know what happened."

"Tell me what happened? How the fuck did my nigga die when y'all wasn't even on the hit yet?"

"I don't know. We was riding down the street when some niggas rode up and started flashin'."

"That shit don't even sound right. Some niggas just fired on y'all for no reason?"

Quincy looked around the van, his eyes pleading for help.

"I think it was some mistaken identity shit," Desmond spoke up. "It happened just like he said. Niggas rode up and started squeezing. We got them niggas, but they got Scooby."

"Who am I talking to? This you, D-Money?"

"Yeah."

"Scooby was like my family, man," Donny said, emotion filling his voice. "I need you to see the mission through. You got the potential to lead an army. Do what you need to do to finish the job. Meet with Lucky and get it done. And I need you to bring Scooby back home so we can give him a proper burial. Damn, this is fucked up. Can you handle that?"

"I won't let you down, boss man."

"Okay. And call me if anything else happens."

Desmond turned to the shooters after hanging up the phone. "A'ight. This shit just put a black eye on our shit, but we still gon' get it done. I'ma drop y'all off to Lucky and I got it from here."

"Where you going? What about gettin' at Polo?"

"I'ma take care of that by myself."

"Yeah right, nigga." Quincy laughed. "You gon' kill that nigga and his shooters by yo'self?"

Desmond gave him a serious look. "I don't play about this shit. I'ma drop y'all off to Lucky and I got the rest."

The shooters gave one another questioning looks.

"How you get to be in charge? We don't even know you, fam," another shooter spoke up.

Desmond eyed the light-skinned kid with gray eyes. His name was Demon.

"You heard what Donny said. Unless you want me to call him and make him explain it again, I think you should be easy. And if we done talking, grab Scooby and lay him in the back seat."

Demon looked like he wanted to say more, but when none of the shooters spoke, he fell silent. When Desmond was satisfied that he had control of the group, he nodded towards Scooby's body laid across the front seat. Demon and Quincy grabbed it and took the body to the back.

The drive to Lucky's house was silent. When they were close, Quincy sent a text to let Lucky know they were close. And instead of waiting around for Lucky to claim his men, Desmond dropped them off at the curb and kept going.

◆◆◆

When Lucky got the text from Quincy, he walked to the front door just in time to find four niggas walking up on the porch. "Where Scooby?" he asked, looking for the leader of the group.

"He dead," Quincy spoke up.

Shock flashed on to Lucky's face. "Dead? I just talked to him earlier. What happened?"

"Niggas got down on us when we left the hotel. Shit just happened right before we came over."

Lucky stood on the porch dumfounded, stunned by the news. When he realized they were looking to him for their next move, he snapped back to the moment. "Damn. Y'all come in. How y'all get here? Was that y'all ride?"

"Yeah. That was D-Money. He dropped us off and going to get at Polo."

This news shocked Lucky even more than the death of Scooby. "Why y'all not going with him? We was all supposed to go together."

"Nigga wanted to go by himself. Since he was in the army, Donny put him in charge. Said he got it and dropped us off."

Lucky stared at the young men's faces for a moment. They seemed dejected and unsure. Then he went back to something Quincy said. "You said an army nigga going to kill Polo by himself?"

"Yeah. D-Money. I think he from Milwaukee. He was the one driving us around."

Lucky got a funny feeling as thoughts of his brother entered his head. "What this army nigga look like?"

"Tall and dark-skinned. Kinda swole like the he just got out the joint. And one of his eyes fucked up."

Lucky's eyes grew wide like he just took a hit of crack. He pulled out his phone and searched for a picture of Desmond. "Is this him?"

"Yeah, that's him. That's D-Money. You know that nigga?"

Lucky nodded as snippets of the conversation he had with Desmond yesterday flashed in his head. "Yeah. I thought he was in jail."

"D-Money definitely ain't in jail, brah. He in that van on his way to murk Polo."

◆◆◆

Desmond pulled into the parking garage and drove around until he found an empty corner to duck off the van. He made sure to hide Scooby's body from prying eyes before grabbing two pistols and leaving the garage on foot. The next mission was getting a set of wheels. He walked to the closest gas station and waited alongside the building until he found a mark. A young hustler pulled up to the pump and left his Audi truck idling. Desmond slipped behind the wheel and headed for Brookfield.

Polo's house was a half a million dollar mini mansion sitting back by a small pond. The house seemed to be sitting by itself, on its own island. There were no trees or neighboring houses for a few hundred feet. Desmond didn't have a way to approach the house without being seen. And he knew the baller had cameras installed. He let out a frustrated breath and tried to think of a way to get to the house. Nothing came to mind. He wished he had taken a shooter with him to cause a distraction. But that wasn't the case. His only bet was to wait it out and see who would leave the house next and try to get inside. He parked down the street and began the wait. Two hours later, he got the opportunity he'd been waiting for. A middle-aged man walked out of the house with two huge Rottweiler. The man walked along while the dogs ran towards the pond. There was a park bench at the edge of the water where the man copped a squat and began messing with his phone.

Desmond grabbed put on a pair of dark shades and lowered the hoodie before leaving the truck. He moved quickly, half-trotting silently towards the man, hoping he kept his attention on the phone. The dogs continued running, barking and playing. When he was about twenty feet away from the man, the dogs stopped playing and looked in his direction. When the man noticed the dogs grow silent, he looked around. Desmond was already in arms reach with a pistol pointed in his face.

"Don't do no stupid shit," he warned, glancing towards the animals. They lowered their heads and trotted silently towards the humans. "Get up and walk to the house. And don't call these dogs or I'ma bag all y'all ass."

The man stood, eyeing Desmond like he was trying to remember his face. "You know who you fuckin wit', brah? If you leave right now, I'ma act like this ain't happen."

Desmond's face turned dark with anger. "You the one that don't know better. Move towards the house before you piss me off. How many people inside?"

The man began to walk slowly. "Just me. But ain't nothing in there. We don't keep nothing in this house."

"Good. Because I didn't come to steal nothing. Now shut the fuck up and stop the dogs from following us."

He turned towards the dogs and barked a command. "Stay."

The dogs stopped in their tracks, eyeing their master and waiting for another command.

"What you want?" he asked as Desmond led him into the house.

"I need to holla at Polo. When do he come back?"

"Ain't no telling. He be in and out."

186

Noise at the back door made the men pause. The dogs were barking and scratching at the door.

"Make 'em stop," Desmond said.

"You gotta let 'em back in. They smart and know somethin' wrong."

Desmond thought for a moment. If they continued making noise, they could draw attention to the house. "A'ight. Let 'em in. If you try any bullshit, I'm fuckin' you up," he warned, pulling out another pistol.

The man smirked as he walked to the door. When he opened it, the dogs rushed inside, growling at Desmond.

"Put 'em in a room" Desmond said, keeping both guns pointed at the dogs and moving behind a table to keep distance between him and the animals.

"Sic 'em!" the man yelled and then made a run for the hallway.

The dogs didn't care that Desmond was armed. They charged as him, ready to tear him apart.

Pop, pop!

The animals whined as bullets to the head dropped them. Desmond took aim at the fleeing man and shot him in the ass.

"Aahhhhh shit!" he screamed, falling to the ground.

"Didn't I tell yo' dumb ass not to try no stupid shit?" Desmond admonished as he approached. "New get yo' stupid ass up."

"I can't, man. Ah shit! You shot me in my ass."

Desmond stepped on his bullet wound.

"Ahhhh!"

"Get'cho ass up, nigga, before I shoot yo' ass again."

The man held the wall and struggled to get to his feet. "Ah shit! Damn, man. What the fuck you want?"

"Y'all got cameras in here?"

"Yeah. And they recording yo' ass right now."

"Delete the footage and turn 'em off."

Defiance shone in the man's eyes. "Fuck you, nigga."

Desmond pointed the pistol at his foot and squeezed the trigger. Pop!

"Ahh shit!" the man cried, falling to the floor.

Desmond pointed the pistol in his face. "Turn them cameras off, nigga."

"Fuck you," he cursed, gritting his teeth in pain.

Desmond pressed the pistol against his crotch. "Last chance."

The man's eyes grew wide as he thought twice about his defiant stance. "Okay. Okay," he mumbled before pulling out his phone and disabling the cameras. "They off. Don't shoot me no more, man. Please."

Desmond looked him in the eyes for a moment. He saw the fear of death in the man's irises. "It don't hurt," he said before putting a bullet in his forehead.

"Yeah, baby! Rich nigga shit! You know how we do!" Polo celebrated as he threw money in the air. He was at Diamond's, a new strip club in downtown Milwaukee, and tonight was the grand opening. Dope boys, athletes, and entertainers filled the VIP. Some of the baddest women in the Midwest put on erotic shows that made niggas come out the pocket and tip big. Polo seemed to have the best seat in the house. Caramel and Cinnamon were two of the baddest dancers in the club and they were currently twerking on either side of him.

"Gimme that bottle of Aces, Kato!" Polo called.

When his boy gave him the bottle of bubbly, he began pouring it over Cinnamon's ass while she twerked. "I got so much money I can make it rain champagne!" he bragged, spanking her ass while the champagne poured down her crack.

"We tip drilling in this bitch!" Kato called, swiping a credit card down Caramel's ass crack while she twerked.

After the ballers had fun and partied like rich niggas, Polo pulled his two favorite dancers to the side. "Cinnamon and Caramel, I need y'all for the night. Come party wit' a rich nigga and let's do all the shit y'all manager won't let us do in the club."

"I'm about my bag, baby. Ain't nothin in life free," Cinnamon said, smacking Caramel's ass and watching it ripple. Wanting to make sure to tease him some more, Caramel bent over and touched her toes and Cinnamon ground her pelvis against her ass, simulating fucking her from behind.

"Money ain't shit to me. Spending that shit is the only way to guarantee you have a good time. Get y'all shit. We riding Porsche truck tonight."

After the women put on skimpy outfits that barely covered their bodies, Polo wrapped an arm around each woman's shoulders and headed for the parking lot followed by a twelve man entourage.

"Kato, you wit' me, fool. I need you to drive. I'ma holla at the rest of y'all niggas in the AM. I got big booty bitches to slay!" Polo laughed as he escorted the women to the silver Porsche truck. They climbed in the back and Polo got in the passenger seat. "Show a real nigga how you get down."

Caramel reached out and grabbed one of Cinnamon's big breasts. "You think he can handle us?"

Cinnamon looked at Polo. "I don't know. You ready for the best pussy you ever had in yo' life, nigga?"

"I hear y'all talking. Show me something," he challenged.

"You ain't doin' nothing but talking either. Show us that money bag," Caramel sassed.

Polo laughed as he pulled a wad of cash from his pocket and began showering the women with it. "That's five racks right there. It betta be worth it."

Money made the women react like actors on a movie set when the director yelled "Action!" They kissed aggressively and rolled around the back seat like they were wrestling. Cinnamon ended up on top, releasing Caramel's breasts from the bikini top and sucking on her nipples.

"Yeah, bitch! Suck my titties!" Caramel moaned. "Bite my nipples."

Cinnamon gave both breasts a lot of attention before sliding down her body and snatching off Caramel's thong. Then she spread her legs wide and showed Polo the swollen lips of her clean-shaved pussy. "You like that fat-ass pussy, nigga?"

"You know I do. Now what you gon' do with it?" Polo asked.

"I'ma suck her pussy, then let you fuck her while I suck the juice off yo dick. Get'cho ass back here."

Polo slid into the backseat and pulled down his pants in the same motion. To make room, he pushed the passenger seat forward before sitting down in the back.

"Let me get that dick." Caramel said, leaning over and sucking him into her mouth while Cinnamon ate her pussy.

Kato could barely keep his eyes in the road as he watched the threesome unfold in the backseat. After Caramel was good and wet, Cinnamon stopped eating her and got Polo's attention.

"Come fuck my bitch and let me taste that dick, too."

Caramel lay on her back and Polo climbed on top while Cinnamon kneeled on the floor. Every few strokes Polo pulled his dick out and Cinnamon gave him head. They continued this until they pulled into the driveway of Polo's mini mansion.

"Y'all c'mon in and let's finish what the fuck y'all started." Polo grinned as he stumbled out of the truck, adjusting his clothes. When he was decent, he wrapped his arms around the women's shoulders and walked them to the door. "Kato, hurry up and open the door, nigga."

Kato stood at the door struggling to find the key. "I got it," he said as the door opened.

"Welcome to the Oval Office, ladies. Follow me to the President's suite!" Polo grinned, eager to get the party started again.

Kato locked the front door as the trio headed towards the back of the house.

As soon as they entered the hallway, a big man dressed in black emerged carrying two pistols.

"What the fuck!" Polo yelled.

"Ahhhh!" the women screamed.

Pop, pop, pop, pop, pop, pop, pop, pop, pop, pop, pop, pop, pop, pop, pop, pop!

Polo and the strippers fell to the ground as bullets filled their bodies. When Kato heard the shooting, he pulled the pistol from his waist and ran towards the drama. As soon as he stepped into the hallway, four bullets to the chest cut him down to the ground.

After checking to make sure no one else came in the house, the killer returned to the bodies and gave them all dome shots before fleeing the gruesome murder scene.

Chapter 19

Desmond wasn't locked up.

That single thought had been running through Lucky's head all night. He had watched the police take his brother into custody outside of Melissa's house. He'd talked to him on the phone while he was in the Milwaukee county jail and visited him on Homeway. He spoke to the lawyer about the charges and how they denied Desmond bail. And now he was free. Lucky racked his brain for the how. Only one answer came to mind. Desmond was working with the police. But how did he get to Detroit? That was the million dollar question. Since he didn't have Desmond's number, he grabbed the phone and called Lasonya.

"Hey, Lucky," she answered, bubbly.

"Where Desmond?"

There was a pause. "Um…. You know Desmond is in jail. The military pol-"

"Stop bullshitting, Lasonya. Desmond was in Milwaukee last night. He was outside my house. Where he at?"

"I don't know what you talking about, Lucky. Desmond is in the military prison."

He chuckled. "So you gon' stick to this shit even after I told you he was at my house last night? I got the niggas that he was with waiting for me at the Intercontinental Hotel. Where the fuck is my brother?"

Lasonya stuck to her story. "It has to be a mistake, Lucky. Desmond is in jail. I talk to him on the phone every day."

Lucky shook his head, getting madder by the moment. And Lasonya was adding to the anger by treating him like he was stupid. "You really think I'm stupid, Lasonya? You think I don't know why you moved out of town all of a sudden the same day that Desmond got snatched up by the military police? I figured it out, so stop lying. Gimme Desmond's phone number or tell me where he at."

"Listen to me, Lucky. Your brother is in jail. Are you high or something? Are you okay?"

Lucky was so mad that he almost threw the phone at the wall. But he controlled himself and played the trump card. "If you don't tell me where Desmond at, the next time I talk to him, I'ma tell him what happened at Trev's house. And don't think I don't remember what happened at the hotel. I was drunk, but I know that was you."

Lasonya was silent for a moment. When she spoke again, her voice lost some of the confidence she displayed while defending Desmond. "Don't play like that, Lucky. You bogus, nigga."

"I'm not playing and I'm not bogus. You bogus for fucking me. Twice."

"You bogus too, nigga!" she yelled angrily. "You think he gon' be mad at just me? He gon' be mad at you too. You his only family and you want to hurt him like that?"

"Tell me the truth then. Where is my brother?"

"C'mon, Lucky," Lasonya cried. "Don't do this to me. Me and Desmond are happy. We're trying to have a baby. Don't put me in the middle of whatever you and him got going on."

Lucky didn't let up. "Gimme his number. Tell me where he at."

Lasonya sat on the phone and cried. "Fuck you, Lucky. I did what I had to do, now you do what you gotta do."

After Lasonya hung up, Lucky threw the phone on the bed and shook his head. She had confirmed what he already knew without actually saying it. Desmond was a fucking snitch. And that wasn't the only thing that had him thinking. Lasonya said she did what she had to do.

"What the fuck she meant by that?" he questioned aloud. Before he could wrap his mind around the cryptic message, there was a knock on the door.

"Come in."

Sharday poked her head into the room. "Hey, Lucky. You woke?"

"Yeah. What's up?"

She stepped into the room wearing a long T-shirt. "Can I have fifty dollars? I'ma give it back to you when I get my check."

He looked her over, judging her intent. Figured she needed the money to buy some dog food. "I'm not about to pay for you to get high."

She walked over and sat on the bed. "Please, Lucky. I'ma give it back. I swear to God. Just gimme twenty five."

He shook his head. "Nah. You gotta get yo' hustle on some other way. I can't help you."

"C'mon, Lucky. Don't do me like that," she pleaded, reaching a hand under the covers and grabbing his dick. "Let me take care of you, baby. I will do whatever you want."

He had a quick flashback of the last time he fucked with his baby mama at the hotel. They had a good time until he caught her trying to steal money from his jeans. "I'm good. Get out my room. I gotta get dressed and go take care of some business," he said and pushed her hand away.

Sharday pled with her eyes. Lucky stared back blankly, showing no emotion.

"One day you gon' need my help." She mean mugged him before leaving the room.

Lucky climbed out of bed and threw on some clothes, contemplating his next move. There were four young killers from Detroit looking for him to give them orders. But he didn't know what orders to give because he hadn't received a call from Donny about the terms of the deal they made. Everyone was at a standstill. Then his phone rang. Donny's name showed on the screen.

"I was just thinking about you," Lucky answered.

"That's the universe confirming what is meant to be, brah." Donny chuckled. "How you doing?"

"I'm making it. One day at a time shit. Been waiting for your call so I could plot my next move."

"That's why I'm calling. I don't know if you heard the news, but Polo got knocked off the horse."

Satisfaction filled Lucky's being for a moment. The weight of the deaths of Melissa and her kids seemed to get a little lighter. When he realized Donny had completed his part of the agreement and it was now his turn, he began to feel a little uneasy. "That's some of the best news I heard in a long time. And I take it this is a collection call?"

"You are correct. I'm sending you a package. It'll be there in a couple of days. I have a special messenger bringing it. Once you receive it, you'll know what to do with it. This is a great opportunity for us to become legends, my man. Take advantage of your season and sow a mighty seed so you can reap a great harvest."

The East Saint Louis Nightmare wasn't a bad dream. It was a person. But not just any person. The local authorities described him as a destructive force, a man with a penchant for violence. According to street lore, he got the name after one of the most gruesome homicides in Missouri history. After a man sold his mother crack, Flacco spent the next two days kidnapping twenty of the man's family members. Mother, father, sister, brother, cousins, aunts, and uncles. The oldest was seventy, the youngest a five-week-old infant. For the man's crime, the East Saint Louis Nightmare held the family at gunpoint and made them eat the five week old infant while it was still alive. Those that didn't take part in the cannibal feast were executed on the spot. Those that took part in the unholy communion were granted freedom. Nine family members died. Eleven walked away. The story had been passed around the streets of East Saint Louis for five years. Even though most people knew who did the gruesome crime, no one dared talk about it to the police for fear of their family being killed next. And now the man behind the myth was about to strike again.

"How many people in the house?" Flacco asked as he took a puff from the Backwood stuffed with ten grams of sour. Flacco could easily been described as a beast. Standing 6'2" and 240 pounds with tattoos covering every inch of his face, he looked like the poster child for vicious gang member. He was sitting in the driver's seat of a black Lexus, watching a white and yellow one story family house.

"A lot, blood. It look like they having some kind of family gathering. A birthday or something," Duke answered.

"Where Kilo and Mili?"

Duke nodded to the SUV parked a few houses away. "They in the 'burban with Rosé and Jordan. They waiting on you to give the green light."

Flacco took another puff of the Backwood and blew out the smoke slowly. A few beats passed. Duke waited.

"Green light."

Duke smiled as he pulled out his phone and sent a text. A few moments later the doors opened on the black Suburban and four men dressed in red clothing hopped out with red bandanas covering their faces. One of them carried a small red gasoline tank. He walked towards the back of the house while the other three stood on the side walk in front and pulled automatic weapons. A few moments, later smoke began billowing from the back of the house. There were screams from inside the house and the front door opened. People began pouring out of the house: men, women, and children.

Clap, clap, clap, clap, clap!

Boom, boom, boom, boom, boom!

Brrrrreaaaaatttt! Brrrrreaaaaatttt!

Screams filled the air as bodies fell to the ground, riddled with bullets. Flacco watched the horror show, a lustful grin splitting his lips. Then he reached in the back seat and grabbed the street sweeper. He walked towards the carnage, letting 12 gauge slugs fly. A young woman was his first victim. She ran onto the porch as the gauge coughed, the slug hitting her in the face and exploding her head. When the people inside the house realized their family members were being murdered after stepping onto the porch, they stopped coming outside and stayed in the house, screaming as the fire spread. Flacco ignored the dangerous flames and walked into the house. Family members were huddled in corners screaming. He turned the automatic weapon upon them and let it bark.

Kaboom! Kaboom! Kaboom! Kaboom! Kaboom! Kaboom!

When the smoke became too much and the fire spread, the killer left the house and fled the scene in the black Lexus. He drove to the trap followed by his goons in the Suburban. After ducking the vehicles in the garage, they piled into the house.

"Did you see how I was fuckin' them bitches up?" Mili asked, his eyes wide with blood lust as he pointed the pistol and mimed the shooting. "I whacked at least four mu'fuckas."

"That shit was nasty," Kilo said. "Fucked up all them people had to die because of one bitch-ass fuck nigga."

"We not done yet," Flacco spoke. "We gonna keep killin that bitch-ass nigga's family until he come back to the Lou. Nigga ain't finna get down on the bloods and think it's over 'cause he run outta town. He gon' fuck around and come back and not have no family members left."

"Just say the word," Rosé said, kissing the barrel of his 9mm Taurus. "I love the way this bitch kick. Make me wanna go fuck my bitch."

"Don't worry, my nigga. We going back out again." Flacco promised as he pulled a cell phone from his pocket. "Hello?" He paused to listen for a moment. When he spoke again, there was emotion in his voice. "Nah, Aunty. Tell me this ain't real. When it happen?" He listened again. "Okay, Aunty. Don't say no more. I'm coming to Milwaukee on the next thing smoking. I'ma find out who killed Polo. That's on everythang I love."

After hanging up the phone, Flacco looked to his killer team with watery eyes. "We gotta squad up, my niggas. Mu'fuckas just killed my cousin in Milwaukee. I want whoever did it whole family to suffer. On my B's, I ain't stopping til I kill all these bitches."

◆◆◆

The drive from Missouri to Milwaukee took five hours. The Suburban full of Bloods arrived in Cream City at a little after two in the morning. Flacco was familiar with the city, having spent four summers at Polo's house while growing up. When Polo got his money right, he moved his mother to the suburbs and today Aunty Cynthia lived in Oak Creek, a rich suburb on the outskirts of the Milwaukee. He parked the SUV in front of her house and mobbed to the door with a grief-filled heart and bloody red eyes. After ring-ing the doorbell, he gathered his bearings, willing himself to be strong in the presence of his aunt's broken heart. But when she opened the door, the sight of her pain was almost too much for the certified goon.

"They killed him!" she wailed, falling into Flacco's arms.

"It's gon' be a'ight, Aunty." He attempted to comfort her. "Let me in and tell me what happened. Who did it?"

She tried to gather herself, sniffing and drying the tears while allowing him inside. "I don't know. But they shot him in his house. They didn't even rob him or nothing. Him and a bunch of other people died. Even the dogs. I can't believe he gone," she said before breaking down again.

Flacco sat her on the couch and kneeled next to her. "I'ma find out who did it, Aunty. Do you got Derek's number? I need to talk to him and see what he know."

"Yeah. It's in my phone. I talked to him, but he said he don't know nothing."

"Call him for me and let me talk. Hearing my voice might help him remember something."

Aunty Cynthia dialed the number and gave the phone to Flacco.

"Hey, aunty. How you holding up?" Derek answered.

"This ain't Aunty Cynthia. This Flacco. Where you at?"

There was a pause on the other end of the line. "Flacco? You in Milwaukee?"

"Yeah. I'm at Aunty's house. Where you at? We need to holla."

"I'm in Milwaukee. At my li'l baby house on 27th and Center."

"Stay where you at. I'm on my way," Flacco said, ending the call and giving Cynthia back the phone. "I gotta go. You need any-thing?"

"No, I'm okay, baby. The only thing I need is for you to find who did this to my son and put 'em in the grave."

After leaving his aunt's house, Flacco headed for the city with his truck full of killers. When he got to Center, he sent Derek a text to come outside. A few moments later, Derek emerged from his honey dip's house. He walked warily towards the SUV, expecting the unexpected. Flacco was crazy and unpredictable. Even though they were cousins, Derek was scared of him. They ran the streets of Milwaukee as kids and Flacco always took things too far for Derek's liking. When the side door opened and he saw the truck loaded with Bloods, he paused.

"What up, cuzzo?"

All the Bloods mugged Derek, looking like they wanted to kill him.

"You call me that shit again, I'ma forget that our mamas is sisters and blow yo' shit back," Flacco threatened.

Derek's face reflected the fear that gripped his bones and shook his body.

"Quit standing there and get'cho bitch ass in," Flacco mugged.

"My bad," Derek apologized as he climbed in the SUV. "What's up, brah? When you get in town?"

Flacco ignored the question. "What happened to Polo? What you know?"

"We still tryna figure out who did it. He had cameras in the house, but they wasn't on. We got a couple niggas in mind that we think did it."

"Who?"

"This nigga Lucky is prime suspect. They used to be niggas back in the day, but shit went sour after he got out the joint. Him and his brother killed a few of our niggas and we hit back. Kidnapped his daughter, but they came and got her and fucked up some more of our niggas."

"Lucky? Lucky?" Flacco said, rolling the name around in his head. "That name sound familiar. Wasn't that the nigga that took that body for him back in the day?"

Derek nodded. "Yeah, that's him. The nigga brother is a Navy SEAL and he be fucking shit up. I think … "

"A real Navy SEAL?" Flacco interrupted, sounding impressed.

"Yeah. Real deal. The nigga is savage. But he locked up for getting some of our other niggas out the way when we tried to get his bitch daughter. I think Lucky did it 'cause some of our niggas killed his bitch and kids. Or the nigga Wacco."

200

"And who is Wacco?"

"Nigga that be getting money. He run CSG. He heard Polo had something to do with his nephew getting killed so he hit back and killed Mariah."

"That's what happened to shorty?" Flacco asked, sounding surprised. "I thought nobody knew who did it?"

"We said that 'cause we been gettin' down on the niggas that did it. We been looking for Wacco, but can't catch him."

Flacco was silent for a moment. "Okay. Tell me about Lucky first. Y'all kidnapped his daughter, so y'all must know where he be or how to get to him."

"We know his baby mama. Bitch is a customer. Fuck with that Ron. But ain't nobody seen her in a minute. We think he moved them out the city."

"She gotta habit, so she gon' have to come back. Me and my niggas need somewhere to lay down for the night. You gon' hold us down?"

"Uh, yeah. Um, y'all can come in and chill."

"Good looking out, family. And after we wake up I'ma need you to take me to where Lucky's baby mama copped from and show me who she got high with. She bound to show up again. She need that shit to live."

After getting a few hours of sleep, Flacco, his Bloods and Derek hopped in the suburban and drove around the city going to all Sharday's known associates and dealers houses. They spent four hours driving around and right when they were about to give up, Derek spotted a slim, dark-skinned woman walking towards a well-known dope house.

"That's her right there!" He pointed.

The Bloods became alert like sharks that sensed blood in the water.

"Get her attention," Flacco said as he pulled the Suburban to the curb.

"Ay, Sharday! Come here, girl!" Derek called out the window.

Sharday eyed the Suburban for a moment. "Who is that?" she called, unable to see.

"It's Derek. Come here."

Alarm shone on her face when she put the name and face together. "I'm good, man," she said, turning around and walking away quickly.

Flacco smashed the gas and pulled the Suburban up on the sidewalk, blocking her path. Then he stuck a pistol out the window. "Get'cho ass in. And I ain't asking. I'm tellin' you."

Sharday looked caught between fight or flight. But when she looked in Flacco's eyes, she knew that flight meant dying. "I don't know nothing about what happened to Polo," she cried.

"Get this bitch, Mili," Flacco ordered.

The Blood jumped from the back of the Suburban and pulled her into the SUV. When she was secured, Flacco drove away.

"Please," she begged. "I don't know nothing."

"I'ma ask you this one time and one time only," Flacco began. "And I really want you to think about yo' response. I know that you Lucky's baby mama. I know my cousin kidnapped yo' daughter and Lucky got her back. If you don't tell me what I wanna know, I'ma rape you and then all my niggas gon' rape you. And we gon' kidnap you and keep on raping you until you tell me what I wanna know. And if you still don't tell me, I'ma go around killing everybody that you ever knew. I want Lucky. That's all. Tell me where he at. Save yo'self the pain."

Chapter 20

"What are you going to do about Lucky?" Lasonya asked. "You can't keep hiding from him. What if he says something to Donny or the niggas he got with him about who you really are?"

Desmond let out a long breath. "I been thinking about that since you told me he called you. To be honest, I don't know what to do. I was hoping to avoid this. I never thought that when I agreed to work with the Feds that he would be working with the same people I'm helping bring down."

"He was mad. Started threatening me and everything."

"He threatened you?" Desmond frowned. "What he say?"

Lasonya embellished. "He was mad that you been lying and threatened to fuck me up if I didn't give him your number or tell him where you were."

An angry fire ignited in Desmond chest. "He said that shit for real? Who the fuck he think he talking to like that?"

"I was surprised that he said it, too. I thought we was better than that. But I didn't get on his level. I stuck to the story and hung up."

Desmond went silent again. Thinking. "You did the right thing. I'm going to have to talk to him eventually. I just don't know when. He won't like hearing that I'm working with the police. Remember, he didn't want me to work with Detective Perry to get Polo."

"But you can't let him control what you do and how you live. If he really loves you, he would understand. Nobody should want to see their loved one sit in jail and suffer. What kind of love is that?"

"I feel the same way." Desmond nodded. "But he got an old school real nigga mentality. And it ain't no talking no sense into him."

"Just because he wasted all that time in a cell don't mean you have to. If he really loves you, he should understand that you did what you had to do. I need you out here with me. We're trying to have a family. He should want you to be happy. If he can't understand that, then maybe you don't need him in your life."

Desmond shook his head. "I hope it don't come to that. We all we got. He's the only real family I have."

Lasonya rolled on top of him, looking him in the eyes. "What about me and Quaysha? Ain't we your family?"

He pecked her lips. "I didn't mean it like that, baby. You and Quaysha my family, too. And once you get pregnant, we gon' really be a family. But my whole life it was just me and Lucky. Having my brother in my life is important to me."

Lasonya continued searching his face. "The Bible says that a man should leave his family and cleave to his wife. I want Lucky around too, but if he don't understand that you did what you had to do, then I think you should let him do him and you do you. Cleave to me. I will always have your back, even when you're wrong. I love you and I'm all the way down with you. One hundred percent."

Desmond smiled and kissed her lips again. "Thank you for loving me, baby. I don't know what I would do without you." When the phone began vibrating on the bedside table, Desmond checked the screen. It was Donny. "What's up, boss man?"

"I need to see you, man. It's important. How soon can you get to Detroit?"

Desmond sat up in bed. "Within the hour. I'm getting dressed now."

"Okay. Meet me at the cleaning service."

"You got it." After hanging up, Desmond turned to Lasonya. "Gotta go, baby. Duty calls."

After leaving the house Desmond jumped in the Infiniti and hit the highway. When he arrived at the cleaning service, he was met at the door by Royce.

"D-Money, what's good, my dude?"

Desmond gave him a pound. "You know you got it. Where the boss?"

"He in the back waiting for you."

Desmond nodded to the two other shooters as he walked towards the office. Donny sat behind the desk waiting.

"D-Money! What's going on, brotha?" he asked, standing and extending a hand.

"I'm good. How you?" he asked, shaking hands.

"Good. Good. When opportunity meets preparation, you have to be ready. Have a seat," he gestured, sitting behind the desk. "I want to thank you again for what you did in Milwaukee and for bringing my nigga back home. Fucked up what happened," Donny lamented.

"I wish I coulda did more."

Donny nodded. "You did what you could. When it's your time, nothing you can do about it. But I don't want to spend too much time on what can't be changed. I want to talk to you about joining my team. I have a permanent job for you."

Desmond's eyes brightened. "I'm listening."

"I want you to be my runner for the Wisconsin job. I want to set up shop in Milwaukee and I need somebody I trust to make the runs. Since you're familiar with the city and you proved that you can handle yourself, I think you are the perfect man for the job. What do you think?"

Desmond was a little caught off guard by the offer. That meant he would probably have to work with Lucky - something he didn't want to do. "I told you I didn't want to trap forever. Plus, those highways are dangerous. I was scared as fuck driving all the way back with Scooby's body."

"You don't have to do it forever. You'll only make the run once or twice a month for a couple of months. Just until we get it popping. I'll give you twenty-five thousand every trip. With that kind of money, you won't have to hustle. Fifty grand a month. Think about that. I need you on this, D-Money. Fuck with me one time and I'll be forever indebted."

Desmond wanted to say no. Wanted to get up and walk out of the office. But he couldn't. Taking the job would get him further in the organization and get him more information to bring the family down quicker. Then he could get on with his life and live happily ever after with Lasonya and have kids.

"Okay. I got you."

Donny smiled like he won a prize. "You my nigga, D-Money. The first drop will be a light one. Just a brick of boy. Drop it to

Lucky and get yo' ass back home and I'ma have that money waiting for you."

♦♦♦

Sharday had experienced the worst pain she'd ever felt in her life. Her hands and feet were tied to the bed post and she was stretched wide. She didn't have on any clothes. Flacco stood before her with a sick and demented look on his face, like he was enjoying her pain. He had already used the cherry from several blunts and cigarettes to burn hundreds of holes all over her body. When she didn't crack, he began beating her with his fists. Both her eyes were swollen shut, her nose broken, lips busted, and several teeth missing. Dried blood covered her face and the bed. And despite her pain, Sharday kept her mouth closed.

"I gotta admit that you a tough bitch," Flacco said, real respect in his tone. "I wish we woulda met under different circumstances 'cause I woulda loved to have you on the team. I'ma remember you and I'ma tell Lucky that you held on longer than I expected. You sacrificed your body for him. I won't let your sacrifice go to waste."

"Pul-leese. Let me go," she mumbled, barely able to speak.

Flacco looked at the needle nosed pliers in his hand and grinned. "I can't do that, baby. I need to find Lucky. He gotta pay for what he did to my family. If you tell me where he is, I'ma end yo' suffering."

"I-I don't know!" she cried.

"I didn't expect you to admit it. But my will is stronger than yours." He said before grabbing hold of her ankle and holding her leg down while using the needle nosed pliers to grip the toe nail on her big toe. He yanked his arm back, blood squirting as he snatched the nail off.

"Ahhhh!" Sharday screamed, trying to kick her leg free. It was no use. She was tied down and Flacco was too strong. He continued snatching her toenails off until one foot had been stripped. Then he moved to the next.

"Okay! Okay!" Sharday cried.

Flacco looked up expectantly. "I'm ready."

"Just don't hurt my daughter. That's all I ask."

Flacco nodded. "Because you showed heart, I won't touch her. Tell me where Lucky is."

Sharday cried as she told him the address.

Flacco pulled the pistol from his waist and walked around the bed, putting a hand on her head in a loving way. Then he kissed her forehead tenderly. "I promise yo' sacrifice won't be in vain," he said before blowing her brains out.

◆◆◆

"I don't like them being in the house when you not here." Laronda said, cutting her eyes towards the living room. The shooters from Detroit were in the living room playing a video game and smoking weed while Laronda and Lucky stood in the kitchen.

"What happened? One of them niggas fucking with you?" Lucky asked, ready to hand out punishments.

"Nah, it ain't that. They just weird. And they keep looking at my booty."

Lucky looked her from head to toe. Laronda wore spandex-like shorts and a sports bra. "If you put on some clothes, they wouldn't be looking."

"But this is my house. I should be able to wear what I want."

"And all them niggas in they early twenties and horny as fuck. Sometimes you gotta think for niggas. But it ain't gon' be much longer. They outta here once I get these niggas a spot of they own."

"I wish you'd hurry up," she said before rolling her eyes and walking away.

Lucky shook his head and walked towards the living room. "Teenagers," he mumbled, checking his phone when it rang. The numbered showed private. "Hello?"

"What's going on, brah?" Desmond said, his voice heavy with stress.

The sound of his brother's voice made Lucky grow hot. "Where you at, nigga? And don't tell me that locked up shit 'cause I know you been lying all this fuckin time."

"I'm not locked up, Lucky. I'm pulling up in front of your house right now. Come outside. We need to talk."

Lucky walked quickly through the house and out the front door. There was a black Ford Fusion pulling up to the curb. Lucky tore down the steps, walking to the car with purpose. He yanked the passenger door open and jumped in before Desmond could get out of the car.

"You working with the police, nigga?" Lucky yelled, asking the question and accusing him at the same time.

"I ain't like you, Lucky. I'm not about to sit in jail if I don't have to."

Lucky's face twisted into a mean mug as he stared at his brother in disgust. "Don't gimme that fuck shit, nigga. Is you working with the police or not?"

Desmond nodded, maintaining eye contact. "Yeah. I'm working with the Feds."

Lucky's eyes showed the pain he felt in his heart. For a moment he was speechless. He had already figured out that Desmond was working, but actually hearing him say it was devastating. "I can't believe you did that bitch-ass shit, Des. I told you don't work with them mu'fuckas. I told you that's some hoe-ass shit, nigga."

Desmond remained defiant, standing his ground. "I did what I had to do. I want to live my life, brah. I want kids and a family, and I can't do that in a jail cell. You should understand that. You should want the best for me if you love me. Lasonya understands. Why can't you?"

Hearing her name brought a snarl to Lucky's lips. "Lasonya, huh? So that's what this about? You fuckin' wit' them peoples so you can get back to that pussy? Don't think she no different than them other hoes out here, li'l brah. 'Cause she ain't all the way one hunnit, my nigga. And you fell for it."

Desmond demeanor changed from trying to get Lucky to understand his position to angry and defensive. "Fuck that s'posed to mean, nigga? What you tripping on my girl for?"

Lucky looked into Desmond's eyes and saw a jealous rage growing. But he didn't care. Desmond had snitched. He was working with the police. He was a rat. And Lucky hated rats. And Desmond's ass deserved to know that he and his girl were both rats. He was a snitching rat and his girl was a hood rat.

But before he could get the words out, a black Suburban parking in front of the house got his attention. Four niggas dressed in red with red bandanas covering their faces jumped out carrying guns and ran towards the house.

"What the fuck is this?" Desmond cursed, going for his gun.

"I don't know. But my daughter is in there!" Lucky yelled as he shoved the door open.

To Be Continued...
Chained to the Streets 3
Coming Soon

Submission Guideline

Submit the first three chapters of your completed manuscript to ldpsubmissions@gmail.com, subject line: Your book's title. The manuscript must be in a .doc file and sent as an attachment. Document should be in Times New Roman, double spaced and in size 12 font. Also, provide your synopsis and full contact information. If sending multiple submissions, they must each be in a separate email.

Have a story but no way to send it electronically? You can still submit to LDP/Ca$h Presents. Send in the first three chapters, written or typed, of your completed manuscript to:

LDP: Submissions Dept
Po Box 870494
Mesquite, Tx 75187

DO NOT send original manuscript. Must be a duplicate.

Provide your synopsis and a cover letter containing your full contact information.

Thanks for considering LDP and Ca$h Presents.

BOW DOWN TO MY GANGSTA

By **Ca$h**

TORN BETWEEN TWO

By **Coffee**

THE STREETS STAINED MY SOUL **II**

By **Marcellus Allen**

BLOOD OF A BOSS **VI**

SHADOWS OF THE GAME II

By **Askari**

LOYAL TO THE GAME **IV**

By **T.J. & Jelissa**

A DOPEBOY'S PRAYER **II**

By **Eddie "Wolf" Lee**

IF LOVING YOU IS WRONG... **III**

By **Jelissa**

TRUE SAVAGE **VII**

MIDNIGHT CARTEL III

DOPE BOY MAGIC III

By **Chris Green**

BLAST FOR ME **III**

A SAVAGE DOPEBOY III

CUTTHROAT MAFIA II

By **Ghost**

A HUSTLER'S DECEIT III

KILL ZONE **II**

BAE BELONGS TO ME III

By **Aryanna**

THE COST OF LOYALTY **III**

By **Kweli**
CHAINED TO THE STREETS III
By **J-Blunt**
KING OF NEW YORK V
COKE KINGS IV
BORN HEARTLESS IV
By **T.J. Edwards**
GORILLAZ IN THE BAY V
TEARS OF A GANGSTA II
De'Kari
THE STREETS ARE CALLING II
Duquie Wilson
KINGPIN KILLAZ IV
STREET KINGS III
PAID IN BLOOD III
CARTEL KILLAZ IV
Hood Rich
SINS OF A HUSTLA II
ASAD
TRIGGADALE III
Elijah R. Freeman
KINGZ OF THE GAME V
Playa Ray
SLAUGHTER GANG IV
RUTHLESS HEART III
By **Willie Slaughter**
THE HEART OF A SAVAGE III
By **Jibril Williams**
FUK SHYT II
By **Blakk Diamond**

THE DOPEMAN'S BODYGAURD II

By Tranay Adams

TRAP GOD II

By Troublesome

YAYO III

A SHOOTER'S AMBITION II

By S. Allen

GHOST MOB

Stilloan Robinson

KINGPIN DREAMS II

By Paper Boi Rari

CREAM

By Yolanda Moore

SON OF A DOPE FIEND II

By Renta

FOREVER GANGSTA II

By Adrian Dulan

LOYALTY AIN'T PROMISED II

By Keith Williams

THE PRICE YOU PAY FOR LOVE II

DOPE GIRL MAGIC II

By Destiny Skai

THE LIFE OF A HOOD STAR

By Rashia Wilson

TOE TAGZ III

By Ah'Million

CONFESSIONS OF A GANGSTA II

By Nicholas Lock

PAID IN KARMA III

By **Meesha**

I'M NOTHING WITHOUT HIS LOVE II

By Monet Dragun

CAUGHT UP IN THE LIFE II

By Robert Baptiste

NEW TO THE GAME II

By **Malik D. Rice**

Life of a Savage II

By **Romell Tukes**

Quiet Money II

By **Trai'Quan**

<u>Available Now</u>

RESTRAINING ORDER **I & II**

By **CA$H & Coffee**

LOVE KNOWS NO BOUNDARIES **I II & III**

By **Coffee**

RAISED AS A GOON I, II, III & IV

BRED BY THE SLUMS I, II, III

BLAST FOR ME I & II

ROTTEN TO THE CORE I II III

A BRONX TALE I, II, III

DUFFEL BAG CARTEL I II III IV

HEARTLESS GOON I II III IV

A SAVAGE DOPEBOY I II

HEARTLESS GOON I II III

DRUG LORDS I II III

CUTTHROAT MAFIA

By **Ghost**

LAY IT DOWN **I & II**

LAST OF A DYING BREED

BLOOD STAINS OF A SHOTTA I & II III

By **Jamaica**

LOYAL TO THE GAME I II III

LIFE OF SIN I, II III

By **TJ & Jelissa**

BLOODY COMMAS I & II

SKI MASK CARTEL I II & III

KING OF NEW YORK I II,III IV

RISE TO POWER I II III

COKE KINGS I II III

BORN HEARTLESS I II III

By **T.J. Edwards**

IF LOVING HIM IS WRONG...I & II

LOVE ME EVEN WHEN IT HURTS I II III

By **Jelissa**

WHEN THE STREETS CLAP BACK I & II III

THE HEART OF A SAVAGE I II

By **Jibril Williams**

A DISTINGUISHED THUG STOLE MY HEART I II & III

LOVE SHOULDN'T HURT I II III IV

RENEGADE BOYS I II III IV

PAID IN KARMA I II

By **Meesha**

A GANGSTER'S CODE I &, II III

A GANGSTER'S SYN I II III

THE SAVAGE LIFE I II III

CHAINED TO THE STREETS I II

By J-Blunt

PUSH IT TO THE LIMIT

By **Bre' Hayes**

BLOOD OF A BOSS **I, II, III, IV, V**

SHADOWS OF THE GAME

By **Askari**

THE STREETS BLEED MURDER **I, II & III**

THE HEART OF A GANGSTA I II& III

By **Jerry Jackson**

CUM FOR ME I II III IV V

An **LDP Erotica Collaboration**

BRIDE OF A HUSTLA **I II & II**

THE FETTI GIRLS **I, II& III**

CORRUPTED BY A GANGSTA I, II III, IV

BLINDED BY HIS LOVE

THE PRICE YOU PAY FOR LOVE

DOPE GIRL MAGIC

By **Destiny Skai**

WHEN A GOOD GIRL GOES BAD

By **Adrienne**

THE COST OF LOYALTY I II

By **Kweli**

A GANGSTER'S REVENGE **I II III & IV**

THE BOSS MAN'S DAUGHTERS I II III IV V

A SAVAGE LOVE **I & II**

BAE BELONGS TO ME I II

A HUSTLER'S DECEIT I, II, III

WHAT BAD BITCHES DO I, II, III

SOUL OF A MONSTER I II III

KILL ZONE

By **Aryanna**

A KINGPIN'S AMBITON

A KINGPIN'S AMBITION **II**

I MURDER FOR THE DOUGH

By **Ambitious**

TRUE SAVAGE I II III IV V VI

DOPE BOY MAGIC I, II

MIDNIGHT CARTEL I II

By **Chris Green**

A DOPEBOY'S PRAYER

By **Eddie "Wolf" Lee**

THE KING CARTEL **I, II & III**

By **Frank Gresham**

THESE NIGGAS AIN'T LOYAL **I, II & III**

By **Nikki Tee**

GANGSTA SHYT **I II &III**

By **CATO**

THE ULTIMATE BETRAYAL

By **Phoenix**

BOSS'N UP **I , II & III**

By **Royal Nicole**

I LOVE YOU TO DEATH

By Destiny J

I RIDE FOR MY HITTA

I STILL RIDE FOR MY HITTA

By **Misty Holt**

LOVE & CHASIN' PAPER

By **Qay Crockett**

TO DIE IN VAIN

SINS OF A HUSTLA

By **ASAD**

BROOKLYN HUSTLAZ
By **Boogsy Morina**
BROOKLYN ON LOCK I & II
By **Sonovia**
GANGSTA CITY
By **Teddy Duke**
A DRUG KING AND HIS DIAMOND I & II III
A DOPEMAN'S RICHES
HER MAN, MINE'S TOO I, II
CASH MONEY HO'S
By Nicole Goosby
TRAPHOUSE KING **I II & III**
KINGPIN KILLAZ I II III
STREET KINGS I II
PAID IN BLOOD **I II**
CARTEL KILLAZ I II III
By **Hood Rich**
LIPSTICK KILLAH **I, II, III**
CRIME OF PASSION I II & III
By **Mimi**
STEADY MOBBN' **I, II, III**
THE STREETS STAINED MY SOUL
By **Marcellus Allen**
WHO SHOT YA **I, II, III**
SON OF A DOPE FIEND
Renta
GORILLAZ IN THE BAY **I II III IV**
TEARS OF A GANGSTA
DE'KARI
TRIGGADALE I II

Chained to the Streets 2

Elijah R. Freeman
GOD BLESS THE TRAPPERS I, II, III
THESE SCANDALOUS STREETS I, II, III
FEAR MY GANGSTA I, II, III
THESE STREETS DON'T LOVE NOBODY I, II
BURY ME A G I, II, III, IV, V
A GANGSTA'S EMPIRE I, II, III, IV
THE DOPEMAN'S BODYGAURD
Tranay Adams
THE STREETS ARE CALLING
Duquie Wilson
MARRIED TO A BOSS... I II III
By Destiny Skai & Chris Green
KINGZ OF THE GAME I II III IV
Playa Ray
SLAUGHTER GANG I II III
RUTHLESS HEART I II
By Willie Slaughter
FUK SHYT
By Blakk Diamond
DON'T F#CK WITH MY HEART I II
By Linnea
ADDICTED TO THE DRAMA I II III
By Jamila
YAYO I II
A SHOOTER'S AMBITION
By S. Allen
TRAP GOD
By Troublesome
FOREVER GANGSTA

J-Blunt

By Adrian Dulan

TOE TAGZ I II

By Ah'Million

KINGPIN DREAMS

By Paper Boi Rari

CONFESSIONS OF A GANGSTA

By Nicholas Lock

I'M NOTHING WITHOUT HIS LOVE

By Monet Dragun

CAUGHT UP IN THE LIFE

By Robert Baptiste

NEW TO THE GAME

By **Malik D. Rice**

Life of a Savage

By **Romell Tukes**

LOYALTY AIN'T PROMISED

By Keith Williams

Quiet Money

By **Trai'Quan**

<u>BOOKS BY LDP'S CEO, CA$H</u>

<u>TRUST IN NO MAN</u>

<u>TRUST IN NO MAN 2</u>

<u>TRUST IN NO MAN 3</u>

<u>BONDED BY BLOOD</u>

<u>SHORTY GOT A THUG</u>

<u>THUGS CRY</u>

<u>THUGS CRY 2</u>

<u>THUGS CRY 3</u>

<u>TRUST NO BITCH</u>

<u>TRUST NO BITCH 2</u>

<u>TRUST NO BITCH 3</u>

<u>TIL MY CASKET DROPS</u>

<u>RESTRAINING ORDER</u>

<u>RESTRAINING ORDER 2</u>

<u>IN LOVE WITH A CONVICT</u>

<u>Coming Soon</u>

BONDED BY BLOOD 2

BOW DOWN TO MY GANGSTA

J-Blunt